MINOTAUR

MINOTAUR

JAMIESON WOLF

QueerSpace

New Orleans & New York

Published in the United States of America by
QUEER SPACE a REBEL SATORI PRESS imprint
www.rebelsatoripress.com

Cover design by Sven Davisson

ISBN: 978-1-60864-409-4

For Michael,
Who led me home.

ACKNOWLEDGEMENTS

The path of the labyrinth has been a long one, and there are quite a few people I'd like to thank.

My beautiful husband, Michael, is always my sounding board when I'm trying to figure out a plot point. He would help me to find my way out of a tight spot when I got stuck in the maze. You have my heart, beautiful husband, and I am so thankful for you.

I was lucky enough to have a wonderful group of beta readers, and the novel shines a little brighter because of them. Thank you to: Christine Moore, Cait Gordon, Derek Newman-Stille, Stephen Graham King, Kate Hartfield, 'Nathan Burgoine, Marie Bilodeau, Dava Gamble, and Jen Demarais.

When I was writing the book, I put a call out to anyone who would like to be a character in the novel. A lot of people wanted to appear in the labyrinth, and I'm so thankful to those people for allowing me to use their names. In no particular order, thanks go out to: Dominic, Jason, Bruno, Myles, Suze, Ekral, Chayle, Gustav, Cheryl, Leo, Gabriel, Deorwyrn, Alvia, Elaine, Kris, Ali, Tanya, Ash, Rob, Nataliya, Eleanor, Joni, Beverly, Dava, Vilma, Kelsey, Nicole, Michael, Maureen, Mich, Sunita, Catherine, Carolyn, Kimberlee, Carrie, Kaylan, Diane, Cindy, Geoff, Meaghan Josia-James, Su Jay, Dawn, Alexander, Lucy, Brian, Gailene, Pamela, Iskra, Mike-Razzle, Cynthia, Sylvia, Dana, Susannah, Cassiopeia, Melissa, Charlotte, Megan, Isabelle, Ginette, Richard, Raven and Helen.

Lastly, thank you to Rebel Satori Press for giving Minotaur a home. I'm so glad that the labyrinth led me to you.

CHAPTER ONE

We were friendly with the dark.

I had come to terms with it a long time ago. There was little light that filtered into the labyrinth, and even those small rays of sun were fleeting. Our eyes had become so used to seeing in the dark but there were things I yearned for that I had never seen. I wanted to see the blue of the sky and there was a particular shade of purple I had only seen in picture books, read in the shadows. My body missed wide open spaces and the feeling of freedom though it had never experienced either.

It's a very quiet life. We had to be quiet, lest we wake the Minotaur. We would hear it roaring in the distance and could feel the ground rumble when it walked. When it did so, we all knew to remain silent and not move. It could hear our voices and sense our movement. We were raised to enjoy the quiet and learned to speak through signing, hand motions, and whispers that sounded like the wind. Some days, I forgot the sound of my own voice.

I was born inside the walls of the labyrinth. I've never been outside of its walls, so I knew its internal pathways well. I've lived here all of my seventeen years and am as familiar with its walls as I am with the dark. I knew how to find the market, which steps to take to see the Oracle, and the best hiding spots to conceal ourselves from the Minotaur.

Often, my friends and I would go looking for these spots deep in the labyrinth where the light came through the cracks, where we could smell the air of the outside world. We would each take guesses as to what was outside the walls, each guess bigger and grander than the last. One of my treasured possessions was a carnelian stone that the Oracle gave me. I liked to pretend that it gave off a soft orange light that reminded me of the sun. I would take the stone to those places where the sun shone in and let it sit in the rays for a bit to recharge its warmth.

The darkness offered many places in which to hide things. For instance, it was not possible to know what another person was thinking by looking at their face; you had to become really good at listening to what people were saying or at how they moved their hands when signing to really know how the person felt. You have to trust your gut in the darkness. The Oracle always said that intuition was a gift. We had to use it if we wanted it to grow.

There were things that you could not do in the dark. We couldn't grow a diversity of food in the shadows. Potatoes grew well, as did some varieties of root vegetables and different types of greens. Mushrooms and rhubarb grew in abundance and didn't need light. Rhubarb made the most wonderful pies, though they were bitter without sugar. We did not have sugar in the labyrinth. Beansprouts and chicory grew well without sunlight. Sometimes we were able to grow carrots in some of the spots that received direct sunlight. There were small streams and tiny little lakes to be found in certain areas of the labyrinth, so we were always able to find some water for our gardens. There were sometimes fish and crustaceans we could eat. They would find their way down from wherever the water came.

You learn a lot about yourself by spending so much time in the darkness. I learned to confront my fears a long time ago. I'm still afraid, but I've acknowledged that fear. I know who they are now and where they came from. It doesn't mean that they've gone away, only that I've shed light on the darker parts of myself and can see my fears for what they are.

Today, I am afraid of death.

Mother has made sure that I'm wearing my best coat. I know that it's supposed to be an intense red colour, but in the darkness, it looks like a deep black velvet. The fabric has stitches in it that make it look as though the coat is covered in stars. I only wear this coat for important occasions. I know why Mother has pulled the coat out today and part of me is glad that she is trying to make me feel good, even if it has the opposite effect.

We are going to a mourning; a celebration of life. I know that death is a part of life and that people are born to die, but when the life is taken from you too soon, it seems unfair to celebrate that life when it hardly had a chance to live. We are going to mourn Persephone, the daughter of Ms. and Mr. Carmichael. Persephone was only six years old and had never been very strong. She had a difficult childhood, plagued with sickness. It's hard to thrive in darkness. Though people were sad about her passing, I was glad for her. It meant that she was no longer in pain. She had not been made for the dark.

My mother whispers to me, "Cheer up, poppet. It's not as bad as all that."

I let out a small breath, a release of pressure. "Why do we have to celebrate her life when she hardly lived one?" I whisper back.

"Because that is what is done, Roanne. She must be celebrated and remembered," my mother says.

I have forgotten what my mother's voice really sounds like. I think I remember bits of soft song when I was younger and if

I concentrate hard enough, I can hear the ghost of that voice. Sadly, it has been so long since I have heard it above a fierce whisper that I don't know if I'm inventing the timbre of her voice in my head or not.

We didn't often gather as one group but reserved those times for weddings and funerals instead. Part of me liked the balance of it, that we gathered to celebrate life and honour death, but part of me wondered if there was ever a time when you gathered for no reason at all. There were often quite a few people in the market, but not the whole town, not all at once.

It was difficult when we all got together like this. We had to be careful to be extra quiet and move slowly so as not to make any noise. We didn't want to attract the attention of the Minotaur. This happened once when we were having a celebration and the children had been playing a little too loudly, despite their parents attempts to quiet them down. That was a day that ended in blood. I can still remember the sounds made by the children that day.

Each of the villagers have claimed a spot for themselves within the labyrinth, a spot to call their own and to afford some measure of privacy. It gives us the semblance of having a home even though none of us really do. Mother lucked out and we have a large section of nearly three hundred square feet. Some of the walls within this section have fallen down over time and we've used these as shelved cubbyholes in which to keep our belongings, few as they are.

Each family's symbol marks the walls closest to where they sleep. Ours is marked with the symbol of a phoenix. Mother says that they are mythical birds that used to burn themselves up and then be reborn from their own ashes. She often says that we will be reborn one day and that we will be able to move out of the dark and into the light. I don't have the heart to tell her that this will never happen. I was born here. The labyrinth is all that I have ever known.

As we are leaving our part of the labyrinth, my mother hands me a jar. "Roanne, come here," she whispers. She reaches into a wooden box and pulled out a jar. That jar seemed like it was full of light but was actually full of glowworms. They radiate a soft but brilliant blue. My mother reaches into the jar with deft fingers, selected a worm and placed it in the jar. It glow happily, sliding around in the jar. She t another jar and worm for herself, returning the source jar to the wooden box and puts it aside. We t the jarred glow worms with us. Each person who lives within the labyrinth carries a jar. They make it easier to see where we're going; it's supposed to symbolize the departed soul finding their way out of the labyrinth by following the light. I can't help but think it a cruel sentiment as we can't ever leave the labyrinth.

We make our way down the long twists and turns of the labyrinth and I'm careful when walking. My arm is hooked in mothers, and my other arm holds the jar with my cane hooked in the crook of my arm. We are soon joined by other families making the expedition to the centre of the maze where the rowan tree grows. My mother told me that it was planted back when she was a little girl and symbolized the strength and fortitude of the people who lived within these walls. I think that's a load of nonsense. While it does take a certain amount of strength to live within the walls, it would be better to have a tree that symbolizes fear because that is the force governing our lives.

I see a few friends amongst the growing crowd as we quietly move forward. Kiles and Riley are always together, as though they are brothers. Riley was taken in by Kiles' family when Riley's parents were killed during the last rampage. Kiles has again done something to his hair, for it sparkles delicately in the softly lit dark. Riley gives me a goofy grin, extending his fist out and open so that all five fingers are spread wide while holding his jar with his other hand. It is our gesture to say hello. I return the gesture, as does my mother.

Janice and Hugo walk by not making any gesture of greeting to me, but Janice does spare me a glance. I see pain in her eyes for an instant and then it's gone, replaced by the coolness that she and I now display towards each other. There are some things that the heart can't forgive, it seems. Janice pulls on Hugo's arm and clutches it, almost making him trip and fall. He stops himself just in time. His jar nearly falls from his grasp, but Hugo rights it at the last second, the glowworms inside his jar flickering for a moment and then shining brightly again.

Everyone glares at them. We all know what would have happened if the jar had fallen and shattered. It would have brought havoc down upon us. One person makes a gesture that is still used today and is well known. The woman holds out her hand and raises a middle finger in Janice and Hugo's direction. A few other people repeat the gesture. Even without words, their displeasure is evident. Janice merely nods and casts her eyes down. She still holds on to Hugo, but not as tightly as before.

We all continue walking, our footsteps as silent as possible. All that can be heard is the occasional footfall and the sound of the wind passing through the maze. There is the periodic sound of a bird that has somehow found its way into the labyrinth, but the birds don't rouse the Minotaur. Only we have that privilege.

Moving through the labyrinth, we find our way quietly to the centre of the maze. Some people wear worried looks on their faces; these are the people who don't like to congregate in case it draws too much attention. The other people exhibit looks of frank curiosity. They may not ever before have seen the girl who is laid out on the altar before the rowan tree.

There is no way of knowing how many people live within these walls. Sure, someone tried to do a census once by canvassing the entire labyrinth, but it proved too vast. One would think that it goes on forever, but I know that it does have limits. Our part of the maze is close to one of the outside walls. I know this because I can feel the wind through the walls when I am walking in the nearby corridors. There are even times when the air smells sweet; I expect it's the smell of summer.

There are about one hundred and fifty people here, gathered closely together. I can see Suze and Ekral. They are standing with their youngest daughter Chayle who looks frightened, her eyes huge and haunted in the glowing light now filling the air. I offer them a smile; a grinning Suze points at me and Chayle looks, her face happily mirroring my own.

The Oracle stands by Persephone's body. She raises her hand in the air in a gesture that clearly means "Stop." There is no chatter to quiet down as we are all terrified of making any noise, so there is little for us to stop. The Oracle nods as if she has spoken. What happens now is a series of hand gestures taking the place of words. We watch the Oracle as she signs, and it looks as if her hands are singing.

'We have lost one of our own. She was taken from us by the labyrinth too soon. Now we send her home, back to the sky from which she came,' her hands say.

She puts both of her hands to the sky; we understand and accept her cue. We all unscrew the lids of our jars. I watch as my glowworm thinks about it for a moment and then flies out, radiating a phosphorescent blue. Hundreds of glowworms fly upward, filling the sky with their light and move as one towards the tree. It looks as though the leaves themselves are glowing. This is supposed to symbolize Persephone's journey into the sky. The glowworms are the representation of her spirit while her body remains here. I've always loved the symbolism behind this part of the ritual. It's like poetry in motion.

We all say our own individual prayers to the deceased. I didn't know Persephone well, but I did know her. She was a friend of sorts, someone that I would say hello to if I ran into her while I was at the market. I try to send her the sound of laughter so that she won't be afraid on her journey, wherever it may take her. Though no one makes a sound, I can hear the internal sigh from all who are here. They are glad the service is over; they can go home.

Except, as people start to move away the air is split open with the most horrible sound. Even though I've lived in the labyrinth for seventeen years, that sound still sends a chill down my spine. It is the same for everyone. I see fear on everyone's face, and those who were already sporting a look of worry are now have terror on their faces. It sounds like metal teeth gnawing on tin foil and screaming at the same time. When the ground begins to shake around us, I know that we have only a few moments.

The Minotaur has woken.

CHAPTER TWO

MOTHER takes my jar and puts both mine and hers in her rucksack. She grabs hold of my arm. Her grasp is tight so as not to lose me in the crowd. I hold my cane tightly to my side so that I don't lose it or harm others as we begin to run. When the Minotaur screams again, Mother's grip becomes painful, but I don't shrug if off. That pain is a reminder that I am still alive.

"We must move quickly," she says, her voice just above a whisper. I can hear the music notes contained in her voice and though I can hear the panic, it is also a joy to actually hear her voice raised above a whisper.

Behind us, others have dropped their jars and started to run for safety. I hear Mother release an angry breath. Though it contains no words, that breath was full of discontent. With every bit of noise that is made, we become easier to be found. We have no idea how big the labyrinth is and no idea where the monster is hiding, but it will find us in mere minutes if the noise continues. I don't blame them though. Fear makes us forget.

Gripping my arm, Mother shuffles us quickly forward. A child begins to cry in the crowd and I can hear the child's mother try to calm it. The Minotaur screams again and the child cries louder. The rumbling of the ground changes. I know that it has changed its course now and it is heading right for us. The walls around us begin to vibrate and I can see them pulsating even in the dark. With each footfall the Minotaur makes, they shake even more, and my mother quickens her steps, knowing that we have only moments. The grip on my arm has become as tight as a vice but I do not complain. The pain means love in this moment.

Mother and I run as fast as we can without making more noise, though I don't know why. There are cries of fear all around us, people calling out to each other, wanting to be close to their loved ones, people shrieking in fear every time the ground rumbles even louder or the Minotaur screams again. Still, we stay as quiet as possible as we pass through crowds of other people. I see Janice but do not see Hugo anywhere near her. Her eyes are wide with fear and when I see her, I reach out a hand to her and pull her closer. We are now a trio. Mother gives us a strained smile.

"There is strength in numbers," she whispers.

A mockery is made of her words when we look at the people trying to flee the unseen foe, yelling, screaming and making too much noise. The air smells like rust and I wonder if someone has fallen and cut themselves open on the rocks. I have come to associate the smell of blood with fear and safety. If someone else has bled, that means that we are safe.

Mother puts her arm around Janice and pulls her close.

"Mother, where are we going?" I ask, my words coming out in a hiss of fear. She stays silent and pulls us with her as she shoves her way forward through the crowd.

"It is almost here," I say, looking above me. I know that we will smell it first and then we will see it in the distance, growing larger with each thunderous step. Janice looks at me and her eyes are even larger than before. I think she has gone into shock. Janice has never done well with fear. She has always had Hugo and me to help her through situations in the past, and recently it has just been Hugo. That was of her own choosing. Still, I am not going to turn my back on someone who was once a friend, probably more than a friend. I remind myself that I am better than her because I am not a coward, but I am not so sure of that anymore.

"We will go to the only place where it can *not* go," Mother said.

She holds on to us and we shuffle forward. I can hear the clink of her jars now when she places them in her bag. She has to use both of her arms to hold on to Janice and me, but I don't think it will matter. The noises of fear are rampant around us. I hear Janice whimpering beside me, she is saying something, but I can't make out her words. Perhaps it is a whispered prayer? Perhaps for Hugo's safety, or for our own. I pay her no mind but grip her hand gently. Her eyes look big enough to swim in. I know she is close to a mental break, and perhaps we all are. I know I broke a little some time ago and have never been the same since.

There is a scream that rips the air apart and the glowworms have flown away from the tree. Even they are afraid of what makes that noise. They flitter around us now, strange blue lights in the air above our heads. I watch their progress; the light that they bring gives me comfort, I do not know why.

Mother shuffles all three of us forward into a stretch of walls that bare the mark of an owl. No mythical bird this time. I wonder what Mother plans to do. Does she not know that there is nowhere to hide? Besides, I wonder who lives here and whether or not they will come back. Mother is almost pushing us now and I grab hold of Janice's hand; she looks like she will fall soon and is very unsteady on her feet.

"Come on!" Mother hisses at us. I let her push us forward. She has grown strong in her fear, and I know that the easiest way forward was to let her push us. Mother gave us one more hearty shove, and we are standing in a dark stretch of the labyrinth. No family lives here. There are shadows in the corner and Mother pushes us towards this dark spot.

"Hurry!" she hisses. Another scream rips through the air, and we knew that the Minotaur is close now. It would be mere moments until it arrived, and I had the same thought I did every time it came: will today be the day I die?

Reaching out, Mother presses one of the owl's eyes and we hear a click that runs through the walls. I can feel a rumbling in the corridor rather than hear it and my body feels like it will fall apart at any moment, whether from fear or from disbelief I am not sure. We watch as a hole begins to appear within the shadows, and I can see a glint of light. I wait for the grinding to stop. I can see wood showing within the dirt and the light has gotten brighter. I'm so unused to strong lights that I have to shield my eyes from it, and Janice must do the same. Mother does not and I wonder if she has been here before.

"Come!" she says motioning with her hands. "Mind your heads going down and stay close to the wall. There is no railing, so tread carefully."

I nod and Mother offers me a smile, but it is strained. There is fear in her eyes that make the smile unsure of itself. I know that she is smiling to offer me reassurance, and I step forward holding on to Janice's hand. She comes willingly. I take a moment to look down at the steps that were not there before, wooden stairs that should not exist but do. I wonder briefly at their existence but step down and then again. My feet are silent on the wood, and I wonder what takes the sound of my footsteps away. I step down again and feel a moment of fear as the ground begins to swallow me. I can feel Janice starting down the steps behind me and my eyes widen at what I see.

I try to hug the wall as closely as I can on the flight of stairs, I try to press my fingers as deep into the wall as they can go. I hear Janice gasp behind me as she takes it all in. The stairs end on a dirt floor but there are throw rugs to protect our feet. I have never seen so much colour as those rugs contain, oranges and reds and blues all twisting together. The rugs are old, and the colours are worn, but it is more colour than I have seen in such a long time. I choose to look at the carpet, to make that my focal point to guide me down the stairs. Once I am on the ground again, I can relax. Being on the stairs unnerved me. I have never been so high up in my life; the fact that I was on a staircase that was going into the ground is not lost on me.

Janice takes my hand, and I almost jump into the air. I turn and smile. "I'm sorry. I'm so unsure of myself."

"I feel the same," she says and smiles back at me.

These are the first words that we have spoken to each other for quite some time, since back when we used to do nothing but talk to each other. The absence of words feels thick on my tongue, as if all the words that I would normally have said to her by now have built up in layers. I try to swallow those words; they won't do us any good right now. I find that when I speak again, a few of the words have remained stuck to my tongue anyway.

"How have you been? I worry about you." I want to shove the words back in my mouth the moment they're spoken.

Janice's eyes harden slightly, but they are also softened by the fear that still runs through her. "I'm…fine," she says. "I have missed you." I don't hear truth in these words. It is as if she is talking to a close acquaintance and not a friend of seventeen years.

I nod to show her that I have heard her words, and I watch

as Mother puts a wooden plank across the top of the stairs. I assume that this is to stop passers-by from finding the entrance and shutting out the light that comes from a grate in the wall. A flame burns there continually. She makes her way down the stairs, and I am struck by how tired and afraid she looks in the shadows cast by the light. She places a hand on my cheek and touches one of Janice's arms. Mother does this from time to time, almost as if she is reminding herself that I am here when she cannot see me.

Overhead, there is another shriek, and I am surprised that we can here it even here, ten feet below ground. It seems to be coming from the walls, though I know that this can't be. I look at my mother with a question in my eyes.

She gestures at the walls around us. "This place was built a long time ago. It's been here since before I was born. Not many people know about it."

"Who was the one who showed you?" I ask. I was still whispering because I didn't trust the sound of my voice at full volume.

"It was your father," Mother said simply, but I see the pain she carries. "We will be safe here for the night. We will know when it is over."

She did not need to explain how we would know when the massacre had ended. It would be when everything was silent once more and the air was not filled with the sound of screams and misery. I nodded. There were four beds down here and a small bookcase filled with books. I went to the bookshelf and chose one at random and claimed a bed for myself, though I had no intentions of reading. When the Minotaur starts screaming, I don't sleep until it goes silent, which means that it had gotten its fill and left.

I looked down at the book and saw that it was a journal of some kind. I sighed. I had no wish to read some prepubescent girl's thoughts. I flipped through and saw that it was not full of lined paper but of graph paper, containing what looked to be drawings of some kind. I tucked the book inside one of the pockets in my dress, interested despite myself. I needed something to occupy my mind while we waited within this chamber. I looked at light that was filtering into the room and wondered if I would ever fall asleep. I sat up on one of the beds and was not surprised when Janice took the bed beside my own. We locked eyes for a moment before she looked away.

It would be a vey long night indeed.

CHAPTER THREE

OVERHEAD, the noises continued.

I had no idea how long we've been down here. Time is funny in a labyrinth. There is no real sense of it, whether you are in the darkness of shadow or the brightness of light. Hearing all the sounds of the people above made the night seem longer somehow. Every scream from a villager, every crash, however muffled, made time seem to slow so that seconds took minutes and hours were forever. My heart was beating as if I was above ground with everyone else. With every scream and each yell, my heartbeat increased. I felt torn between wanting to help and needing to stay safe. A body landed right on the covering of our hideaway and the sound of the body hitting the ground was impossibly loud as it echoed in the chamber. The sound was so loud, it fel like my heart had stopped.

I looked at Mother and Janice and they both shared the same panicked look. My mother's skin had gone pale white. I know that both of us were wondering who had met their end above us. We all looked away from each other and I tried to find something to distract me from the noise above us.

I took the book out from time to time, but it didn't hold my interest. I just kept slipping it in and out of my pocket for something to do. I was entranced by the paper; it was old and yellowed and looked as if it would hold secrets of long ago past. I wanted to put off reading it in case it was just a collection of family recipes. I could see that there were drawings of flowers in the margins, and the writing was spidery and aged. I slipped it back in my pocket again, I would look at it later.

Janice was sitting on her bed and was lightly rocking back and forth. Her eyes were open, but they didn't appear to be looking at anything. I was worried about her. Mother had taken a bit of yarn and her crochet needle out of her rucksack and was busily working on what looked like a sweater in a dark purple yarn. I listened to the crackle of the fire from the grate, and I could hear everyone's breathing. It was making me anxious. Finally, I spoke.

"Are you okay?" I ask Janice. While I did not whisper, I did keep my voice pitched low. I didn't want to shock her out of her reverie.

She blinks in surprise. "Oh, Roanne. I don't know how I am at the moment." She continues to rock back and forth but not with the same speed as before. I decide not to make her stop the motion; whatever brings her comfort at this time is useful. Her eyes look impossibly large, almost as if her face is a mockery of itself. Janice looks as though she's trying to force her words past her wall of grief, and it looks like every word pains her.

"That's okay." I tell her. I reach out to pat her hand because it seems like what we would have once done when we were friends. I expect her to pull away at my touch but to my surprise, she reaches out and clamps her hand on mine and her grip is strong.

"I'm sorry."

I decide to plead ignorance. "Whatever for? You didn't ask the Minotaur to come here anymore than Mother or I did."

"No," she says. "I'm sorry for...what happened."

Two words. Only two words to sum up the vast space

between us that has grown so large it seemed impassable. It was as if an invisible body of water existed between us and neither of us had learned to swim. Sometimes, when I saw Janice in the labyrinth, I saw a film of water covering her in the darkness. If she happened to pass under a chink of light, it looked as if her skin were glowing.

I only nod. I do not try to fill up that small space that was left. That silence told the language of the water between us, and I could hear birds in the air for a moment and the lapping of the water against a rock. Then it's too late, the water has moved by quickly, and my words are left within me instead of upon the surface of the water.

Even so, I close my eyes for a moment and try to mentally communicate the words that I couldn't say to her. When I open my eyes, I see that it didn't work. Her gaze has gone blank again, even though she clutched at my hand.

"I'm sure he's fine," I say

She starts. "What?"

"Hugo. I'm sure he's fine."

A loud scream comes from above. It is a woman's voice, and we could hear her pleading and begging to whatever was after her. I knew that the Minotaur could not be reasoned with and that it was fruitless to try. It did not understand mercy and the only thing to do when you found yourself in its path was to hide. I felt guilty hiding down here with Mother and Janice. I felt that I should be up there, fleeing and fighting with everyone else.

I look around and I can see my mother watching me. She shakes her head slowly. "I can tell what you're thinking," she says softly. "I thought that the first time I hid down here. You can't think that way. You know was well as I do that in the labyrinth, it's everyone for themselves when the Minotaur comes calling."

Janice whips her head around and my mother continues to knit. "You saved me though," she says. "You took me with you."

"Wouldn't have done so if you weren't holding on to my daughter's hand. As you were, you had to come with us." Mother stood and put her knitting away into her rucksack. She came closer to us and looked at Janice with a cold expression. It was one I had seen a lot as a child and thought of it as 'the look'. "Mark my words: If you ever tell anyone about this place, I will know and I will make you pay."

Janice reacts as if she had been slapped. "Why do you hate me?"

Mother let out a small snort of a laugh. "I don't hate you; I hate what you did to my daughter, and right now that's pretty much the same thing."

Janice nods once to convey that she understood the message and then she looked away from me, her face showing the fear she felt as plain as day. I take her hand and give it a soft squeeze and Janice looks at me again, smiles weakly and looks away. I have lost her to her thoughts. I wonder how long she will be able to find room in her head, what with all of her thoughts taking up space.

Mother comes to sit next to me. I lean against her and I draw comfort from the repetitive beat of her heart. I can even feel its tattoo against my skin and, though I don't fall completely asleep, I do let slumber take me to the edge of sleep several times. Each time I am woken by a scream from above. Eventually, I just sit there with Mother, letting my eyes half close and feeling the beat of her heart.

I have no way of knowing when the screams stop; I've passed into a state of waking sleep. My body is awake, but my mind is asleep. It's nice being amongst so much light, and the flickering flames have lulled me to a half sleep when my mother shakes me gently.

"It's time to go back upstairs, Roanne," she whispers.

"Okay, Mother." I stand and feel the ground move for an instant. It then rights itself, but I still grab hold of my mother's arm. She lets Janice fend for herself and I don't protest. I am greedy for my mother's love right now.

We make our way carefully up the steps and I almost hug the wall. I can hear my mother in front of me, the creak of her leather bag loud in the closed-in space. We make our way to the top and she moves the wooden door. We carefully and quietly step out into the musty air of the labyrinth.

My mother closes the wooden door and makes sure to slide some earth onto the wooden circle then she stands and we both regard Janice. She looks at us with large glassy eyes and she nods once as if putting a period on the whole night's ordeal. She does not reach for my hand.

I return the same nod and then take my mothers arm again. We let Janice make her own way home. She is no longer our concern. I try to tell myself that. I've been telling myself that for months now. It's difficult letting go of someone when they used to be a part of your everyday life. I pretend that I don't feel like I've lost her. This is no different from any other day when it feels like we've always lost before we've begun.

The first thing I notice as we turn down one of the labyrinth hallways is the smell. It smells like rust and wet earth, and I know that there is carnage coming. There always is after the Minotaur has paid a visit. I am always glad that I can't see the soil we walk upon. There has been so much blood spilled over the years that it would no longer be completely brown. I imagine it looking more like powdered rust to match the smell.

We turn another corner and find ourselves in one of the largest areas of the labyrinth. When it was built, it would have been the spot where the Minotaur would be waiting for the hero. There was even a pedestal where it would have stood. Whenever I saw it, I wondered why someone would make a labyrinth and assume that the Minotaur would stand upon a pedestal in the first place. It was a beast that was beyond wild. It would not have done what the gods had wanted.

This was normally where our market was. The Minotaur normally avoided this place when it came on one of its rampages, perhaps remembering some long-ago resentment. Looking across the market, it seemed as if the Minotaur had changed its mind. The stalls were overturned and crushed, a couple of wooden carts had been shattered to pieces and people lay dead on the ground, their blood still seeping into the soil. I saw Gregor gathering bodies and putting them in one of the remaining carts. A few others looked on, too shellshocked to help or even move. There was no talking going on, but there was so much whispering that it sounded as if a soft breeze had filled up the market square. We all knew that it would be some time before the Minotaur returned, but we were still afraid to talk at full volume.

Mother went to help some of the people who were still in shock. I went to Gregor to help with the dead. It seemed only right since I had been hiding with Mother the entire time. I went over to him, the soil spongy underneath my boots. There was so much blood here, it was all that I could smell. The scent of rust and soil were in my nostrils now and I knew it would be a while until I could smell anything else clearly.

I tap Gregor lightly on the back. "Did you want help, Gregor?" I whisper.

"That would be lovely." He pointed at one of the bodies. "Cynthia Graham tried to protect her children." He let out a sigh and I saw there were two other smaller bodies beside hers. "Shame. At least they are together." Even in his whispers, I could hear the thickness of emotion.

"At least," I said, patting his shoulder.

We carried all three bodies and placed them gently inside a cart. The wheels had already been oiled so they wouldn't make any noise. I lay them so that Cynthia is cradling her children, young Charlie and even younger Rose. Their father, Alain, was killed during the last Minotaur raid. She had been trying to do right by him and while the children were quiet and often sullen, they were polite and kind. Or they had been.

The labyrinth takes a lot from all of us. It just depends on what we have left to give.

CHAPTER FOUR

MOTHER was trying to calm Jed Carmichael and his wife Annabelle.

She had been hit by a falling rock and had lost a lot of blood, but she looked as if she would be okay. I watched as Mother took a needle and thread out of her rucksack and heated the needle over a flame. I had to look away when Mother started stitching the gash across Annabelle's leg closed. I knew the needle had pierced her leg when I heard a sharp intake of breath, but other than that she let out no sound of pain. We learn from an early age not to make any loud sounds, even during moments of shock or pain. We were taught to cry silently and let no sound escape our lips.

With my back turned, I looked at the others who were sitting with their own injuries or in shock and unable to move. I went over to help Ben who was kneeling with his wife's head in his lap. I could tell by the way that Chloe was breathing that she didn't have much longer left to live, but Ben was running his fingers through her hair and whispering to her. His face was close to hers and I could see the tears that he had already cried. I wondered if he knew that he didn't have much time left with her. I hope he was telling her how loved she was. I picked up a shirt that had been discarded and rolled it up into a makeshift pillow. I kneeled down and gently placed it under her head. Chloe grasped my hand before I could stand, and I looked into her eyes. They were filled with the stars, and I knew that if I looked at them too long, I could get lost within them.

She pulled me closer. "He waits for you," she whispered. The words came out in a fierce pained breath, and I could tell by the way her breath smelled that her time was close. "He may not know it, but it's you he's waiting for."

"Thank you." I knew from experience that it was best not to argue with people who are dying. It's easier to let them go in their own way. If this involves letting them say things that don't make sense, then so be it. I knew that she wasn't all there right now. Though Ben wasn't ready to let her go, Chloe was already looking into the hereafter.

I patted her hand and then gently took my hand back from her. I touched Ben's back, but he was so focused on his wife. I moved on to help someone else. I saw Jason. He was sitting and looking into the darkness that surrounded us. There was no sun and no moon, only the darkness. Jason looked as if he were trying to see beyond the dark, as if he could find a way past it.

He saw me coming and turned toward me. There was stubble across his jaw though I knew that he was still young. His face looked wary, as if he couldn't see me and was afraid of what might be walking toward him. I spoke softly. "Hello, Jason."

"Roanne." He whispered my name, letting out the breath he had been holding. I cold see a dark smear of blood on his face and there was a cut on his shoulder bleeding through his shirt. "Roanne." He said my name again as if he was confirming it was me.

"My mother is stitching people up," I told him, laying a hand gently on his leg. "I'll make sure she comes to see you next."

He nodded, but I wasn't sure that he had heard me. It was often like this after a Minotaur attack. I could still hear the lethal sound of its screams in my ears. "Why do you think they did that?" he asked.

"Did what?" I whispered.

"That." He pointed up at the dark blanket that covered us. Where there should be a sky for us to see, there was only the dark. "Did they not think that we'd like to see the moon and the sun? Or the stars? I'm tired of looking at nothing but the dark." There was pain in his voice. I wondered if this was the first time, he was uttering these thoughts out loud, and it hurt him to say them out in the open.

"I don't know," I said simply.

"Did they think we wouldn't like to see the sun? Or the stars, Roanne? The beautiful blanket of stars." He reached out a hand as if he could catch a star. "I wish that I could see the stars."

I wondered if my mother had any alcohol in her rucksack. "What makes you think they're even there?" I asked. I wanted to keep him talking so that he didn't think of the pain.

"Well, they *have* to be," he said. "I mean, all the photography books show the skies lit up with stars. Hell, even children's books show the sky filled with stars."

There were a lot of things that had been left within the labyrinth. Tools and household items like kitchen plates and cutlery, small pieces of art, but there had also been a lot of books left behind. I had no idea who had left them, but I assumed it had been the people who had built the maze. There were a lot of books. Others had speculated on why they had been left here, scattered all over the maze and found by the explorer or the Oracle as they roamed the labyrinth's many twisting walls. Mother preferred that I stayed close to home, lest I wasn't able to find my way back home and she lose me. I did do some exploring and had seen the books that Jason was talking about. He had been born in the labyrinth just like me. I wondered what else he wanted to see.

"I suppose you're right," I said.

"Did they not think that we'd like to see the stars?" he said for third time. I knew that he was in a state of shock, and I knew that he needed more help than I could give him. "What kind of maze has a fucking roof?"

"They needed a way to keep the Minotaur in."

"Or was it *us* they wanted to keep inside?" Jason asked.

I shook my head. I didn't know how to answer his question. I walked onward to see if I could comfort others in some way. I heard my mother's footsteps and could hear her comforting Ben who was crying full on now. I wondered if Chloe had passed on to what came after. I only hoped that there was sunlight, wherever she was.

I moved on and had to step over fallen debris. I moved large pieces of rock only to find that Bruno was lying beneath one pile. He was bruised but seemed unhurt. I helped him to stand and walked him to one of the stalls that miraculously remained standing. I knew that Mother would help him with whatever he needed. I saw Kiles sitting with Riley and, though Riley looked hurt and had a large gash on his forehead, he had his head on Kiles' shoulder and Kiles had his arm around Riley. Love could heal almost anything. I knew this to be true. The only thing that love couldn't heal was death, though it did keep the memory of those we'd lost with us, rather like an afterimage of a ghost.

I felt guilty that all of these people were in pain while I had been able to hide from the Minotaur, I had been able to stay safe. I knew that Mother would have said it was me or them, that if she'd had the choice to do it again that she would have made the same choice, but that didn't help ease my guilt.

I heard Mother behind me, talking to Jason. "Here now, this gash should heal without stitches but let me clean it for you."

"That's a waste of good moonshine, Sophie," Jason said

She had obviously taken the booze she kept in her rucksack out to clean wounds. "It's no trouble. I can always make more." She whispered. My mother made her hootch out of fermented potato skins that she grew in a patch of the labyrinth not far from our home. It got enough glimpses of sunshine that filtered through the cracks in the ceiling. The potatoes were small, but they were useful.

She had found the instructions on how to make potato vodka in a book that was kept in the library. She had explained it to me once when I was younger. I knew that she pulled the yeast needed for fermentation from the potato skins themselves, then she boiled the skins for a few hours before fermenting them. Potato vodka didn't need sugar, but it did have a strong potato flavour. It didn't matter; people took what they could get down here.

Jason drew in a sharp breath, and I knew that she had placed the cotton swab soaked with moonshine onto the cut. Jason didn't make a sound, but his breathing told me all I needed to know.

"Thank you, Sophie," Jason said.

"No thanks needed. You come and find me if you need anything, all right? Let me know if the wound starts to bleed again."

I hear her footsteps and then feel her arms wrap around me. "How are you, poppet?" She whispers into my hair. "Are you okay?"

I shrug. "Better than any of these people."

She kisses my head. "That's as it should be." Mother releases me and instead takes my hand. "I do not regret my decision. Let's go see if anyone one else needs help. Why don't you go and find Gustav? He'll need help gathering the dead onto the carts and the bodies need to be taken to the burial site."

I nod and my mother and I walk into the darkness. I can still hear Jason's words in my head. I wonder if I will ever see the stars.

CHAPTER FIVE

WHEN we return home, I am exhausted and covered in blood. Though it's dark enough that I can't see the blood, I can smell it and feel its cold wetness as my clothing presses it against my skin. I stand in the entryway of the little warren of walls that is our home, and I am tired. I feel dead on my feet, and I wonder if I will ever get the smell of earth and blood out of my nose.

Mother looks at me with worried eyes. "You should go to the river and bathe. We'll both go. We can bring a glowworm jar."

"Aren't they supposed to be used for special ceremonies?"

"What's more special than seeing the water and getting clean? We're bathing after a long day. That could be considered a special ceremony all its own." She winks at me, and I give her the ghost of a smile.

"Okay."

I know that I can wash my clothes at the same time as myself to get most of the blood out of them. I am glad we're going, and that Mother has suggested we use a glowworm. It will make it easier to rid our clothes of blood when we can see it, however fleetingly. We walk slowly, and mother takes my arm so that I can keep my cane hooked in the crook of my elbow. I let her lead. She knows where to go. Mother knows the areas that are best for bathing and away from prying eyes.

There are watering holes and small rivers that run through the labyrinth. I don't know if they were there when the labyrinth was built, but over time, nature has found a way. Even though the maze is in the middle of nature, it always finds a way in. Seeing the watering holes, the small trees that crop up throughout the labyrinth, gives me hope. It makes me think of a world outside, one where we can be free, where there are no walls and where it is possible to feel the grass between your toes. Such simple pleasures are the stuff of dreams.

We quietly make our way out of our enclosure. I notice the phoenix on the wall outside of our space and I wonder if it does anything like the owl symbol. There is no time to ask Mother because she takes my hand and leads me forward. The hallways of the labyrinth are quiet. Everyone who is left has gathered together with their families, having a silent celebration that they are still alive. I've read books where celebrations are a joyous and wonderful thing, where people are laughing and there is song. Our celebrations are not like this. They are quiet and sombre, almost ritualistic in their fashion. We don't know any other way, I guess.

Mother leads me down one hallway and I see the marking of a bee, then an otter followed by what looks like a seagull. Then I spot a heron, tiger, and an elephant. I do not know how long we've been walking. I normally go to the swimming hole closer to our home. I can find my way to the water there, even with no glowworm, I know it so well. It has a little pinprick of sun that shines through the ceiling and when I stand in the water quickly washing myself, I like to pretend that I'm bathing in the sunlight. The watering hole is large enough for two or three others and we have long since gotten used to this. We have no modesty with each other. I wash myself as quickly as I can, nodding in greeting if someone else arrives at the water while I am there but I keep my eyes averted out of respect. It's amazing what you can see when your eyes become used to the dark.

The body of water that my mother is bringing me to must be larger because I can hear it before I see it. It is a soft hissing whisper. I wondered what could make such a sound. We took a few more turns around walls and then came upon something I never thought I would see in my lifetime. I can see a small waterfall flowing over a pile of rocks about two meters high. There are women sitting on top of the rocks, dipping their feet into the flowing water. I see Ali whispering with Nataliya and Tanya. As we move closer, I nod to them and begin to disrobe. Each of them nods back to me, their eyes seeming too big in the dark. Everyone has this kind of look about them after a Minotaur attack. Each attack reminded us of our mortality, and it was never an easy pill to swallow.

I go to the waters edge with Mother and leave my cane there. Mother helps me disrobe and carefully step over the rocks to slide into the water. It's the first time I've been able to completely submerge myself in water for months. I know that this bathing area is normally for women who are older and more refined. I wonder if this is my mother's subtle way of telling me that I've grown.

She takes out the jar with one lonely glowworm, but it still puts out a fair amount of light. With its glow, we take our turns washing our clothes and getting out the worst of the blood. With the light of the glowworm, we can see most of the spots. The others will fade with time. When the clothes are washed, we lay them out on the stones in two small piles. I know that when we get home, we will hang and lay out our clothes. It will take some time for the clothes to dry which is fine with me. I don't know that I ever want to wear the red dress that looks as if it is covered in stars ever again, though of course I will have to. It's not like I have a whole wardrobe of clothing to choose from.

Mother peers at me with that look in her eyes, the one that says she knows something but wants me to say it on my own. I'm not going to help her with this one, I see no point because Mother will pull it out of me anyways. I put my head under water and open my eyes underneath the surface. Everything is dark shadows and the green of dark emeralds. There is a book about jewelry in the library. I have studied those pages many times and have often wondered if the stones that people wore used to have heat, or were they cold? I think rubies and citrine would be full of warmth while sapphires and agate would be the cold of water. Emeralds always struck me as a warm stone, too.

When I resurface, Mother is looking at me with that look again and I wonder what she expects me to say. I have experienced a lot of death today and that is nothing new for life in the labyrinth. I watch as Mother's nostrils flare, a sure sign she is about to speak, and what she says surprises me. "Can you tell me what happened with Janice?" She whispers.

This is unexpected and it catches me off guard. "What?" I try to think something more to say but she can hear the panic in my voice. I'm whispering, my voice even quieter than usual, as if Mother has taken all my words from me. She has never asked me what happened. All she knows is that Janice has hurt me. That's all I was willing to tell her.

I shake my head. "I don't want to talk about that."

"You're going to have to at some point," she says. "You can't keep carrying around all the hurt that you have. I know about hurt, poppet. It eats away at a person, even if you've forgiven the person which I don't think you have."

Trying to appear haughty while you're in murky green water is not an easy thing to do. I try anyway. "We're no longer friends,"

I tell her. "Isn't that enough?"

"It's not," she says simply. "Not when you're holding on to the hurt so tightly that it's killing you."

"I don't know what you mean."

"I watched you last night. I watched both of you. What you did say and didn't say to each other. You looked thrilled to be holding her hand as you made your way down the stairs but let her hand go when you got to the bottom as if you were repulsed. You can only love and hate people at the same time if you have had a grievous hurt," she says to me. "I watched how your face melted when she took your arm, but how you looked at her when you let your hand leave hers. There was a hardness that appeared as if you were putting a wall in place."

I do nothing but blink in response. There is nothing for me to say because she has seen everything in my face from the night before and she is right. There is no need for me to confirm this. I dunk my head under the water again, wanting to lose myself in its green depths once more, but I fear what is waiting for me above the water. The green depths looked as if they hid their own multitude of secrets and I didn't want to be one of them.

When I broke the water's surface again, the look on Mother's face had softened. This throws me. I wonder why she's looking at me like that. I wonder if she was waiting for me to say something, to tell her what had happened with Janice, but she doesn't press me. Instead, Mother reaches out and takes my hands in hers and gives them a squeeze. "I hope that whatever she did you can forgive her eventually. You can't hold on to all that anger, especially in here. The labyrinth eats away at you, and you don't want to have that sped up by having the anger eat away at you too."

I blinked because there was nothing I could say. Mother had

always had a way of seeing into me. I supposed that had to do with the fact that I came from her. Knowing your child was like getting to know a part of yourself. I was very much like Mother. I wondered what pain she had to let go of? What pain had she held onto until it had eaten away at her? I could see this reality reflected in her eyes. They were eyes that knew my pain without me having to say a word about what had happened between Janice and myself. I guess all mothers are good at that, I wouldn't really know. What I did know was that my mother could see into me. I took comfort from that now, even though it was often a source of frustration.

We finish bathing and Mother pulls two robes from her rucksack. We put those on, and she wrap our clothes in another cloth that she brought for this purpose. Our boots we hook around the end of one of our fingers and Mother put the glass jar with the glowworm back in her bag. With her free hand, Mother reaches out and takes hold of my own free hand and we made our way carefully over the rocks. The trip back home was a little bit more precarious as we did not have the light of the glowworm to guide us, so we go slowly. We are used to going slowly in the labyrinth. There was only one time when you ran and that was when your life was in danger.

As we made our way home, I try to keep track of our direction and the different sigils that I saw (elephant, tiger, heron, seagull, otter, bee) but I can't pay attention to the twists and turns of the walls. Would I be able to find my way back here? Would I be able to do it on my own? I thought of showing Janice the bathing spot and that thought sent needles throughout my body, so I pushed it from my mind. Perhaps Mother was right, and I did have to let go of the pain. I would think on how to do that.

The walls started to look familiar, and I recognize certain

pathways and knew that we were almost home. When we pass by the market, I see that all signs of destruction had been wiped clean and the stalls had been repaired. They stood empty and waiting for the next market day.

I look at my mother. "Do you think Cheryl and Leo will be at the market tomorrow?" I ask her.

She shrugs her shoulders. "I don't know. They seemed pretty shaken up. Cheryl has already lost most of her family in previous Minotaur attacks, this just brought back all that pain she's already been through."

"But she has herself," I say. "At least she has her life."

"Yes, but some people are too afraid to live." Mother squeezes my hand. "You have to remember that we live with fear and it's a strange bedfellow."

"Is that why we hid?" I ask gently.

Mother nods. "That is part of the reason. The other reason is that I did not want to die tonight. Are you going to hold that against me?"

"No, of course not. I didn't feel like dying tonight either."

We make our way home and Mother gently puts the glowworm back in the jar. It glows brighter than it had for a moment and then softens. Mother closes the door, and our little cavern of rooms is darker again.

Laying our clothes out on the stone that we use for a table, Mother heats a pot of water over a small flame we keep burring. When the water is warm, she sprinkles in some powdered valerian root. I can smell it as it simmers. When the water is warm enough, she pours the water into two small mugs and passes one to me. "Drink," she says. "We could both use a good night's sleep."

I nod and take a grateful sip. I let it cool a little as I put on my clothes for the next day. They will be what I wear to bed, so that I am ready to go at a moment's notice if needed. We never know when the Minotaur will come to call, and we must be ready.

Mother and I lie on our piles of clothes. They are what makes our pallet to sleep on, that and some soft leaves we found near one of the watering holes and some grass that we found near the market stalls. We try to settle, and yet I can still feel my heart going, can feel its steady tattoo inside of me.

I let the beat of my heart lull me to sleep and feel my mother's hand take my own. As sleep claims us, my last thoughts are of Janice and the way her hair used to fall over her face. My last thoughts are of her eyes as I let her go.

CHAPTER SIX

THE morning comes and I am still alive.

A small part of me hopes that one day, I will not wake, but then I feel guilty for taking that thought out into the light. I get angry with myself because my next thought after each time I wake is what would happen to Mother? We are all we have; she is my whole world inside these walls. Without her, I lose the anchor that keeps me grounded. Otherwise, I would be floating against the ceiling, never able to find a way out.

I sit on my pallet of old pieces of cloth and leaves and the air smells of lavender for a moment before I smell the scent of soil that is never far away. I stifle a groan and stand, only to find that Mother is at what passes for our kitchen counter. She has steeped some tea that she made from leftover pieces of rhubarb leaves over the small firepit that she keeps in the corner.

"How long have you been up?" I ask her.

"Long enough. Cheryl came looking for you. She has what you were looking for last week."

"That's wonderful," I say, already looking forward to going to see Cheryl.

"What is it this time?" Mother asks.

"It's a reminder of how life used to be."

She shakes her head. "This is the only life you've known."

"Then this will help me dream of a new one," I tell her.

She gives me a smile. "I'll come with you then," Mother tells me. "I need a few things. Did you want me to carry some of your items?"

"That would wonderful. I don't know if I have enough pockets," I tell her.

She takes the items I have left on the table and puts them in her bag. She hands me my cup of tea and pours one for herself. "Did you need more time to wake up?" she asks. "We don't have to go right away."

"You know as well as I do that the good items will go quickly, especially after a Minotaur attack." I reach for my cane. It's always nearby, leaning against one of the walls.

She nods and we make our way carefully towards the market. We aren't the only ones. There are others who are further ahead than us, but that's okay, Cheryl will be holding my item for me, making sure to keep it hidden from view.

I've seen in books what other people thought markets were, places where you could go and buy food and clothing. There is some of that in our market, yes, but the majority of things on sale are from the past and they may or not make sense in the world as it is today. Things like hair clips and lost pieces of jewelry. These are items found deep in the labyrinth left by the people who built this prison. I've always wondered why they left all of that stuff here. While a lot of the objects have made our lives better, why would they not take the items with them when they were finished building the walls and the ceiling of this place?

We are nearly at the market when I see Dominic talking to Gustav. Dominic is showing him one of the maps he keeps within his coat. There is always the sound of paper moving when Dominic is around. I wonder if he has some extra maps or if he has drawn any more? The only way to find your way sometimes is with a map and, as Dominic is always exploring the hidden reaches of the labyrinth, the maps are always changing. He knows almost every corridor by heart and some of the maps he carries will lead intrepid explorers to the far reaches of the labyrinth, places that only he has been. Dominic often disappears for months at a time and then reappears with thrilling tales to tell of sights that he has seen. He also carries maps from far off places that I have seen or read about in books, and I will never see in my lifetime. I don't like those maps; I prefer the ones that he has drawn. I don't like knowing how to get around a place that I will never visit or see when all we have is within these many walls and corridors.

When I approach him, Dominic's face breaks out into a wide smile, and he approaches me with arms held open. I step into them and let him wrap his arms around me. I don't let that many people get close enough to hug me. Mother gets away with it by virtue of the fact that she gave birth to me and we have a great friendship, but I find letting others into my personal space a difficult thing to do. I knew that it was hard enough having the walls of the labyrinth around us, but I needed walls around myself, too. I didn't get hurt that way. I let him hold me just for a moment and the comfort that he provides gives me solace. I've known Dominic for a long time, since I was a child. For a time, he was a stand-in father for me, but that was some time ago.

He gives me another wide smile. "How are you, Ronnie?"

Dominic is also the only person to call me Ronnie and live. "I'm okay." I tell him.

He takes my chin in a couple of fingers and tilts it this way and that. He's done this before, so I know what he's doing. He is looking in my eyes. Dominic says that the soul of a person is visible through the eyes. He says that while the soul lives somewhere within the body, it sees through our eyes and that we can learn so much by looking into another person's gaze. I try to blink so that he won't see anything, but he's too good for that.

"No, you're not. But that's okay too." He tilts my head once more and then lets it go gently.

I try to distract him. "Where have you been this time, Dom?" I whisper. I try to inject joy into my voice and yet there isn't any there, more a bone-crushing fatigue.

He purses his lips for an instant and then lets them smile again. I appreciate that he's not going to force me to talk about why I'm not okay. He knows that it will come in time. "Wait until you see my new maps, Ronnie. There are such far off places. Did you know that there's a floating garden nearly three days walk from here? There are flowers such as you've never seen before."

"How can they grow in here?" I ask him, trying to keep the eagerness out of my voice.

"The ceiling has some cracks in it and light flows down to the plants," Dominic says.

"But who planted them there? How would they know that they would get enough light?"

He shrugs. "Alas, I don't know. All I can do is show you how to get there."

"Which she will not be doing," Mother says gently at my side. She gives Dominic a soft smile, but it does not reach her eyes. She has never approved of Dominic's vagabond lifestyle and thinks that he's taking his life into his hands every time he leaves us.

"But she can have my map," he says. "She won't get lost that way."

"There are other ways of becoming lost besides directions," Mother says.

He leans in to give her a gentle hug. "How have you been,

Sophie?" There is tenderness in his voice.

"I have been managing," Mother says. There is little to no tenderness in her voice. They have had this conversation before. "The same as always. What brings you back?" She can't help herself. There is hope in her voice. I have heard it often.

"I've come home," Dominic says.

"For now," Mother says.

"For now," Dominic agrees.

She nods. There is an understanding that passes between them even without the depth of words. Perhaps there is more depth without them. Either way, Mother takes his hand as we walk further into the market. I look for Cheryl and Leo and spot them. I leave Mother to walk the market. People have done what they can to rebuild it. It takes time to get to the point when it's a quietly bustling market and they've only just started again. A lot of vendors aren't here; they are too afraid the Minotaur will come back. I know that it won't come back for some time. We have a few days at least, a month or two at most. It's harder when the Minotaur comes after a month's time. We can be lulled into a false sense of security that is shattered in an instant.

We don't sell things, not really. As we have no currency to speak of, the market works on a trade and barter system. There are foodstuffs, like rhubarb and rhubarb pie. Those are made by Alvia and are very popular. There are other things like root vegetables, little containers of fish and even larger fish that have been killed and descaled. Those are very dear and usually only traded for when someone is having a special occasion. I often think of surviving another day as a special occasion, but that's okay. I'm not fond of fish.

Cheryl and Leo's respective stands hold the most marvelous of objects and I go straight to their stalls every time I go to the market. Cheryl has books and things written on paper, including receipts, that she has found in her travels. Like Dominic, she walks all over the labyrinth, the two of them often travelling together for safety.

I have always been entranced by these pieces of paper. Signs of another life lived before my own. I wonder how they came to be left here, but more than that, I wonder to whom they used to belong. Mother calls them flotsam and jetsam, but I don't care. To me, they are pieces of a life lived with choice, unlike the life that I am living now. We have only one choice in the way we live now: survive.

These paper objects speak to me of decadence, when people had time to write things down and keep their memories in their pockets, like notes of distant appointments, things they wanted to remember. I don't know who left everything here, but I'm glad they left something. To me, all the flotsam and jetsam show me that there was a life before the labyrinth, a life without a Minotaur that ruled over everything. It makes me believe in the possibility that this might happen again; it might not be in my time, but I must believe that there will come a time when the labyrinth crumbles.

Cheryl hugs me gently. "How are you?" she whispers. "It feels like I haven't seen you in a long time."

"I know what you mean." It's always like this after the Minotaur comes. Time is no longer relative. It ceases to matter in a place like this.

"I have some new things I've been saving for you," she says.

Her table is filled with a few whole books, and one that had been as ripped in half. I look at the cover and wonder if the story is worth reading if I can never find out the ending. Would I always be wondering what happened? I suppose that I can make my own ending. I touch the cover of the book. It shows a woman's face half hidden in shadows as she turns towards a man. The title is *Sophie's Choice*. I wonder if she made the right one. There are a few other pieces, like what looks like a stack of receipts punctured through the middle. Cheryl has placed them all on a string like a necklace. I wonder what kind of animal pierced them all. What kind of beast would have that deadly of a claw or tooth?

"No, no I have a few things set aside for you." Cheryl says with a smile when she sees me looking at the items on the table. She reaches under the table and pulls out a small, wrapped parcel. She places it on her table and unwraps it slowly, revealing what looks to be a diary. It even has a lock on the cover and the small key is still attached. I reach out to pick it up and am comforted by its weight. I turn the key and the book falls open. There are only a few words written on the first page: *Too late to go back. Must remember about tomorrow.* I skim through the rest of the journal to find that it is blank.

"Where did you find this?" I say, my voice light and hopeful.

"One of my new haunts. I found it tucked under a tree root as if the person expected to be back soon. And look, this fits in the little loop on the side." She slipped a pen into the loop. "I tested it, and it still works. It has a lot of ink left." She takes it from my hands, closes it all up and then hands it to me.

I frown. I know that I don't have anything worth the value of this journal. I think of the bits and bobs that I have in my bag, the meagre candle stubs, an empty jar filled with what look like semi-precious stones, a hair barrette I found, and a few bottle caps that I discovered in amongst the stones and the dirt. I don't even bother to reach for the diary.

"I can't accept this, Cheryl. It's too dear."

[43]

"You're dear to me, so let me give this to you. If you want, you can trade for some of the books that you've been eyeing." She keeps a small selection of books, and they always go quick. People are desperate to escape any way they can.

I nod and accept the gift. It is a rare treasure and her friendship an even rarer treasure still. I reach out to squeeze her hand and she gives me a soft hug which I allow. As she pulls away, I see her smile brighten. "I'm so happy that you're doing better," she says.

This stops my heart for a moment. "What do you mean?" My voice is a fierce whisper, but Cheryl doesn't notice it. The urgency of the whisper doesn't register and I'm thankful for that.

"After what happened with Janice?" she says. "I was really worried about you for the longest time."

I grip her hand tight but try not to hurt her. I think I succeed but I'm not too sure as Cheryl's eyes widen. "How long have you known?" I ask her. "Do others know?"

She sees my concern for what it is, blind fear. Gently, Cheryl pries my hand away from hers and when I move to pull it back, she takes both of my hands in her own. I am surprised by how warm she is when I always feel cold. She looks into my eyes and even in the shadows of the labyrinth, I can see that hers are a blue grey that Mother would call hazel. When she shakes her head slightly, I see them change from blue grey to silver and back again.

"No, not unless you've told them." Cheryl gives my hands one final squeeze before letting them go. I miss the warmth immediately.

"Then how do you know?" I ask this out of curiosity. I also wonder if there is a part of me that shows what I am not ready to share.

Cheryl thinks for a moment, and during her silence I can hear other people around me whispering and talking, bartering and making deals. I can see others exclaiming silently by shaking their hands above their head as the sign for jumping up and down with joy. I watch as Deorwyrn picks up a new shawl and rubs his hands along the soft yarn before throwing it over his shoulders and pulling it close around him. The sight of that much joy brings me happiness.

When Chery speaks again, I am startled, so drawn in by the moment that Deorwyrn was experiencing. It felt almost improper being a witness to that much joy when there is so little to be joyful about within these walls. "I think it was in the way that you looked at her," Cheryl says. "I think the only way I can describe it was that it was like you were looking at the sun. Does that make sense to you?"

I nod. "It makes perfect sense." I tell her. "I wasn't aware that I was so glaringly obvious."

Cheryl puts a hand to my cheek, and I lean into it a bit. "I spend my days looking at people and reading them, trying to figure out if I will get what I'm asking for or if they will move on to another stall where someone isn't asking so much. I know the way people look at each other. Don't worry, your secret is safe with me until you're ready to share it."

I blush despite myself. I can feel my cheeks colouring. Mother says that cheeks redden but I've always thought that it's only my heart becoming more visible on my face. "Thank you."

"Now let's go look at those books you wanted to see. I know you've got your eye on the collected works of William Shakespeare. Don't know how you can read him, though. I tried a few pages and couldn't manage it."

I had borrowed a copy of *A Midsummer Night's Dream* from the library. The play felt like what we were living through. I wondered if we would all wake up at the end of a long night only to find that this had all been some kind of dream. Shakespeare spoke to a part of me that I didn't often acknowledge. "Shakespeare knows about pain," I told her. "But he also knows about love and magic."

"Well, we could use some of that in a place like this," Cheryl said. "Come on and let's go get you some Shakespeare," She told me with a smile.

I was surprised when I smiled back.

CHAPTER SEVEN

MY bags are so full now they are almost bursting. New books and my journal add weight, but it's worth it. I can't wait to lose myself in the works of Shakespeare. However, he will have to wait. There are other treasures to find.

The bottles that I have brought to trade are gone already, but I still have a few items in my rucksack. I always stop by Leo's stall. There is never any way of knowing wat he will have. He captures magic much like Cheryl does. As far as I know, he doesn't explore the labyrinth like Cheryl and Dominic. However, he always manages to find items that fill me with wonder.

Today his stall is filled with an array of rocks that he has carved into different shapes. I see a fish, what looks like a monkey, a cat and a dog. There are others, some shaped like snowflakes and others shaped like flowers. We don't get snow in the labyrinth so I'm pretty sure that he drew them from the pictures that he saw in a book from the library. It has all the seasons in one book. I have never seen any other season except darkness.

He sees me coming and he gives me the most beautiful smile. It always makes me stop. What would he have to smile about here? Then I look down at his offerings again and realize that anyone who would make such beautiful art would be able to find their own happiness. When I look back at him, I see his eyes. They are seeing me, but they are looking *into* me too. I wonder what labyrinth he carries within himself. I know that we all carry our own journey within us as well, as we walk along on the one that is made for us. I once read a story that said the stars held the part of our lives that were predetermined. As I have never seen the stars, I can only hope that there is nothing predetermined about mine.

Leo takes something out from of his smock pocket and moves to hand it to me. It is wrapped haphazardly in a few sage leaves and tied with a bit of twine. I reach for my pockets for the rest of my treasures to trade. I pull out a blue robin eggshell, still whole. Whatever was left inside has since been drained. When I found it, there was a small hole punctured into the shell. I marvelled at the existence of such a thing, never having heard a robin's call. I think that a robin's song would be joyous. I've only ever heard crows within these walls, though how even the crows came to be in here is a mystery. No one has ever been able to find a way out of the maze. I wonder what brings the crows here. Are they lost in the dark like us?

I press the robin's eggshell gently into his hands and he cups it like a precious jewel. I wonder what he'll do with it. He tucks it gingerly into his pocket and gives me a warm smile. "Thank you for this treasure. Where did you find it?"

"Near the library. Around that small stream that runs behind it?"

"I know it well. I go there when I want to hear the sound of something else aside from silence. The sound of water calms me."

He placed a little object into my palm. The leaf he had used as wrapping was a large sage leaf. I loved the smell of the leaves when they were crushed underfoot. Even now, I could smell its smoky scent. The Oracle often used sage leaves in different ceremonies. For some reason, they always made me think of my father.

"I think you'll like this," Leo says.

I unwrap the leaf and look down at what was nestled inside. It's a small carving of a hummingbird. He has carved it out of quartz, and it shines so brightly. I can see bits of the original coating of rock that he has chipped away at to create movement in the wings. It looks almost like the hummingbird is flapping its wings as what little light there is reflects on the stone. He has even put it on a thin chain.

I look at him, a blush rising in my cheeks. "I cannot take this, it's too dear," I tell him.

He touches his hand to the pocket that holds the robins egg shell.. "Today you brought me proof of new life within these walls. That's worth everything and more."

I can feel my skin blushing again and I look down for a moment, then look back up and take in the colour of his eyes. They are a beautiful green and look like jade in the shadows. "Thank you," I say. "The necklace is beautiful. I will wear it with pride."

He nods and then fastens it around my neck, his skin warm against mine. I'm struck by a moment of longing, and I wondered if things were different whether or not there would be something between us. I cut that thought off before it has the time to grow into fullness. I won't give my heart to another, not now. It's still trying to find its breath again from what Janice did to it and to me. At the thought of her, my heart spasms a little and I push that pain deeper within me. I hope that it will further my resolve not to love again.

He adjusts the chain and looks at the hummingbird that now hangs from my neck. "There," he says. "It's beautiful."

"Yes, it is," I say, pretending not to see the way he's looking at me. I almost feel the need to curtsey as I take my leave from him. Leo unnerves me, but in a good way. I don't feel like I deserve to feel good, but I can't help the thrill of joy as I walk away and feel the hummingbird as it settles around my neck.

I stop at Joni's booth. She has new root vegetables and rhubarb. I give her a small bottle of my Mother's moonshine as trade. Joni throws in another bushel of root vegetables, and I nod my thanks. "There are carrots in there, too," she tells me. "I have to grow them by the watering hole that gets the rays of sun through the cracks." Joni smiles down at them like the carrots are her children. "They're beautiful, aren't they?"

"Yes, they are," I tell her.

"They took so long to grow, but they carry a sweet taste of the earth." The way that Joni is looking at me changes. "How have you been, Roanne?"

Why is everyone so concerned about me? I wonder. "I'm fine."

"You got through the last Minotaur attack all right? Your mother is okay?"

I look around and see Mother and Dominic looking at the fish that Mich has, laying in sage leaves to keep them from spoiling. They are freshly caught, and I know that Mich can find them in one of the many watering holes that have popped up over the years. It always amazes me how nature will always try to take back what belongs to it, regardless of what we put in its path. Mich and Dominic are taking while Mother looks at Dominic with love in her eyes but resolve in her stance. I wave at her, and she turns and waves at me, a smile breaking out on her face.

"She's fine. Dominic has returned again." I roll my eyes.

"That should make things interesting for a while at the very least."

"I would think so."

"And how are you?" She asks. "You must have had a hard time during the attack, what with the Minotaur taking your father…"

I watch as she blushes and my immediate reflex is to harden my gaze and make her look away, but I can't bring myself to do that. Everyone has lost someone during the attacks. "Yes, I did think of him," I say. "I always do. The dreams come at night, mostly."

I know that she understands this, and I can see a darkness in her eyes that mirrors my own. She lost her aunt during one of the last Minotaur raids, the woman who raised her after Jon's parents disappeared during a previous attack. She carries her pain well and I know that she is a woman of strength. The labyrinth has made sure of this.

"Yes, they do. Let me know if there's anything else I can do, or if you need more. Okay?"

This last word is uttered in a question, almost an invitation, that invites me to open up to her and bring her even further into my world. I nod. "Thank you." I walk away from her, putting a wall up between the offer of kindness and myself. I don't know what it is that makes everyone want to bring me into their confidence, but it's easier for me to remain careful. The heart takes a long time to heal, and I can't afford to let it get hurt again. This is the lesson that Janice has given me; it's easier for me to stay as far apart from people as possible, even though I am right across from them. I opened myself to her and now have a wound full of shards of glass. I can hear them tinkle and clank as I walk.

I have been removing them one piece at a time. I know that eventually there will be no pain, there will be no shards of glass that make me bleed internally. I will hold on to the last shard for as long as I can in order to keep myself safe and to remind me of what people are capable of. It's what my father's passing taught me. He always said that we couldn't learn just by being kind. We learned the most when we hurt or got hurt. It was then, he said, that we learned the deepest truths of ourselves.

I decided to head over to Mother and Dominic. I sometimes liked to imagine what the market would really sound like, filled with people and noise, hustle and bustle, the feeling of light on my skin. I looked up, and for a moment I thought that I could see the sun; but then the world came back to itself, and I knew that I was in the labyrinth, where I always was. This was the reason I loved to lose myself in books. They gave me worlds that I could carry with me when even the darkness is too dark.

Mother and Dominic are sharing a quiet laugh with Mich. Something he said must have cracked Mother's hardened exterior, or it may be Dominic's hand on her back. I knew that she couldn't stay angry at him for long. They are like the moth and the flame, but then when the flame takes hold of the moth, the wings fall away to reveal a butterfly. They were meant for each other, even if they drive each other slightly crazy. Also, I knew that she had never been as happy with my father. I know that we were the people he loved most in the world. My father just didn't know how to show it.

We don't talk about my father a lot.

I'm not sure why. At first, when my mother was healing after he went away, it seemed the right thing to do was not to ask questions so that Mother could focus on getting better. Later on, it had just become habit, and I would wonder about what wasn't being said late at night when I lay down on my pallet.

Mother is actually smiling when they turn and make their way to me, and she puts her arm around me for a moment. I breathe in the warmth. The bathing pond seems like it was another lifetime ago. I think of everything that I have always wanted to say to my mother but all that comes out is, "I love you Mother."

She smiles at me and kisses my cheek. "What's brought this on?"

I shake my head. "Just felt like saying it," I whisper.

Dominic leads us towards our enclosure. He knows the way as well as we do, and though we don't say anything on the short journey, there are many things I want to ask. Like, how long are you staying? Will you tell us when you're leaving this time? Or do you know how long it took me to put Mother's heart back together again after you left last time? I don't ask any of these things. I know that it would be fruitless to do so. My mother's heart is in Dominic's eyes, even I can see that. Much as I know that he can't help exploring and making his maps. Much as I try to find other worlds inside the books I read, he explores to see how big our world really is.

CHAPTER EIGHT

When we get back to our enclave, Dominic starts pulling maps out of his coat.

It's amazing to see how much he'd created since he left us the last time. He keeps taking pieces of paper and tree bark, little bits of ribbon and the occasional piece of cloth out of his coat, every item covered in lines and symbols. I recognize part of the labyrinth, a certain bend of the walls that were close to my home, but there are other pieces of maps that I don't recognize. Some of them look like they belong in a different world, their lines indicating that the spaces were wide open. I wonder if he has seen the stars at all, but I am afraid to ask him. He has travelled all over the maze, exploring every section of it that he could, but always comes home. He told me once that Mother was his touchstone, that she brought him luck.

"Sometimes I wonder why you bother coming back at all." This was my mother's reply every time he called her his touchstone.

"How can I survive out there alone when you hold half of my heart?"

Mother always melted at his words, though it took longer for her to melt each time. Even now, when she looks at him with such love in her eyes, there is a sheen of ice between them that I could see, and I'm sure that Dominic could feel. He is not a stupid man. He knows that every time he left us, he risked not being accepted back the next time. I admire him, though. He has an endless thirst to discover. He knows more about our world than anyone else, except for Cheryl. She never goes as far as he has, though. Cheryl always tries to stay close to home and never stayed anywhere in the labyrinth that was new to her overnight. Dominic didn't have any such misgivings. I called him brave once and he gave me a sage look. "Bravery has nothing to do with it. It has to do with a *thirst*, Roanne. Do you see?"

I tell him I do, though in reality I don't. I didn't have anything in my life I truly thirsted for except for the books that could take me to different worlds within myself. I had plenty of love for the words in my books, but do I thirst for them? I don't really know what thirst is, though perhaps I thirst for Joyce. I am not thirsty now and my mouth is parched. I prefer it that way. It's like the desert. I am afraid of what could make me thirst for something and what that thirst could do to me.

We enter our enclave of walls quietly and put down the bags filled with our treasures from the market. Dominic and Mother take the fish they got and put the fish in a wooden box filled with coals. Dominic takes a flint and puts a few sage leaves inside the box. Our enclave fills up with the sweet heady scent. He built this smoke box for Mother. It's really the only way that we can keep fish for any length of time in the labyrinth. It makes the fish edible and taste like sage and sweetgrass when it's finished smoking. There are lots of people who eat their fish raw, but Mother and I would never eat it that way, the very thought of it makes me ill. Smoking the fish cooks and preserves it so we can keep it longer. After smoking for a few hours in the smoke box, Dominic or Mother will wrap the fish back up in more sage leaves so they stay properly preserved.

When Mother bemoaned only being able to keep fish for

a couple of days before it had to be taken to the trash pile on the outskirts of the labyrinth, Dominic thought of making the smoke box. It took him time to gather the materials and the tools he needed, but he was successful. The smoke box works like a dream. It would be hot enough to smoke the fish in a few hours and then it would last for up to two weeks, as long as it was kept dry in the sage leaves. I especially liked the last bits of the fish, where they had crusted over. Those pieces had a lovey crunch to them that I found satisfying.

Mother sat in the corner of the room on the pallet of leaves and cloth. She took her knitting out of her bag again. I wondered if she was making herself a new sweater. It certainly looked like it. Looking at the yarn, I could see bits of every piece of thread and string that she had been able to spin into her yarn. She was always gathering bits of thread and string she found and turning it into something beautiful. You would think, looking at the yarn, that it would be ugly as the yarn was all greys and whites with the occasional bit of colour in the mix. However, when you took in the completed sweater it looked like it was made of clouds or of the earth itself. We didn't worry about things like fashion, as seen in the couple of magazines we found. I wondered why they would bother. Fashion didn't matter here. All that did was making sure your clothes were durable enough to last. Mother's sweaters were pretty much indestructible.

As she sat knitting, she kept looking over at Dominic, almost to reassure herself that he was really here and not figment of her imagination. I wondered if she ever thought of father in the same way, lusted after the memory of him but I knew that if she did this, it was where I couldn't see it. My mother didn't like to show weakness in front of me, believing that she had to be strong enough for both of us. It's funny, I thought the same thing, not showing any perceived weakness in front of her so that I could be strong enough for the both of us. It's why the whole thing with Janice stung so much. I cried silently for hours while my mother held me. I was not strong enough then.

To amuse myself, I go to my pallet and take out the small book that I found in the underground room. I had flipped through it before, but never really gave it any examination except to look at a few pages, barely taking in any words during our time below ground. It's a thick little book, easily over three hundred pages. I turn a few and it looks to have been someone's diary. They've filled the pages with rough block letters. I wonder who wrote this? I read a few pages, and it all seems trivial to me.

I flip through the book randomly and notice something that I didn't before. There are little symbols written on the side of each of the pages. When I take a closer look, I see that they aren't merely symbols, they are stick figures. Their position changes with each turn of the page. I take a moment to wonder about their placement and what would happen if I flipped the pages. I gather the pages in my right hand and let the pages flip though my fingers rapidly. The little figure comes alive on the page. I watch as a little man walks until he comes to a wall. There's a keyhole in front of the little man and he points to the wall and pulls a what looks like a key from the surface. He holds it victorious, and I wonder where the wall is or whether or not this is even a real thing instead of an illustration. It's when I flip to the last page of the book that the world seems to stop around me. I take in a breath and look around to make sure Mother didn't notice. There is a small drawing of a Crane. I let out a sound that is part sigh and part astonishment.

I know from talking to the Oracle that the crane symbolizes wisdom and knowledge above all things. She said that they could be good secret keepers. "Always trust a crane." She told me once. "They have been around long before us, and they will be around long after us. They will take our secrets from us, so we don't have to take them to the grave."

"How will I know one when I meet one?" I had asked her.

"They'll likely see you first. They are wise that way."

I thought of the animals that marked some of the walls, like the phoenix near our enclave, the owl that we hid by during the last Minotaur attack and the heron that graced the walls and the other animals that Mother and I passed by on the way to the watering hole. I wondered where I could find the crane. It would make sense that there would be one here. What else did you need but wits and wisdom to survive inside these walls? Well, maybe a healthy dose of moonshine. Mother made good moonshine using potatoes and a few other elements. I'd only had one sip but got quite drunk. There were others that made moonshine in the labyrinth too; anything to take themselves away, even for a short while. None of them tasted very good, but you didn't care about taste in the labyrinth. You cared about staying alive.

I knew that I would have to go and see the Oracle when morning came. I looked up when I heard Mother put her knitting away. She stood and went over to Dominic to check on the salmon. It would take several hours for the fish to smoke; it had only been smoking for just under an hour. The fish was safe inside the smoker and there was little danger of the fire moving beyond the confines of the box.

Mother stood and embraced me, wrapping her arms around me. She squeezed me tightly. "Don't stay up reading too late," she whispered. "I know how you like to read your books."

"I won't Mother." I did something I don't normally do. I kissed her softly on the cheek. She squeezed me tighter for a moment and when she pulled away from me, I could see the sheen of tears. I wasn't worried because she was smiling. I wondered at the power of a kiss and the magic it held over someone or the spells it weaved, long after the kiss was gone.

I lay on my pallet of leaves and pieces of cloth and tried to get comfortable. In the semi-darkness, I took the little green book out again and made the little stick man run back and forth, toward and away from the wall and the secrets that it held. Finally, I put it nearby and lay there, feeling the slow warmth that was coming from the smoker. It was wonderful not to be cold, at least for a few hours. It had been a long time since I had been able to feel warmth of any kind.

I closed my eyes and tried to let sleep take me. It takes a long time and when I was wondering if sleep would ever come, I felt its pull and let it take me to complete blackness. When I was asleep, I could be with Janice. I wondered if she dreamed of me too. I knew that the dreams pushed the shards that remained in even deeper, but I still looked forward to them. My dream self couldn't wait to see her and when the darkness of my mind cleared, and I found myself on the beach we'd been walking on, except she wasn't there.

Where Janice should have been waiting for me, there was only a barren and empty beach and the sound of waves lapping against the shore. She had left me completely. I knew that then. It was one thing for her to be gone from my life, but now she was gone from my dreams too. It felt like a cruel kind of goodbye all over again.

In my dream, I cried but all I could hear was he noise of the waves in response.

CHAPTER NINE

THE Oracle knew I was coming.

When I arrived, the smell of tea permeated the air. She made the tea from sage and other flowers which grew around the labyrinth. She said that the tea was supposed to help clear the mind and the spirit, and it would help to open the third eye. I didn't have the heart to tell her that I didn't believe in any of that stuff, but I let her talk anyway. Her voice brought me comfort. When Mother was in a state after my father passed, it was the Oracle who looked after me. We've never spoken of that time, nor have I spoken of it to Mother. She was there in body, but she wasn't really in the room with me. She would stare blankly at the walls and occasionally mumble something. At night, I could hear her softly crying to herself. After the third day of this, when the silence was so loud, I thought my head would explode, I heard the soft whispering of the Oracle.

"What have we here?" She had waved her hands in front of Mother's face and received no reaction. "Oh, Sophie," she whispered. "It's not as bad as all that." She snapped her fingers in front of my mother's face and though she flinched slightly, she stayed absolutely still, looking at the wall in front of her. I wondered what secrets it was showing her. The Oracle gathered my mother up and took her to the infirmary. It's really just a part of the labyrinth where people go to rest and recuperate from shock. That happens a lot within these walls. I'd seen the look on Mother's face on many others. There were nurses there who would burn sage and spoon feed them warm broth made from root vegetables. I had no way of knowing how long Mother would stay there.

I was actually shocked to hear the distinctive steps of the Oracle returning. She came into our rooms and looked at me with kind eyes. I trusted her instantly. The Oracle had this effect on people. "What are we going to do, little one?"

She looked after me for the weeks it took for Mother to get better. She felt less a mother to me and more of a wise old friend. The Oracle was full of all kinds of stories which she would whisper to me at night until I fell asleep. She had told me one about a crane. I didn't recall all of it, but it had been carrying someone else's secret, and the weight became too much for the crane to bear. I pictured the crane with its bill on the ground and the crane could not lift it. This mental image fascinated me.

She was full of stories and comfort, albeit the no-nonsense variety. She would not tolerate falsehoods or unkindness, which suited me fine. She was content to let me do my own thing unless it put me in danger. Thankfully, there were no Minotaur raids during those weeks. Quietly, I mourned my father. I wasn't sure what he meant to me or if I even felt love for him. I suppose I did, but we were never ones for showing love or affection to each other. That was Mother's reign, and she did what she could to show me the love that every child needs, that is before she went catatonic. At the time, I knew that she was mourning in her own way. I didn't know how to grieve a man whom I never really knew.

One night, when the chasm felt too wide, the Oracle held me while I cried. I cried silently, but it was a deep cry filled with longing for a relationship we never had, for a love neither given nor received. I cried because I had no words to express what I was going through. There were only tears, snot and a silent wail that I'm sure only the ghosts could hear.

The Oracle and I never spoke of that night. There was no need to, but we both silently acknowledged it from time to time. She had seen me at my worst and still respected me. That earned her my lifelong respect.

The scent of the sage tea brings me comfort. It's the scent I most associate with her. I weave my way through the labyrinth walls that make up her place, knowing the route well. She is seated at a table that she fashioned out of the trunk of a tree. It had grown near one of the watering holes and had fallen with age. Who knows how long it had been within the walls? It sprouted bitter fruit, so it was no great loss, but the Oracle gladly took the tree after leaving an offering at the tree stump for its gift. She had shaped a table and chairs and had made a kind of pallet for her bed, filled with the customary cloths and leaves. "I don't like sleeping on the ground like an animal." She replied when I asked about her bed. "It's bad enough I have to live like one, I don't have to sleep like one too."

The Oracle told me once that sage leaves required a lot of light. "Just like us, sage cannot be grown in complete darkness."

I thought of the sage fields that ran along part of the labyrinth where we got our sage from. "But if it needs sun to grow, how can there be so much of it? That doesn't make any sense."

She had given my shoulder a pat. "You are so analytical, Roanne. We need light to live, too, and yet we continue to thrive. You were born here and have lived in the darkness for your whole life. Yet you continue to grow."

She had laughed softly at my confused face. "Roanne, sometimes, things just are the way they are. How do we thrive, like the beautiful sage? We just do."

The Oracle hands me a cup of tea when I enter her rooms. She claimed one of the spots of the labyrinth that turned in on itself; she loves the layout because she is always hidden. She says that anything mystical should require a little bit of work, otherwise what was the point. To the Oracle, magic required privacy The place suited her. She had been able to get a spider plant to grow with abandon. She had planted the original to grow in one of the cavities in her wall and it had taken to it like wildfire. It covered most of her walls. She would mist them with a little water bottle that she made for herself. Her rooms were full of warmth and life, and it was like a personal protest against where we were and what the Minotaur had taken from all of us.

"Thank you," I tell her, motioning at the tea.

"No thanks needed. It's just tea. It's one of life's small but great pleasures."

I sit down on the ground in front of the table and sip my tea. "Well, thank you just the same." I say giving her a wink. The Oracle lets out a quite laugh.

"Who taught you to be so saucy?" She gives me a wink which makes me smile.

"I think that would have to be you." I tell her. I get more comfortable on the ground. I love looking at the Oracle's face. It's a roadmap of lines and valleys, nooks and cracks that tell of a life lived. "What was it like on the outside?"

She waves a hand. "I don't want to talk about that," she tells me. "It depresses me some."

"Can't you tell me one thing? I've never been outside these walls." I motion about me and I know the Oracle understands.

She sighs and pushes my tea towards me. "Drink up," she tells me. "There's more where that came from. How's your day so far?"

"Fine," I tell her. I hope that she doesn't tell me the same story about the fact that we are living on forgotten time. The world had gotten more unforgiving as of late.

"You seem lost in yourself today, child."

"I'm hardly a child, I'm seventeen."

"I'm near seventy, so you're a child to me. What has you wandering within yourself?"

She often talks like this. The Oracle is all about the internal journey that each of us are on. She says that for every step that we take in the physical world, we are also taking a step in the spirit world. The Oracle once told me that not many people ever become aware that they live their entire lives walking in two places at once. Only a few have opened their physical *and* spiritual eyes. I believe her because I must believe that there is more than what we have in the physical world. This world around us filled with walls and pathways full of confusion. I've never known anything different, but there has to be something more than this. Rather than answer in a dismissive way as many people do, I tell her what is on my mind. If I'm honest with her, she's honest with me.

"I found this," I say, pulling out the little green journal.

Her eyes widen as she takes it. "I recognize this. Where did you find it?"

I keep myself from looking away from her. "I found it in the room below the ground. Mother took me there during the last Minotaur attack."

"She taught you to see through the eyes of the owl?"

I nod. "Yes."

"Good, I was worried about you all during that night. I'm glad your mother had the sense to hide you away."

"It wasn't just us though. Janice came with us."

Her eyes narrow at the mention of Janice's name. "How did you feel about that?" she asks.

I shake my head. "I don't know," I tell her. "On one hand, I was overjoyed to have her safe with us. It felt like old times and for a moment, I could pretend that nothing had happened, except for the fact that she was worried about Hugo for the entire night."

The Oracle waves a hand in the air and the scent of sage is wafted into my face. I breathe it in. It calms me and I look at the Oracle. I can see the genuine kindness in her eyes but there is also wisdom there and words left unsaid. She wants me to look within, this is always her answer, that looking within will help me see the world in different way. I shrug. "I don't know where Janice fits on my path anymore. I'm not sure what to think of her. One moment I want to hold on to her and the next moment, I want to push her away."

"That's understandable," The Oracle says. "Your heart is wrapped up in how you feel about her. It's natural to feel love and hate at the same time." She taps the green cover of the little book. "What did you find within the book? Was it enlightening?"

I nod. "Look what I found." I show her the animation and the last page that shows a crane. "You told me once that cranes are holder of secrets. Can you tell me where to find the crane? Would it hold a key, like the owl held the stairs that led below ground?"

The Oracle nods. "Indeed, but have you read what is within the book? Or were you just more entranced by the little walking man?"

I can tell by her eyes that she already knows the answer. I take a sip of the sage tea. "I flipped through it, but I was more concerned about the walking man," I tell her honestly. "Should I have read it?"

"Well, did you not stop to think that this little book holds secrets of its own?"

It had never occurred to me to read through the book. Something else has occurred to me, though. "You recognized it. When I took the book out, you looked as if you had seen it before."

"Well observed, Roanne. I have indeed seen it before. The books always show up when one is ready to begin their own journey. It seems to be the way, at any rate."

"You say books as if there is more than one."

"Indeed, there is. There are three of them. They will reveal themselves to you in time. It was that way with me, so very long ago. The books only show up when one is in need of them."

"You speak of them as if they are magic."

"And why shouldn't they be? Everyday acts can be magical. Reading a book and absorbing someone else's words is an act of magic. Walking is an act of magic and will in tandem. Talking is an act of magic if our words hold power or we choose them with intent. It's always been this way."

I take in these thoughts so that I can go over them later. I think of the blank journal that Cheryl gave me and wonder if, after reading what is within the green book, whether or not I will have my own things to write. "What about writing?" I ask her.

She nods as if she approves of my reasoning. "Words have power, no matter how we use them." She takes my hand and places it softly on the green book with faded gold lettering. "You were meant to find these words just as the person who wrote them was meant to write them. If they inspire you to write words of your own, then that is a marvelous thing, and they will hold power for you."

She goes to one of the many cubbyholes she's made in the walls in between the spider plants growing on the walls. She pulls something out and brings it to her table. When she places it in front of me, I'm not sure what I'm looking at. "What's this?"

"This is a fountain pen and a bottle of ink. You can always make more ink; I can show you how. It's the easiest potion you can do. It's a magic all its own, making your own ink with which to write. Magic doesn't have to be difficult, it can be simple, you see?"

I nod to show that I did see. Only I didn't, not really. She gave me a knowing look. "No, you don't, not yet. But you will. Take these as my gift to you. Also, remember words have power. Now, come with me. Leave your tea."

"Where are we going?"

"I'm going to show you where the crane is. It would take too long to explain its whereabouts."

CHAPTER TEN

WE walk among the walls.

I look at the other (tiger, beaver, wolf, bear) while we walk into an area of the labyrinth that I had never been. I saw more animals (elk, spider, seal, dog, whale) and I knew that without the Oracle I would never find my way back. I try to keep track of every turn and every twist of the walls, but there was no way. It all blurs together except for the animal signs that stood out even in the dark; the black a stark relief to the almost yellow of the walls. The walls were even grimier here and there didn't seem to be anyone who lived in this part of the labyrinth. I could be wrong though, there were always those who wanted to go their own way, so I was glad to have the Oracle with me.

Finally, after what seems like forever but has really only been minutes, we come upon the crane. It is in flight, its black tipped wings outstretched along the length of the wall. I look at it and notice how the black iron which shapes the crane is shiny here. There is an absence of people touching its surface and so time seems to stand still here. Indeed, I don't hear any voices. I wonder how far away we are from the core of the labyrinth. I look up at the Oracle.

"Don't worry, I know exactly where we are. I've noticed that you've tried to keep count of the animals, that's good. Always be aware of where you are and always pay attention to whatever you may see. Did you notice anything else of significance as we made our way here?"

The Oracle likes to test me in this way, saying that truly seeing things was a form of magic all its own. "I noticed that some of the walls in the labyrinth have crumbled. Over back…that way?" I point right from where we had come. "It looks like they started to crumble from age and not from a Minotaur attack," I tell her.

"Good, Roanne, that's good. I'm glad you've been paying attention. Now what does the book illustration say that we have to do?"

I open the book, flip through the pages and watch the little man walking up to the to the wall where there is a small keyhole. I watch as he points to the wall and pulls the key out from the wall as if it were a sword. I look at the wall and there doesn't appear to be a keyhole anywhere. I look at the crane's eyes, thinking that it might be like the owl and the button that Mother pushed. I put my fingers around the eyes that are unblinking in the dark.

"That's a good idea," the Oracle says. "But you have to think about what it is that the crane does."

I shrug. "They're the secret keepers." I tell her.

"Yes, but think simply." The Oracle motions at the feathers. They have been finely wrought in iron and if I look at them a certain way, it seems as if the iron will bend from the wall and the crane will take flight. Each feather has been so finely detailed, but there is one which doesn't look like the others. It stands out because its end is round while the other feathers end in a pointed tip.

I look at the Oracle, she nods, and I reach forward to pull the rounded feather from the wall, but it won't budge. I pull again but the key doesn't want to come free. "I think it's stuck."

"Well, it has been a while since these walls were built," The

Oracle says. "Who knows how long this crane has been waiting here to bestow its secrets to the one most deserving?" She offers me a smile. "Did you want some help?"

I nod. "Yes please."

She smiles and places her hands over mine. "Never be afraid to ask for help, Roanne. Though you think you're alone, there are plenty of others that would be willing to help you."

I nod and then we begin to pull. I don't want to pull too hard fearing I could break the key, and the Oracle says, "Easy does it, Roanne." I always wonder if she can read minds. She seems to know what I'm thinking. I wonder if this is some innate talent that all Oracles have or if it's unique to her.

We pull gently and eventually I can feel the feather start to wiggle in its slot. I move it back and forth and it starts to free itself a bit at a time, moving further and further with each pull. It suddenly comes free without warning, and we topple backward, and my hand is now holding the key which is shaped like a curled feather. The end that was lodged into the wall is shaped like a key.

Looking at it, I know that we must find the keyhole. I look back at the bird and know that I won't find a keyhole in the bird's eyes, just as I know that I won't find anything within its other feathers. I begin to search along the rest of the wall, knowing the hole must be around here somewhere.

"Use your eyes, Roanne," The Oracle says. "Use all of them. The keyhole wouldn't be that easy to find."

The Oracle talks a lot about using our third eye to see within. I think this is all nonsense, but I play along. I close my eyes to see what I can see, mostly just to humour her, but to my surprise I can hear something that I couldn't before. A small noise, almost like someone softly whispering, fills the air around me. I don't know if the Oracle can hear it. I open my eyes, and I can't hear the sound anymore. Maybe I need the darkness to hear the sound? I need to remove everything my eyes tell me is there so I can hear what is not.

I close my eyes again and can hear the quiet whispering once more. Keeping them closed, I move slowly towards the whistling sound, shuffling my feet carefully forward until I can hear the sound even more clearly. It sounds as if something is singing for me and I find myself almost swaying to the sound, as if I'm in a trance. In a way, I guess I am. I hold out my hands until I touch the wall and begin to feel along it, the whistling getting louder and louder. Finally, it sounds as if I'm right on top of it. I start to run my fingers over the wall, trying to feel the keyhole with my fingers. The pinkie finger of my right hand gets stuck in something, and I open my eyes, and look down.

It's stuck in a part of the wall that's a little away from the crane, but standing back to look at the spot, I realize the hole actually looks like the one of the seeds scattered on the ground in front of the crane sigil. I wonder at the significance of this, the keyhole being a seed. I put that in the back of my mind and take the feather key. Placing it in the hole, it fits perfectly, and I turn the key. I hear a click, and I pull gently. A small part of the wall opens and for a moment I think there is nothing within the hole, but then I see a glint of light. I reach in gently and my hand touches something. I wrap my hand around the mystery item and pull it out. It's another small book, smaller than the green book. It's a dark royal blue with gold writing on the cover which has faded with time, much like the green book.

I hold the book out for the Oracle. I look at her for the first time and her eyebrows have risen high up on her face. I'm not sure if it's a look of shock, suspicion, or amazement. She takes the book from me and examines it from front to back, flipping the pages just as I did the little green book. She nods and hands the book back to me. I close the small door and turn the key again. I put both the key and the book in my dress pocket.

The Oracle gives me a sage nod, and I nod back, unsure of what I'm agreeing to. "It looks like you have a lot of reading to do," she says.

CHAPTER ELEVEN

I take my time wandering back.

It's easy to feel isolated in the labyrinth, even with so many people around you and separated only by walls. Everyone's journey is different and all of us handle living within these walls in our own way. While I normally like to keep to myself, I do occasionally seek out the company of others. Sometimes I get tired of my own internal voice.

The Oracle walks me back to an area that I recognize. The walls here are covered in moss and I've played amongst them many times. The Oracle leaves me and heads back to her enclave of walls. She gives me a kiss before she heads away. I give her a quick hug and before she leaves, she gives me one of her smiles that say so much.

I see Carrie. She's always wandering the by the same wall and each time she visits it, she leaves something she's found: a pebble, a leaf, a small piece of glass. She has built quite the monument. It looks like it's grown out of the ground and along the wall. If you look at the monument from a certain angle it looks as if it's moving, as if it's made of water.

I approach her, happy to see someone I know. I watch as she takes a leaf, a red one full of points, almost like a star. She places it and steps back to observe her new addition. Only then does she let a smile cross her face. She hears my footsteps and turns towards me. She offers me her smile and holds out a fist and then extends five fingers, the loudest hello that she can do in this place. I return the gesture.

When I am close enough, she envelopes me in a hug. I allow this to happen. I try to tell myself that being held by someone is a good thing, that it doesn't remind me of Janice. I return the hug. It's the least I can do. "That's a pretty leaf," I tell her, pointing at the star-shaped leaf that now rests as if it's floating down a body of water.

"Thank you," Carrie says. "I found it down by the small brook that runs in front of the library. I thought of pressing it in a book, but then I knew that it belonged here. He would have loved it."

I nod because I'm not sure what to say that hasn't been said already. Carrie visits the spot where she and her husband fell in love. They whispered that they loved each other for the first time while they were walking by this wall many years ago. Carrie told me that they stopped beneath the shelter of the tree that grows nearby and professed their love to each other. She's always building the monument, adding a different piece every day. Looking at it, I think her husband would have loved it.

"How long has it been?" I ask her.

"Five years," she says.

My tongue can't help itself. "Why do you visit here every day?" The words come out in a rush. "Why hold on to those memories?"

Her face softens and she pats my shoulder softly like my mother would. "I can keep him alive in my memory this way and this is a memento mori made out of love, *for* love." She takes a moment to think and find her words. "For the memory of love that I had."

She lost her husband in the same attack when I lost my father.

The Minotaur had taken much from both of us. "Yes, but why build this?" I motion at the pebbles and the leaves. "What is its purpose?"

Shaking her head, Carrie gives me a brilliant smile. "If this brings someone else joy, then that's a wonderful thing. If they stop and take a pebble or a leaf, then they have brought my love for my husband with them into the darkness," she says. "In this way, our love lives on and is a gift for everyone here."

Carrie gives me another soft hug. "Your heart will heal just as mine did."

I nod and blink away tears. I don't know how she knows about Janice, and I don't ask. "Thank you."

"It takes time, Roanne. You must allow yourself to grieve. Then you will be able to breathe again."

"How do I know who I'm grieving for?" I ask her. "Am I grieving the father I never knew? Or the love that I've lost?"

"You can be grieving both of them at the same time. Grief knows no boundaries and there is no definition. We all grieve in our own way," she pauses. "Are you heading back toward the market? I could walk with you."

"That would be lovely," I tell her honestly.

Though I've seen her walking by that spot in the labyrinth every day and we know each other well, I've never considered her one of my friends. I do now. That she would take the time to help me with the feelings I'm having when she lost the love of her life says a lot about who she is. I resist the urge to take her hand as we walk towards the market. We keep a companionable silence, the noise of our footsteps the only sound. It's nice having someone who you can be with and not feel the need to say anything. There is something comfortable about a silence that you don't have to fill. It makes the silence that exists within the labyrinth almost bearable. For some reason that I can't name, I feel closer to her than I have to anyone in a long time, even Mother. I think it's because we don't feel the need to speak, our mutual silence brings us closer together.

When we get to the market, I notice that other stalls have opened up. People are holding up signs advertising their offerings rather than shouting out their wares. The market is small enough that they don't even need the signs, not really. Ash is there selling small little dolls she has made. She says that the dolls are meant to guard us against harm, and they're small enough to fit in your pocket. I already have two of her little dolls. I don't know where she gets the fabric she uses to make them or where she finds a needle and thread, and I don't ask. She crafts them from old pieces of cloth she finds and bits of fabric or string. I love her little dolls. They bring me and so many others a spark of joy.

Carrie and I stop by Ash's booth, and she hugs us both. One thing I've noticed is that people are very prone to hugging after a Minotaur attack. It's like with each hug, we're fortifying our defenses for the next time, as if with each hug, we build our personal walls that we have around us stronger and stronger so that we can withstand what tries to destroy us. Even though I don't like people touching me, I allow these hugs. I will fortify my walls.

Looking at the dolls, Carrie picks up one dressed in coveralls with a thatch of black hair. "Did you make these with the pair of pants that I gave you? The ones used to belong to Giles?"

Giles was Carrie's husband, and I'm shocked to hear that she gave away a piece of his clothing. I wondered what it took to give away something from someone whom you loved. Then again, Mother and I have nothing left of father except the memories he left us with, so I can't really judge.

"Yes, thank you for those," Ash says. "They were the perfect pieces and just what I needed. See, I've used some of the pieces on other dolls."

Carrie sees my confusion. I've never been good at concealing my thoughts. "I'm wearing Giles's pants, see?" She points down at what she's wearing. "Only they were too long. He was so much taller than I was. I cut off the ends and gave them to Ash, so she has fabric to use for her craft." She takes another doll. "I'll put one on Giles's wall, so that he has one too. What do you want in return for these dolls?"

Ash shakes her head. "Nothing. You've given me plenty. Take them as a gift."

"You're too kind." Carrie says. She places a kiss on Ash's cheek and gives her a smile. It is the happiest I have seen Carrie in quite a long time. "I will go place this doll now, so that Giles will have something to amuse himself. I will also have a doll of my own to remind me of him."

We watch her leave and Ash gives me a look that says so much without any words being spoken. I see the sadness and the pity for Carrie in those eyes. After talking to her, I don't feel sadness or pity for her. I know that Carrie is just grieving for Giles in her own way.

"Do you think she'll ever get over it?" Ash asked. "Losing her husband like that?"

I think of Carrie's words to me mere minutes before. "Grief takes time," I say.

She shakes her head. "We don't have time for grief in here," she says. "You have to let go of it and move on. Otherwise, the grief just eats at you."

I think of the glass shard that had been pushed so far down

into my heart that I can feel it when I breathe. "I know what you mean."

Ash hands me a doll. "Here," she says.

"I don't have anything to trade for it with me. I can come and see you later with something."

"Just take the gift and say thank you. I heard about what happened with Janice. I always thought she was a stuck-up bitch." She hands me a doll with a tuft of black hair made from yarn, a face from of a scrap of denim, and a dress made from what was once someone's flowered blouse or dress. The amount of detail that she has put into this small doll is amazing. She has even drawn a face using something passing for paint. I don't know from where she's sourced her supplies but at the moment holding the small gift, I don't care.

"Thank you," I say. I make a mental note to go and see her with a small present later. Maybe one of my books or a piece of cloth. I don't like to owe anything to anyone, even if the small doll was a gift.

"Don't mention it. She did a shitty thing, but you're better off without her."

I wish I felt that way. I thank her again and place the doll in the pocket of my dress to keep it close. I hope that it will guard me against the pain that I'm feeling. Better yet if it could help me let go of the shard; I don't know if I've yet learned everything that I need to from the pain. Mother always says that pain is one of the greatest teachers we have and that as much as pain hurts us, it also teaches us so much about ourselves.

I reach out and hug her voluntarily. Just a soft, quick hug, no more than a quick breeze of a hug, but from the answering squeeze Ash gave me, I know that it is enough. I look back towards the walls which contain my home. I should go home, see if Mother needs anything, but I know that she needs time with Dominic. As much as she needs to love him, I know that she will want time to have the right number of words with him, too. Sometimes anger takes on many forms, especially if there is love involved.

I walk towards the sound of water. It's not the great sound of one of the bathing holes, but rather one of the small brooks that run through the earth. The natural world will always find a way in and thank goodness for that. We would have no water otherwise except for the dew that collects on the plants growing within the labyrinth.

The hushed sound of laughter is loud in my ears. I run towards it like a moth to the flame and I turn a wall corner to find that Kiles and Riley are both standing covered in mud and are laughing fit to burst. "You two can't be left alone for a minute."

Kiles smiles. "That's not true. We can be left alone for about ten minutes on our own, honest."

"It's not our fault that we're naturally drawn to trouble," Riley says.

"Shows what you both know. Trouble isn't drawn to you. Both of you are trouble given shape and form."

"You say that like it's a bad thing!" Kiles says.

"I'm wounded fair lady, simply wounded!" Riley says in a theatrical whisper.

"Want to see something amazing, Roanne?" Kiles asks.

"I don't need to see what you're offering," I tell them. "I've seen them both before and they aren't that amazing."

Riley gives me a look of astonishment before laughing silently again. I don't know what laughter really sounds like. I only know this pale imitation of laughter that we have now. Looking at Riley's face, I can envision what real laughter would have sounded like and I imagine it sounding like music.

Kiles gives Riley a knowing look and nods. Kiles turns to me and says, "Come with us, Roanne. We want to show you the sun."

CHAPTER TWELVE

I have no idea where Kiles and Riley are taking me, and I'm not surprised at this.

They have a way of knowing places in the labyrinth no one else has seen. They were the first ones to show me one of the gardens that had grown wild. It had grown in a dense pocket of walls which formed a maze within the labyrinth. The garden received rays of sun that peeked through the roof of the labyrinth, and the plants that grew there were some of the most exotic I had ever seen. When they showed the garden to the Oracle and Beverly, our medicine woman, they both were filled with joy. The garden held plants that neither of them had seen for a long time and using the plants in that garden, they were able to begin making needed medicines. Kiles and Riley were heralded for that.

They also liked getting into trouble sometimes. There was the time they disturbed a nest of moths. No one knew for how long the nest had been growing, but there must have been thousands of moths. There were a few weeks where the air in the labyrinth was filled with the sounds of wings flapping, and there was less light than usual because the moths seemed to absorb what light there was. You would fall asleep and might wake up to find you were covered with moths that had taken rest on your sleeping form.

Everyone knew that they didn't mean any ill by their actions, but they annoyed people more often than they gave cause to be joyous. I loved them for their never-ending positive attitude. It seemed there was always something to be joyful about when those two boys were around. They had only fans and enemies; there was no in between. Thankfully, I was one of the former. I had known them for years, ever since I caught the two of them kissing after school. I was leaving the library that also doubles as the school when there are children young enough who need to be taught. Eleanor was a fine librarian and a gifted teacher. She said that she had come from outside of the labyrinth and could tell us what the books got right and what they got wrong. I wondered why anyone would want to come into the labyrinth and whether she knew the way out. She never answered those questions and would remain silent, giving a glare as cold as stone until you changed the subject.

I saw Kiles and Riley kissing on one of the paths which led away from the library. They had tried to tuck themselves into the shadows, but I was very good at seeing into the dark. I was taking the long way home that day as Mother was in a fit of sadness. These spells came upon her every so often, and I knew that she was really concerned with how I would thrive in the labyrinth, but I didn't want to be around her when she was in one of her fits.

I saw Kiles first as Riley had his back to me. Kiles broke the kiss and when Riley turned to see what had distracted Kiles, he saw me. We watched each other for a moment; I looked at them with their hands intertwined and they looked at me with my cane. Both of their faces were filled with worry. Then I smiled and shrugged. It made no difference to me who they loved. I had always been taught that love was the greatest thing in the world, especially in our sphere.

I had gone home that night not knowing that I had just

made lifelong friends. The next day, Kiles and Riley found me at school and sat on either side of me. They stopped the others from pinching and teasing me. They kept other children from stealing my cane and occasionally they would use it to smack each other, but only when I didn't need it. They were the complete opposite of me, and I had never seen two people smile so much. Not many people had much to smile about within these walls, but as I got to know them, I realized that they smiled because they had each other.

I was keen to see what they wanted to show me this time. I was always too afraid to really explore on my own and Mother wouldn't come with me. I could have asked someone else to accompany me, but there weren't many people with whom I was comfortable exploring. I really had to *trust* them, not just know them. Janice and I had gone exploring and had discovered a few different things that the labyrinth kept hidden, before things had changed.

Kiles punches my arm. "Stop doing that."

"Doing what?" I ask. "I'm walking."

"Your face gets all cloudy when you're overthinking," Riley says. "It always looks like it's full of a furious storm."

"That sounds like a really good poem," Kiles says looking at me. "You should write down what Riley said, I think he may have something there."

They both knew that I wrote, and they loved to tease me about it. They meant well, but they were hurt that I didn't let them read what I'd written. The only person who I'd shown was Janice and look how well that turned out. "You're being stupid," I say.

"Better stupid than dead," Kiles says. It was a familiar refrain.

"So you keep telling me. Where are we going? We've been

walking for quite a while."

"Don't worry, we're almost there," Riley tells me. "Not that much farther."

We turn around one wall, and it seems to turn into itself. It forms a curved wall that leaves a small gap. Riley motions for me to follow. "It's a bit of a tight squeeze, but it's so worth it." He says, moving carefully forward. I look at the opening with some trepidation. "Don't worry, I'll be in front and Kiles will follow behind. We won't let anything happen to you."

I nod to let them know I understand. I watch as Riley goes in, turns back to me, smiles and holds out his hand. I give my cane to Kiles and take Riley's hand. I half step forward and let Riley gently pull me at the same time. Then I am standing beside Riley and Kiles comes behind me. Kiles hands me my cane. I don't know what I'm supposed to see, but as my eyes adjust, I realize that it's not completely dark. I wonder what is providing the light and make a questioning face at Riley. He smiles at me and motions with his hand to come closer.

I do, following him into the half-lit darkness. We turn around a corner and I all I can do is stand still and take the room in. The room is a cylinder shape and all along the walls there are glowing rocks. They look to be filled with lava, and their shine moves and morphs and changes. The whole chamber glows softly from the light of the rocks. I stand there just looking at them and taking in the sight. I reach out to touch one and I'm surprised when I find that it is cold. I expected it to be hot to the touch, like holding a piece of flame. It's like I'm standing in front of the sun itself.

I think about taking a small piece off the wall, but I don't. It's one thing to use glowworms when we need to, but to have a permanent source of light is to welcome trouble. The Minotaur reacts to light, and it seems to draw him to us like a moth to a flame. This is not always the case, much like the other night. Sometimes, the Minotaur is just hungry.. I wonder why we all run when the Minotaur shows up. He's like a dog with a ball wanting to chase what moves in front of it. He is the dog, and we are the ball.

I look at Kiles and Riley and nod, smiling. There is not much room in this small chamber, and it feels bigger than it is because of all the light given off by the rocks. I could stay in here for much longer, but I'm keen to get out of this small space. It reminds me of places I've hidden. I wonder if I could find my way back here to this place when the Minotaur came, but I would never leave Mother on her own. We could both squeeze in here, but I much prefer the owl room. At least there, the sounds of carnage were muffled.

When we are back in the shadows, my eyes are still full of sunlight. I look back towards the rock crevice and none of the light shines out into the labyrinth. It's a miracle, like finding a star that has fallen to earth. I was a little unsteady on my feet so Kiles and Riley each took me by an arm to steady me. We walked a few steps away from the crevice and they let me go when I was walking well again.

"What did you think?" Riley asks.

"Do you love it?" Kiles asks.

I love that about both of them. They never bring up the fact that I walk with a cane, and we never discuss it. They never ask me what happened, whether I was born this way or if something had occurred, and they never call me broken. I a friend to them both. Most people see the cane first. Kiles and Riley just see *me*.

I nod. "I loved it beyond what mere words can say."

We walk slowly back to the market. It was the area that always drew people, where people gathered, albeit quietly. I wonder why since we are all in hiding anyways. Maybe it's just the need to be around other people. To me, if I want to meet anyone, it would be back there in the sunlight-filled crevice. I could actually see them, take in what they truly looked like before I got used to seeing them in shadows and shades of grey with the occasional bit of light. They had given me a true gift. They had given me light when I thought all that we had was darkness.

I look at their eager faces and feel such fondness for them. I would even go so far as to say that I love them, but I think they already know that. Why else would they give me such a gift? Finally, I answer.

"I can't ever repay you for this," I say. "It was truly amazing. I've never seen anything like it and had no idea that there was something like that room in the labyrinth."

Riley looks pleased. "Isn't it amazing? We just wanted to take you away somewhere. Do you think you could find your way back there?"

I shake my head. "I don't think so, but I'd rather have you both with me to show me where it is. Or we can always go somewhere else next time. You know more of the labyrinth than I do. Besides, it's more fun with friends."

They both look shocked to hear those words from my mouth. I know that had a lot to do with how guarded I am; I didn't want to be hurt and I want love at the same time. I think it's the paradox of the human condition, really. Even in our world, in this dark and earthy tomb-like space, people need love. Even people like me.

I turn away from them, feeling the tears start. Kiles squeezes my shoulder. "Let it out, Roanne," he says. "You don't want to hold onto the hurt she caused you forever. She's not worth that and the hurt will eat away at you bit by bit until nothing is left."

I look at him and wipe away the tears that have fallen. "I don't know how to let it go," I tell them. "I feel like I deserve it somehow."

"No, you don't," Riley says. "No one deserves that. Absolutely no one."

They had been there when it happened. They had seen everything and yet they still talked to me and wanted to know me. "Thank you," I tell them.

"No thanks needed," Riley says. "We got your back."

I link my cane in my arm as we three hold hands and walk together. We don't say anything, there's no need. One of the things I love about Kiles and Riley is that the air is full of things that have already been said instead of things I didn't want to say. There wasn't a need to fill the air with words because they had already been spoken.

CHAPTER THIRTEEN

MOTHER and Dominic aren't there when I get back home.

Dominic likes to take Mother on long walks where they would have hushed conversations. Mother would sometimes yell at him with as much passion that a whisper could muster. I know that they love each other, but there is a lot of anger in my mother. I think she is still angry at Father for getting killed by the Minotaur. It must be hard to go on living for yourself sometimes, but it is even more difficult when you're living for someone else, even if they are a ghost.

She is angry that father is gone, and angry that Dominic takes his life in his hands as well as her heart every time he leaves to go exploring. We know the labyrinth better now because of the work he does; we know some of its secrets and some of the things it contains, the multitude of gardens and waterways available if one is willing to venture far enough, etc. Thanks to Dominic, we know that there are signs of other people living or having lived in the labyrinth, though none have ever shown themselves. When I was a child, we were told that no one but us lived in the labyrinth. As I grew older though, there were signs of other life within these walls. One of my friends found a shoe that could have belonged to anyone, but no one would lay claim to it. I once found a barrette made out of metal and something that looked like crystals. None of the usual people I traded with recognized it. It was only when Dominic went father than any explorer had gone before him that he could confirm that there were other people within the labyrinth.

Mother didn't mean to be angry with Dominic; it was just that she hated to be alone and I knew that she wondered whether she would see him alive agin. There were dangers inside the walls of the maze aside from the Minotaur and she had already lost one husband to the Minotaur. Regardless of what my mother and Dominic were to each other, she didn't want to lose him, too

I wondered if there were groups of people living unseen within the walls of our labyrinth. Would they ever make themselves known? We had enough troubles as it was without other people showing up. There were too many people as it was, or at least it seemed like that to me.

I vow to take the time alone to open the little green book that had led me to the key and eventually to the little blue book. I put both of them together, for they seem to be brothers. Why else would they be hidden the way they were in the labyrinth? What do they contain?

I start with the little green book. It's bigger than my whole hand outstretched, whereas the blue book is small enough to fit in my palm. I flip the green book open, and I find that it's a history. Someone has taken the time to write about the construction of the labyrinth. It seems to cover everything from the conception of the labyrinth itself to the sigils that mark its walls (though not the secrets that they hold) and the type of stone that was used. It doesn't show me the exit, though, which is something I realize that I was hoping for by the time I finish reading it.

I look around me to make sure that no one is near and take a glowworm out of the jar and place it in another so that I have light to read by. Their light is not bright enough to tempt the Minotaur. I take out the journal and the charcoal that I got from

Cheryl's stand. As I read, I begin to make notes, so in a way I am making a third book. I don't know if any other books are hidden in the labyrinth. I do hope that either the green book or the blue book will give me a clue as to what the key does.

I look at the key by the light of the glowworm. There are markings on the key. It has the end that looks like a feather, but all throughout the key, there are streams of colour, lines like veins running its length. The feathers shape is made from black iron, like the sigils, but there are other colours here too. The veins and the feathers are the same colours as the books, but there is also one other colour. There is green, blue, and a brilliant red. I try to picture the red book in my mind and conjure up the image of an old and dusty journal, much like the books I have now.

I take a moment to flip through the little blue book and see that it's not a journal, but rather that someone has written a story of some kind. It's typed out like all of the other books I've read. I wonder why it was hidden. I can't help but think that these two books are linked and that though one contains a story and the other someone's thoughts, they are both equally important. They must be, why would both of them be hidden?

This makes me think of Mother. She knew about the room that was below ground after she pressed on the owl's eye. The Oracle had known where the crane was, too. What did they know about the other animals contained within the labyrinth? What tricks did those animals play? I thought of the ones I had seen (bee, otter, seagull, heron, tiger, elephant and more) and I wondered if each of them held a secret, or were some of them just animals? The little green book had led me to the Crane. I wondered if it or the blue book held any more secrets for me?

I heard Mother and Dominic's footsteps close by. I only just had time to put everything in my bag and to grab the book of

Shakespeare's works so I could pretend that was what I'd been reading. I don't know why I was keeping this from Mother, but I wanted this to be my secret for now, at least until I read what was in the books. I feel bad about keeping my activity clandestine, but I want to find out what the books say before I share it with anyone else.

Mother comes in and sees me reading Shakespeare by the light of a glowworm. She smiles at me and gives me a hug. She smells of flowers. I wonder if Dominic has found a new garden close by. She was smiling, so that was good. Their talk must have gone well, at least this time.

"Be careful, Poppet. Reading for too long will hurt your eyes," Mother says.

"I've read in the dark all my life," Dominic told her. "It hasn't hurt me any."

"And yet, you have trouble finding your way home," She says this with a smile, so I assumed she was teasing.

"Hush now, let me work on getting dinner ready. I'm afraid it's just vegetables and fish again tonight. They didn't have much on offer at the market," Dominic tells me softly. He looks down at the book I'm reading. "Shakespeare? A marvellous writer and well worth reading. Good choice, Roanne. I've always admired the way he could tell a story. That man could travel without leaving his mind. I know you have the same aspirations." He ruffles my hair, mostly because he knows that I hate it.

Mother and Dominic work at putting dinner together, setting a pot to boil over a low fire we had in the corner of our encampment. I watch them as they move about and to me it looks like they are dancing. It's strange that a couple who argue all the time can be so in love with each other. Maybe Janice and I should have argued more? I'm unsure of what to think about that. It's not in me to argue with those I love.

I am reading Shakespeare's play *Much Ado About Nothing* and it strikes me that for a play with nothing in the title, a lot happens in it. I prefer Shakespeare's comedies. We need whatever laughter we can find in the dark.

Mother rinses the dishes in a jug that we keep for this purpose. It has a wooden cover and inside I can see the water looks like tar as it moves in the shadows. Mother dunks the dishes in the water for a rinse, then dries them on her skirt. The dishes will be clean at least, even if they are covered by the same dust which covers our clothes.

They plate the fish, and we all sit on the ground around the table. I place the glowworm on the table between us. It makes the dinner and the people sitting around it almost happy. I pass Mother the pot of vegetables, carrots, and radishes, and I take the fish from her. I'm surprised to find that I'm hungry. Perhaps it's my general moroseness regarding my state in life, but I am rarely hungry. The only thing that can tempt me is certain sweets. My mother knows this but there is little if anything sweet within these walls.

I take a portion of fish and add is to my carrots and radishes. I like it because the meal looks wholesome and full of colour, though slightly dulled because of the dark we live in. I like to imagine what it would look like in the light. The glowworm helps a little, but it's not enough. There is never enough light.

There is little talking when we eat. I often feel the air is filled with words not said and conversations yet to be had. It's like with Kiles and Riley though, the silence is not uncomfortable. Finally, Mother breaks the silence. She turns to me and smiles. "I feel like we left you alone all day," she says. "What have you been up to?"

I shrug. "Not very much," I tell her. "I saw Kiles and Riley."

Dominic grins and I can see his teeth in the dark. "What were those two up to? They're always looking for trouble."

"Not always, only most of the time," I say.

"Did the three of you get into trouble?" Mother asks She knows Kiles and Riley well.

"We just went exploring." I want to keep the crevice filled with light to myself. It feels like a secret shared between Kiles, Riley and me, aside from which, they had asked me to keep the cervice a secret. It felt brighter to me because of the fac that it was a secret, almost as if the shine grew brighter in the darkness of my mind I wonder if I will just become filled to the brim with secrets and eventually float away. I wonder if I'll be able to see the sun then, or if I will just end up floating forever on the ceiling of the labyrinth.

"You were careful?" Mother asks. "I know that those boys go to so many different spots in this godforsaken place that many fear to tread."

"It's okay Mother. We just looked at different rock formations." I figured a little bit of the truth wouldn't hurt.

"Well, as long as they kept you safe, then that's okay. I worry about you in here Poppet."

I let out a small sigh. "I worry about everyone in here."

Dominic put a hand on mine. "Don't carry that kind of burden, Roanne. You don't need to worry about anyone else aside from yourself."

I raised an eyebrow, a gesture that I was sure was lost to the darkness for its subtlety. "Really? Not even you and Mother?"

"Okay," he smiled at me. "You can worry about your mother and me, but that's it. You already look like you carry the world on your shoulders, you don't need the added weight of everyone else upon you."

I had never thought of it like that. "Okay," I said. "I won't."

We finish the rest of our dinner just as the soft footsteps of a visitor can be heard. Mother is putting the dishes into the wash pail when Hugo walks into our enclave of walls. He stands there awkwardly, and I can tell he unsure of the welcome he will receive. I don't know what to do except stare at him dumbfounded.

Mother eyes him warily. She knows that he was involved in the drama that happened with Janice, but not what part he played. "Yes, Hugo?" she asks.

"I was wondering if I could speak with Roanne." His voice is softer than a whisper and he shakes with every word. I can tell he was aware of the kind of welcome that he would receive.

"I don't know if I want her going anywhere with you," Mother says.

"It's okay," I say quietly.

Dominic gives me a look of knowing. "Are you sure?"

"Yes, it's okay," I say again. "I won't be long."

I avoid looking at Hugo as we leave the walls and pass by the phoenix. I run my hands along the wrought ironwork of the birds' wings and continue onward, still not looking at Hugo. I'm not upset exactly, but I don't want to look at him until I hear what he has to say and why he's here. I don't know Hugo that well so I'm not sure if he's here as friend or foe. I don't know what his visit to me is supposed to mean, if anything.

I lead the way, knowing that he will follow. I don't want him to have any control over the situation. I need to maintain that control because it was something that Janice took from me. She took everything from me, and I'm still not sure how I feel about talking to him. I can feel the shard in my chest sink deeper within me.

I stop walking when we reach one of the small brooks flowing through the labyrinth. Nature always takes back what was taken from it. Nature always finds a way. I always walk to the water wherever I can find it because its sound, however soft, brings me comfort. I spent a lot of time just sitting by this brook when Janice and I parted. It seemed right to bring Hugo here, too.

I stand, not looking at him and waited for him to speak. I know I am being difficult, but I am not about to make it easy for him. I can hear him taking deep breaths, trying to ready himself to speak. I look at him out of the corner of my eye and he looks tortured. This is far from the calm version of him that I saw when we were all walking towards the celebration of life for Persephone. That seems so long ago, and it is odd that I hadn't seen him since. I wonder if Hugo and Janice had been holed up together somewhere. I tried to tell myself that I didn't care, but I knew I was fooling myself. The shard throbbed in my chest, and I tried to ignore it.

"I came to say thank you," Hugo says finally.

I am a little shocked. It isn't what I had been expecting at all. "Whatever for?" I ask. I look at him finally. His dark eyes looked back into mine and his dark brown hair was falling into his face. He brushes it with his hand, the curls springing back to where they had been before. He lets out a breath.

"Thank you for the other night," He says.

"I didn't do anything the other night." I still didn't understand what he was on about.

"Thank you for saving Janice," he says. "She told me what you did the other night when the Minotaur attacked. That you took her into the hidden room with your mother." He sees the look of panic in my eyes. "She didn't tell me where it was or how to get to it, don't worry. She did tell me that you saved her and tried to make her comfortable."

"More like she latched on to me and wouldn't let go," I say a little waspishly.

"Even so, you took her with you," Hugo says. "You didn't have to. You could have left her where she was or thrown her off. It's what I would have done."

I'm actually shocked to hear this. "What do you mean?"

"If she had done to me what she did to you, I would have thrown her hand off my arm, let alone spend an evening with her in an underground room. I would have left her to fend for herself."

I'm even more shocked to hear this, but I don't let it show on my face. I don't want him to know that he's made an impression on me, that he has actually found a way through my armor. I look away from him so he can't see the surprise in my eyes, so that he can't read how what he has just said has affected me. "I didn't realize that she told you anything about what happened."

"She wouldn't tell me at first. I had to pull it out of her and little bits of it came but not everything. I finally told her that I would leave her if she didn't tell me."

"Why do you care so much about what she did?"

"Because she still loves you. I had to know what happened to make her pull away from you."

I'm so stunned I don't know what to say. I think of my journal and pen and how, if I had them with me, the words would fly out of me, desperate to be on the page and display my thoughts back to me. Right now, with no pen and paper in sight, the words are stuck in my throat, and I breathe and breathe again so that they might fly out when I exhale.

I manage to squeeze the words out. "She no longer loves me. No one who did what she did could love me." I look back at

Hugo and see only kindness, not judgement, in his eyes. They are so human and so warm that it's no wonder Janice always found her eyes drawn to him.

"Sometimes we hurt the ones that we love the most," he says. "It's something my mother used to tell me when I was hurting from some slight or insult. I know she loves you. I see it in her eyes every time she talks about you."

Again, I find myself at a loss for words. The shard feels a little looser in my chest, however. "Tell her that she can stop loving me," I say. "I don't love her anymore."

"We both know that's a lie. I can see it in *your* eyes right now."

I guess my walls weren't built strongly enough if he can see my emotions that clearly. "It hurts," is all I can say. "I don't want to hurt anymore."

"Love hurts sometimes."

"Is this another of your mother's sayings?" I ask him.

"Yes, it was. She was always fond of her sayings; she told them to me often enough. I think she always knew that she was going to die young, and she wanted me to be prepared for what life had in store and to give me guidance for when she wasn't here."

I knew that Hugo's mother had died quite young. She was only thirty. Her celebration of life had been horrible because Hugo, who was only ten at the time, had been wailing silently in front of us all. I remember that night. His mouth was open, tears were sliding down his face and he showed every aspect of screaming but no sound escaped his lips; just because we didn't hear him make any sound didn't mean that all of us didn't hear his scream inside our own heads.

"She was a remarkable woman," I tell him. "I liked your mother. She always had a kind word for me, and she often lent an ear when I was in need of one."

Nodding, Hugo says, "She was good like that. She tried to help everyone."

"Is that why you're telling me about Janice? You want to help?" I try to keep the steel from my voice.

"I suppose so," Hugo says. "I wanted you to know that she still thinks of you even if she can't say it…and I wanted to thank you."

I nod. "You're welcome." I don't think there is anything left to say, and I move to go, but Hugo stops me with a gentle touch.

"Let go of your hurt," He says. "She's not worth holding on to all that pain."

I let out a mostly silent snort. "But you're in love with her," I tell him. "How can you say something like that?"

"No one is worth holding on to the pain they caused you. You need to let it go, Roanne. You carry enough pain as it is."

"How do you know what I carry?"

"I know pain. I can see it in the way you pull away from touch, or the way you carry yourself when you think no one is watching. The pain is weighing you down, Roanne. You need to let it go. No one is worth that," he says again.

I nod, no words finding their way past my lips. There are tears sliding down my face, but I don't make any move to wipe them away. What would be the point? He gives my arm a squeeze and walks away into the darkness of the labyrinth. I stand there, feeling the shard with every breath. It's loose inside my chest and if I breathe in deeply and exhale, I can feel it release further.

Standing there, I make up my mind. I close my eyes and reach inside of myself with my mind. I can see the shard lodged within my lungs. I can see it twinkling in the darkness of my body, trapped between the bones of my ribs. I admire how beautiful it is, but how hurtful it has been to me already. With deft fingers, I pry the shard free, careful not to nick or tear anything within me more than it has already been torn. It looks like a slice of diamond or even the stars, and I hold it in my hands for a moment, letting the light that filters into me through the pores of my skin shine upon it.

There is a pain that runs through me that causes my eyes to open and the picture in my mind fades. Fresh pain rolls through me and I begin to choke, I drop my cane and clutch my throat uselessly, trying to massage my throat open once more. I fall to my knees in the dirt, the sound of water nearby growing louder because it's so close to me. I hold myself up with my arms and retch into the dirt, trying to free what is in my throat, trying to breathe, trying to get air into my lungs which have already been hurt so much.

With one final cough, I feel whatever has been choking me slide free and I open my mouth to let it fall out. It lands in the dirt and twinkles up at me, almost as if it is winking.

I look at the glass shard and marvel at it. I pick it up to determine if it's real and it is, the glass cutting into my finger. I look at it knowing that I will never tell anyone of this, that I can't.

I stand shakily, clutching the shard of glass in my hand. I make my way to the water, careful not to get to close. I hold out my hand above the water and open it up, almost as though I am presenting a greeting, and let the shard fall into the water below.

I stand there for a moment wondering at what just happened and then begin to make my way home.

CHAPTER FOURTEEN

I felt different walking back home.

There was a gaping hole where the shard had been. I can feel the air moving through it and realize how much my pain was suffocating me. I reach up to touch the spot in my chest where I'd seen the shard. It had been right behind the breast plate. I take a deep breath in and can hear the rattling of my breath as it moves through the hole. I knew that it would take time for it to heal, and that was okay. I had time now.

I knew that the healing wouldn't happen overnight, but the majority of my pain had been expunged from me. If I hadn't seen the shard, I would not even believe it myself. I wondered if the change in me was visible from the outside, or if something in me had begun to shine. I wondered if the hole that had been left open was wide enough for a seed. I thought of a myth I had read in the library. Eleanor had let me read the book one afternoon. In the myth, a woman had not heeded her brother's warning. She had swallowed a small seed which had brought darkness to the world. I wondered if my seed would be different, if I had swallowed a seed that was full of healing white light. It felt as if something was growing inside me now that it had the room to grow.

With each step I took, I was walking away from the shard which had been my constant companion for so long. A part of me wanted to go back and retrieve the shard from the water, believing that I somehow deserved the pain. I knew that this was wrong of course.

When I arrive back home, Mother and Dominic are sitting in our living area. I know this space has been called a living room from looking at books in the library. We didn't have a whole room, so I call it our living area. We have a thick pallet filled with leaves and vines that we use as a seat during the day, and it became my bed during the night. I am fortunate; most people in the labyrinth slept on the dirt floor. Mother has her own pallet in her section of the enclave. We were fortunate to have such a large space to call our own. It makes it feel like a home of some sort, though the word *home* makes me think of comfort and security, and there is little of that to be found within these walls.

I sit down beside my mother, and she wraps her arm around me. With her free hand, she is reading one of the books I received from Cheryl. There are parts of the living area where light filters in, enough to read by. Mother is reading a book called *To Kill a Mockingbird*. I don't know why you would want to kill a harmless creature. I will have to read it once she's finished.

Dominic is pouring over some of the maps he has created. He looks concerned, but I want to speak up regardless. He was always telling me that a question not asked is a missed opportunity for knowledge. I sit there, contemplating whether or not to voice my question. I listen to the sound of people talking and can hear my mother breathing beside me. I can hear the gentle sound of her heartbeat, and I am lulled by it. I hear one of the birds that live within the walls let out a soft and musical note that sounds like song.

"Why do we live here?" I ask quietly.

Mother puts her book down and Dominic stops looking at his maps. "What do you mean, Poppet?" Mother asks.

"I mean, why do we live here? Surely somebody before us has found a way out. Some people who live here have found their way *in*, so surely, we can find our way *out*?"

"The maze doesn't work like that. Once you're in the maze, you can never get out. That's the way it works, you see," Dominic says.

"No, I don't see," I tell him. "Haven't you been able to find a way out of here with all the exploring you do? Hasn't anyone?"

Mother lets out a sigh. It's full of sadness and I feel a little bad for bringing this up but, I need to know. "Sweetheart, we've been through this all before."

"I've looked for a way out," Dominic says. "I was born in this labyrinth just as you were, and I've been looking for a way out for decades now. I know that there is a way *in*, but I don't know that there is a way *out*."

"Maybe you haven't gone far enough?" I say meekly. "Is there anywhere you haven't been?"

He lets out a little laugh. "There is everywhere that I haven't been." Standing, Dominic holds out his hand and I take it. He leads me to the front of our enclosure. Looking out at the walls of stone that are in front of him, he scans twists and turns of the labyrinth. "I have been trying to find my way out for as long as I've been in here. When I entered, I had a leather rope attached to my belt so that I could follow it back to the entrance. I remember exploring a little ways for a few minutes, but when I tried to go back and bring others with me, I pulled on the leather which should have been taunt and it was lose. I followed the leather rope as far as I could, making sure not to pull it any more towards me, I did not want to erase my path to the start of the maze." There was a panicked look to his eyes even now, though he had been in the labyrinth for so long, it was hard to remember a time when he wasn't in my life.

"What happened when you found the entrance?" I asked, somehow already knwoign the answer.

Dominic shook his head. "I never found it. When I found the start of the rope, it looked like it head been torn or gnawed or like it had been cut. Looking around me from where I stood that day, I realized how far I was in the labyrinth and no closer to finding the entrance."

I nodded. Everyone who had come into the maze never found their way out again. It was as if the walls themselves were the gatekeepers of it's secrets and they didn't want just anyone knowing what they were."

I nodded and took his hand. I didn't want to hug Dominic, but I did want to offer him comfort in some way. He deserved that much.

"You know that there are hundreds and hundreds of walls in front of us that make up the maze?" He said this softly as if just realizing it himself.

"Yes," I tell him.

"Well, there are also hundreds more, thousands more. The maze defies size and shape and concept. I have travelled to many different places, some miles from here and others days away. I have never been able to find an exit," he says. "I have never found a way out."

"But there *has* to be a way. There just has to be." I try to stop my voice from sounding wary, but I am not successful. The labyrinth feels too close, too dark after I let go of the shard. I wonder if this left over emotion from the shard that I carried with me for so long. For a split second, I wish for it back as it seemed to be taking up all the room in me, leaving little for other emotions. I know that leaving it to the water was the right thing to do, but I don't like these emotions. I am not fond of fear.

Dominic sighs and looked at me full on. He always does that with me; look at me in the eyes so that I could see his true self. That was one of the things he had taught me, that people always carried who they really are inside their eyes. That if I really wanted to know who a person was, all I had to do was maintain eye contact. That was hard to do in the shadows of the labyrinth, but not impossible, seeing as we were close enough to each other to whisper. I'd seen the secret that Janice was carrying even if she couldn't say it. I could see it lurking there within her, growing before the words had to come out.

"I've looked high and low and everywhere in between," he says. "Why do you think I've been exploring the labyrinth so much? I've gone farther and further into the depths of this place than anyone else before or since. I've discovered wonders and amazing sights, I've seen rivers and oceans of space, gardens full of exotic flowers, animals of every description, but I have never been able to find a way out."

"How are you able to find your way back every time?" Mother asks. I know that she worries that Dominic won't be able to find his way home. I was worried about that too, but I knew that he had to go on his adventures much as I felt the need to write. I write when I was moved to, much as Dominic explored when he needed to.

"I just follow you home," he says. Dominic looks at the both of us. "Wherever you are, I can find you. You are both my touchstones, and my heart is with you." He looks at my mother first and then me.

My mother blushes. "That's impossible."

Dominic shrugs. "It doesn't make it any less true." He kisses her hand, and I let them share a moment between themselves. It feels like a gift to see this love in front of me, especially now that the shard has been pulled from my chest.

When Dominic looks back to me, his eyes have grown serious. "I don't know how to get out of here. No one does. I urge you not to go looking for an exit. It's a fruitless journey. I've been looking for years, and I have yet to find anything except wonders."

"Then how did we come to be here?" I ask.

"No one knows, ," Mother answers. "There are myths of course, those are rampant around here especially with all the things that we've found. All those books and items must have belonged to someone. The question of who they were has haunted many people." She ruffles my hair. "What makes you ask these questions?" she asks. "This isn't like you. Did Kiles and Riley say something?"

Truthfully, I've been thinking of it for a while, especially since finding the books. I want to ask who left them here and why did they hide them, but I don't ask. Instead, I say, "I'm okay Mother. I just wanted to write a story about it."

"Don't use too much paper," she says. She's right to warn me, blank paper is scarce in the labyrinth. That's why having a whole journal, even with a few sheets filled in, is a big deal. I clutch my bag to me.

"I won't Mother," I say.

She nods and goes back to her knitting, leaving her book face down beside her and Dominic goes back to his maps. Part of me wonders if he is trying to draw the whole layout of the maze so that he can lay it out and look at every twist and turn it contains, giving himself a different view at the world he seems to know so well.

I carefully pull the green book, the one that started me on my weird quest, out of my bag. While they are both distracted by their tasks, I delve into the book. I resist flipping the pages like a flipbook again and instead turn to the first page. The handwriting in the journal is scratchy and the ink looks aged, but it's still readable.

I explore the little green book. It's a long read, but fascinating. It really does relate the history of the labyrinth and its construction from the ground up. It talks of the materials used and the plans made. I had assumed that the labyrinth had been here since time began, that it had been found and sealed up again, but the fact that it was actually built by someone is astounding to me. There are a few words bolded or underlined, but mostly the writing just flows over the page. It talks about improvements to the stone to be used and the method of building the walls. It says nothing about the Minotaur. I can only assume that he was added afterwards.

I had thought we lived in an old Greek maze, that we were living in a creation which time had forgotten, although that can't possibly be the case. What about everything we've found, all of the books and clothes and sometimes a child's toy? It had to have been created by someone more recently in time.

It's a curious book, full of lists of materials and what they used during the construction, how they would cover the maze, etc., and it cuts off after about fifty pages, however there is one line at the end that makes my heart stop and then start again. I wonder if Mother and Dominic can hear my breathing or my heart, they have both grown so loud in my head. I look at the words again and marvel at them, tracing my fingers over the letters.

I have planned the exit.

CHAPTER FIFTEEN

I *have planned the exit.*

A thrum moves through my body, and I look up to see if the world has changed or if time has suddenly stood still, if Mother and Dominic know that I have discovered something. They are the same as they were, Mother absorbed in her knitting and Dominic in his maps, each of them in their own little worlds. They didn't notice the shift that happened in mine.

After those forty pages, the rest were left blank. The history of the labyrinth was incomplete. I wondered why there was no mention of the owl room or the other animals found all over the labyrinth. Surely those were created when the maze was built? I carefully flip back through the pages, but there is no mention of the animals, only notes on the building materials and the types of supports required, the land formations at the time and the soil composition. All very boring stuff. I think of the owl room, and I know that Mother said it was my father who had shown it to her, but how did he know of its existence?

None of this makes any sense. Who drew the little stick men on the edges of the pages? They must have known what the crane concealed. Perhaps they were the ones who put the key inside the wall? My head is full of questions, and I want to get up and walk, to move and feel the air around my skin, but I don't. I stay put and stay still. I do not want to draw attention. I close the book and long to pull out my journal to make notes.

However, as soon as I close the little green book, I know that I need to delve further.

I open the book again and I flip through the rest of the blank pages one by one and notice something. There appear to be indentations on some of the pages that look like writing. I trace my fingers along the indentations. I'm trying to figure out what they are and where they came from. I wonder if I take my charcoal and rub it over the pages whether or not it will show me what is hidden?

I turn back to the other pages, and I look at the drawings that are interspersed throughout the words. I can see partial plans for the labyrinth, drawings of different animals in different inks, small doodles of leaves and insects along the edges of some pages. There is one very convincing drawing of a glowworm, and I wonder how long they have been used here within these walls. I also wonder what story is contained within the blue book. I will have to wait for a moment of privacy before I dive into that. I also wonder if there is anything important to be found in the indentations on the previous pages. I slide the green book back into my bag just as Mother sits down beside me.

She strokes my hair. "You're so quiet, Poppet. Are you okay?"

I shrug. For lack of anything to say to explain my silence, I say, "I'm just thinking about Janice."

Mother turns to look at me, her face hard. "Don't spend another moment thinking about her."

"It's okay," I tell her. "I was able to let go of a lot of the hurt this morning." I don't tell her about the shard that is now in the water. It's not necessary. "I let out a lot of the pain I've been carrying."

She rubs my hands. "Good, Roanne. You don't want to hold on to any of that, she's not worth it."

I know she's hoping that I will tell her what happened, that I will finally share with her what Janice did. She was the one who found me crying so hard that I could not speak, sobbing so silently that I'm sure I looked like some kind of banshee. Even though the cries and the screaming were silent, she could hear them, and she could see them in my eyes. I didn't speak for a full day afterward and I wouldn't move from my pallet, choosing instead to turn my back on everything. All my mother could do was to cover me with a blanket and whisper calming words to me softly. I think at one point, she took me into her arms and rocked me, but I can't be sure. I don't remember much from the day or so after everything happened.

Now isn't the time to go into that. I don't know if it will ever be the time to tell my mother what happened. I've shared little bits and pieces with Kiles and Riley, but of course they were there, a lot of people were. I'm just thankful that Mother and Dominic weren't, that they didn't witness what happened and that no one has thought to let my mother in on what took place that day. I'm thankful to everyone, even if I have difficulty saying it. I think of Cheryl in the market, how concerned she was for me. I should go back and hug her warmly, or try to, instead of just accept her hugs. I have to say something to Mother, anything. I'm not sure what and am about to speak some words of nonsense when an ear-splitting shriek fills the air.

I know it's the Minotaur, I can feel it in my bones, but the scream is different this time. We have become used to its sounds and thunders, but this wail sounds different. It sounds to me as though the Minotaur is in pain. I wonder what has happened to it, what has caused this sound to escape its maw. I shiver and Mother pulls me close, then Dominic is on the other side of me, their knitting and maps forgotten. I think of the little blue book and the words that it contains yet unread, I grab my satchel and check for the books. I can feel the green book sitting next to the blue book and my journal, and I hear the clink of the key. The most important things I have are contained in this bag and regardless of whether the Minotaur attacks, I will take it with me. I place the strap around my shoulder, tightening it as a precaution. I do not want to leave what I've learned for someone else to find.

The ground shakes beneath us and we all huddle closer as if it is our closeness that will save us. Mother's grip on me is like a vice and I'm thankful that Janice isn't around to use her vice-like grip on me. I don't know if I would take her with me now; I no longer feel that I deserve the pain that she left me with. I wished Hugo well with her.

The ground shook again and the Minotaur let out an eerie scream that sent shivers along my skin. This scream goes on for some time, echoing off the walls and ceiling of the labyrinth. Then the screams became shorter and more guttural and my whole body knew fear. I looked at Mother and Dominic, but they just shook their heads. I could see my eyes in theirs and all were filled with fear. The Minotaur had never made such noises before. It had always been the same type of screams just before it came to feed. These were far more horrible, and after the shivers subsided, I started really listening to the different sounds that the Minotaur was making.

As the screams continued, changing from the short harsh bursts back to wailing screams, it occurred to me where I had heard these sounds before. I thought back to what had happened with Janice, to what she had done to me, and the mess she had left me in. I remembered lying on the ground, the cold earth pressed against my cheek, as I screamed inside my head. At that moment, I could hear my wails as they grew louder and louder and reverberated through my body like waves. I had screamed inside of myself for what felt like hours, my screams quieting to whimpers until I remembered what had happened all over again and my screams increased once more.

I had made sounds like the ones that the Minotaur was making right now which let me to another realization.

The Minotaur could be *hurt*.

As Mother clutched me harder and harder the longer the screaming went on; I wondered who or what had possibly hurt the Minotaur. How could you hurt something which had withstood the passage of time and had never died? Mother said that the Minotaur had been alive since before time began. How did it end up here? Did they build the labyrinth to keep us trapped here, or was its purpose to trap the beast?

All these thoughts and more ran around in my head. I made sure that my thoughts were loud to drown out the sound of the screams. The one thought I kept swirling back to however was that the Minotaur could be hurt; *the Minotaur could be hurt*. It didn't matter how, what mattered was that it was possible. It wasn't this massive indestructible colossus. It could feel pain just like we did. I wondered, what had caused it?

After a few hours, the screams stopped and the ground shook once more, a violent thrashing that shook the labyrinth. I heard a few walls fall and one person cried out softly. I stilled, waiting for the Minotaur's attack which usually followed such a sound. There was nothing but the sounds of the wind, the flap of bird wings, and the occasional whimper from the Minotaur that sounded like a sigh. Then, like the wind, the sound of the whimpering went away.

We stayed in our embrace of three for a moment longer. No one seemed inclined to let go. That we had heard the Minotaur scream and no one had been hurt, no attack had come—this was unheard of. I couldn't believe it. My heart was easing its frantic beat, and my breath had finally calmed.

I look at Mother and Dominic and panic is still alive in their eyes. I know that it is alive in mine, too. All the while, I was thinking the same thought and it repeated over and over again in my mind: it can be hurt, it can be hurt, it can be hurt. It was like a mantra which brought me relief. Then the rational part of my mind brought all of that to a crashing halt with another thought.

To hurt the Minotaur, I would have to find it first. There is no way of knowing how big the labyrinth is. Dominic had been studying and drawing maps of it for years and he said that it always went beyond what he had seen. As a young child, I couldn't believe that the labyrinth was so big, but my years within it had shown me that it went on as far as the eye could see and then some. I'm not brave or foolish like Dominic, Kiles or Riley, and there was never any way that Mother would let me explore that far. Also, I was afraid of what the labyrinth could hide.

I hold on to my mother and Dominic, feeling safety in their grasp and knowing that, for now at least, we were safe.

CHAPTER SIXTEEN

I was coming back from the market when I saw Gabriel.

He was talking with Sunita. She was gesturing and whispering loudly. I knew what they were talking about. It was all that anyone could talk about. The were speculating on what had caused the Minotaur to scream so loudly and for so long. It was the same subject on everyone's lips, and I couldn't blame them. It had been almost more frightening to hear the sounds of the Minotaur without the attack which usually followed. It had been on the lips of many in the market today. They wondered if it meant that the next attack to come would be more fierce or more brutal.

Sunita turns when I approach, and for a moment I saw a look of fear on her face, then it relaxes. Her look of fear disappears, and she smiles. It was amazing how much joy made her look beautiful. "Oh, Roanne! It's you!" she says.

I give her a small smile in return. "I'm not the Minotaur," I say.

"I'm sorry, I know that you're not. I'm just so jumpy!" she says. "I wasn't able to sleep a wink last night, I kept waiting for the Minotaur to come after us. It always has when it makes noises like that. I can't understand why it didn't attack us," she says in wonderment. "Why didn't it attack us, Roanne? Do you have any ideas?"

I shake my head, keen to keep my theory to myself. What good would it do to raise people's hopes when we had no expectation of finding or hurting it? "I have no idea," I say. "Maybe it was mating?"

Gabriel makes a face. "I hate the idea of that beast mating," he says. "It's bad enough that we must deal with one of them, the thought of two of them leaves me cold. I keep looking up to see if I can somehow spot the Minotaur, but all I can see is darkness." He brings the violin he holds closer to his chest, almost as if cradling a small child.

We all think of Gabriel as the composer. There are no strings on the violin, but that doesn't matter. When I watched him play, sliding an imaginary bow across the non-existent strings, he moves with his whole body. It doesn't matter that we can't hear the music. What matters is that *he* could. Whenever I saw him playing, I would watch his body move and sway to the music, and if I asked him, he would quietly hum the melody. Gabriel thought more in terms of musical notes than with words. The notes, placed just so on the page, made more sense to him than letters which formed words and human speech. He was just more comfortable with music. Notes had no way of hiding thoughts or telling tales. They simply were.

His violin is his touchstone, his comfort. I don't know where within the labyrinth he found it, but I did know that he was one of the few who had somehow found his way into the labyrinth from the outside. Gabriel said that he had been lost and that the labyrinth had made him more lost still. It didn't bother him much. Gabriel said that he had never been very good at directions and was always getting lost in the world of before. When he first arrived, people wanted to know more about the world beyond. However, over time Gabriel had lost memories of his travels, like he left small pebbles of thought to safeguard them but now couldn't find them.

I have known Sunita for a long time. We had gone to school together but never really spoken to each other. We were friendly even if we weren't friends as such. People kept to their own and to those close to them. It was just the way things were done within these walls. I wish I had known her better. I knew that she had a brother and a mother who were taken by the Minotaur and that she lived with her father. She had been kind to me after what had happened with Janice. She had been there and had seen everything that took place. We had never spoken of it, and I preferred it that way. It was not a time I wanted to revisit too often, especially now that I had let go of the pain. I was a little afraid that talking about it would shape a new shard to replace the old one, the wound was still so freshly healed. I suppose it would be easier to talk with her about what happened. She was there after all, and it would be easier than telling my mother. Thankfully though, she had never broached the subject. I wonder if it made her feel as uncomfortable as it made me.

I respect her a lot though. She doesn't treat me as a broken thing after the abuse of that day. A lot of people began to talk to me as if I were senile or somewhat crazy, using gentle hand motions and lots of sad looks to punctuate their words. Sunita didn't treat me any differently than she had before. I felt that she saw me, *truly* saw me, which is rare inside these walls. It made me bemoan our lack of a relationship, but that feeling dissipated when I made a promise to myself to make more of an attempt at friendship with her.

"I'm not sure why it didn't attack us," I say. "We were lucky though. It's never done that before in all my years inside the labyrinth."

"You know," Gabriel says. "I think that was the first kind of music I heard."

"What, the Minotaur's screams?" Sunita asks.

"Yes," Gabe ran his fingers along the wood of his violin. They keep running over a nick in the wood that looked like teeth marks. "I don't remember much from before, but I think I worked in music. When I first came into the labyrinth, I didn't hear the birdsong or the babbling of the water. I heard the screaming of the Minotaur, only I didn't know what was making the sound at the time. To me, it sounded primal and hypnotic, and I felt that my own internal screams matched its outward ones. I could feel the notes within me as it raged. The crumbling of the walls of the labyrinth were the bass and the quiet noises of people in panic were the undercurrent of notes. As I walked into the labyrinth, it was like my body was becoming alive to music as it hadn't before."

He often spoke like this, saying that he heard music in the most unlikely of places, but this was the first time that I heard him speak of the Minotaur in such a way. Perhaps it was because of talk like this that made most people want to say away from him, but I understood him. There was nothing more musical to me than when I moved my charcoal or lead across the page and was able to get my thoughts flowing from my head and onto the paper. In a way, I thought that we were both composers, but I kept my music to myself, content to let my thoughts out on the paper instead of in music no one could hear. I wondered if Gabriel wrote down his compositions or if they remained forever in his head. I pictured his mind full of notes that have never been played, much as mine was often filled with words yet to be written.

"That's wonderful," I tell him. "It makes the Minotaur sound almost beautiful."

Sunita made a face. "I would never think of the beast as beautiful."

"Not the beast itself," I say. "But the sounds it makes."

She made another face. "Nope, not going to happen. You two are both artistic in some way and I'm just a realist and a survivor."

I blush. It feels wonderful to be included in the same company as Gabriel, though I don't know if I deserve the comparison. "Thank you, Sunita," I say. "That's kind of you."

"Nothing kind about the truth," she says. "Walk back with me to the market? I heard that Ash has some new stuff at her stall. I'd love the company."

I know that Sunita doesn't like to go anywhere alone, and I often feel the same way, however Mother always tells me that I have to be comfortable in my surroundings. I can't be afraid of what hasn't happened yet, she says; I should only move forward and look back at what I had accomplished.

We all began to head back, Gabriel leading the way. I could tell from the way he was walking that he was composing something in his head. His steps change when he was doing this, and it looks as if he's stepping out each note so that it took hold in his mind. I know from past observances of him that he is lost to us for a little while. I don't mind. I love it when he gives in to his creativity. There is so little to be joyous about in the labyrinth. Who am I to begrudge him the song that was playing in his head all for a few moments of conversation?

Sunita and I walk slowly behind Gabriel. When she reaches out to take my hand, I let her. She is also not one for hugs, but I'm grateful when she takes my hand. It feels like we were finding a way to bond after being adrift in the same ocean for so long. In this moment, walking along the pathways surrounded by walls that went on forever, it feels like Sunita is my life preserver and keeping me from being swept away into the water.

With every step we take, I feel a tsunami waking within me. I feel safe with Sunita but even so, I am afraid that the tsunami could overtake us both. I look at her out of the corner of my eye and see that she is looking at me, her own face full of concern. I want to look away, to run, to scream at her. She is my preserver, and she could save me from myself. I stop walking and lock her in the eyes. If I don't say anything, I will lose the words within myself. Though I appreciate the fact that Sunita didn't say anything about that day, it appeared that being so close to someone who had witnessed the events that had taken place had somehow loosened my tongue.

She squeezes my hand. "It's okay, Roanne."

I take a breath. This was the last thing I had expected. "What's okay?"

"I know that you're still messed up about what happened. That's okay. It must bother you being so close to me."

I shake my head. "I don't know what you mean."

"I stood by and watched her. I didn't do anything. I let her treat you like garbage in front of everyone. That's not right. I don't know how you can stand to be around me right now. I would make myself sick if the roles were reversed."

I wonder how long she wanted to say this, how long she had kept these words inside her. If it were me, I knew that I could keep the words within me, let them build until they were a whirlwind of consonants and vowels filling my head. That was in fact what was happening now, but I couldn't focus, there were too many things I wanted to know, to ask.

I said the only thing I could get out from between my lips. "Why me?" The words sounded weak. "What I mean is, why did she turn on me?" Sunita gave me a shrewd look, and I know that she would hear the words that I hadn't been able to get out, the question I wanted to ask but couldn't bear to hear answered: *I thought she loved me?*

Sunita nods as if she heard me speak the silent question. "Janice has always been selfish," she says. "She has always wanted more, especially what she couldn't have. She's all take and no give, that one. I'm surprised that she kept you around for as long as she did. I was beginning to wonder if she had found a way around her own issues, but she couldn't do it in the end, could she?"

I shake my head, though that makes the words in my head break apart. I can feel the sharp jab of a letter k as it graces my eyeballs, the soft swipe of an o as is runs down my cheek. I take Sunita's hand and give it a squeeze, not sure if I can find the words or if I'm afraid that the words will fly out of my mouth when opened. Sunita squeezes my hand back and I know that she understands without me having to say anything.

When we come upon the market, we find it busier than I've seen it in a long time. There are more stalls open than ever before; normally, people take turns setting up their stalls, knowing that too many people moving noisily at once will draw the attention of the Minotaur. It's always been understood that having so many of us here at once is dangerous, that it could mean the death of one or all of us. Seeing so many here at once is frightening and terrible to me and when I look at Sunita, I can tell that she feels the same way. She takes my free hand and when she squeezes it, she almost hurts me. I don't mind the hurt. It takes away the fear.

The whispering has grown louder too. Normally, it sounds as if a soft but lazy breeze is wafting about us. Now, it sounds like a rushing wind, and it fills the market until it is almost too full of words. I watch the motion of the vendors and the people choosing their wares, hear the fierce whispering and walking and I look skyward to the blackness and wonder where the Minotaur is. This much noise would have normally brought him down on us. Then as I watch them, something occurs to me.

"The Minotaur didn't attack us," I say in a soft whisper. "It screamed and didn't attack us. They are no longer afraid," I tell Sunita. "They have forgotten their fear."

CHAPTER SEVENTEEN

WE descend into the market.

People crowd around us almost immediately. They look happy and even excited. There is too much talking and too many people acting as if they are on some vacation instead of in the belly of the labyrinth with a monster that has terrorized us a moment away from attacking. I see Dava, Vilma and Kelsey rallying around Dava's chair. She can't walk but manages to get around in a rocking chair that Dominic put together for her. It has wooden wheels that allow her some movement. Vilma and Kelsey are pushing her chair in circles and the three of them look as if they are in a moment of such sheer enjoyment that I can't find it in my heart to disturb them. I can only look on in wonder and a growing sense of fear.

A little further away from us, I see Meaghan with her son Josia-James. He's riding on her shoulders and looking around with what can only be described as joy. He looks like a boy who is discovering life for the first time. There is a light in his eyes that is dangerous.

The others crowd around. Elaine and Kris are on either side of us and they're shaking our hands as if we have done something amazing. They aren't the only ones. Others are hugging, some openly dancing. I want to scream at them, yell at them. I feel frozen in place. Sunita has taken my hand again and I can tell that the same words are running around in her head: *we must stay silent, we must keep our heads down, we must not make noise, we must whisper and make sure that are voices are not heard.*

These words were drilled into each of us when we were young. Eleanor made us recite the pledge of the labyrinth at school every day until we could recite it from memory. There are other rules we had to learn, too. I look at all of these people, people I know and love, and wondered why one moment of silence had made them all lose their sense. I look at Kris and his wide smile falters for a moment when he sees the look in my eyes. I tend not to look at too many people in the eyes, it seems to frighten them. Most people think that my eyes see too much. Mother says that people aren't frightened of me exactly, only the fact that they can see themselves in my eyes when I look at them.

"What are you doing?" I whisper. It is the only thing I can think of saying.

"Didn't you hear the Minotaur?" he asks me. "He bellowed and he did not charge!" He was almost laughing. "It has always come after us when it lets out those screams!"

"Those were different," Sunita says. "Why are you acting like this is some sort of celebration?"

"Isn't it though?" he says. "We're all still alive. We're all still here and no one has died. There is no blood on the ground or the stone! It did not charge us, and we are alive!"

I realize what he looks like now. His face looks like a child on Christmas morning, at least according to the picture in the library. Kris's eyes are filled with hope, something that I haven't seen in anyone's eyes for a very long time. Only when I look at Sunita do I feel comforted. Her eyes are filled with fear, just like mine.

I hold on to Sunita's hand and we try to untangle ourselves from the crowd that had grown in the market. Sunita almost pulls me along and I let myself be pulled; I want to be far away from here. I want to run, and I will if I have to, but it will cost me later. It will cost me now if I don't run, so I step as quickly as I can, holding on to Sunita's hand and the other using my cane to hobble along. I am almost running, trying to run, but it will have to be good enough. Sunita has an urgent look on her face, and I have a feeling that it mirrors my own. I nod and try to walk faster, although I am not moving more swiftly, the intent to do so makes me feel as though I am. We stride out of the market, and I turn towards home, hoping that my mother is there, and then I hear someone laugh. The sound is clear and clean and joyous. It is silenced almost immediately.

The air is soundless for a moment and everyone is still, fear finally alive in their eyes. Sunita and I keep moving, knowing that we have only moments. I wonder if we can get near to the owl; will its eyes give us sight throughout the night once more? The air has become still, and I know that people are waiting, and I find myself almost wanting the Minotaur to show up to demonstrate to all the merry makers that their behaviour has caused our ruin. I push the thought away as soon as I think it, not wanting to think the words into reality. I march onward when I see my parents at the edge of the crowd. When my mother sees me, she lurches towards me. Sunita moves people out of the way. My mother seems impossibly far away until she isn't, and she is clutching at my hand. I wonder if she will take us to the owl room, I don't know if I could find the way. Sunita puts her arm on my right shoulder, whether to steady me or herself, I do not know.

We stand there holding each other and all I can hear is Mother and Sunita breathing. I can hear everyone breathing, in both dread and anticipation. The moment grows longer and longer until in the market someone let out another louder, obnoxious laugh. We wait again and for a moment nothing happens. There are no Minotaur hooves that come blundering down from the black sky, there are no screams that fill the air and make the ground shake. The sense of fear that I have lived with all my life, that feeling that there is always something awful behind the next corner, begins to dissipate. I hold on to it, not wanting to let it go, knowing that this sense has kept me alive for seventeen years. I wrap it around me like a shawl or blanket, not willing to let go of it yet.

Mother, Sunita and I walk away from the crowd, which is growing louder now. There is too much noise, too *much*. It's bound to make something happen. We stand and wait, our breath coming faster now. My heart feels like it's going to beat out of my chest. My mother is crushing my arm and Sunita my shoulder, but I don't mind the pain. It's a reminder that I am still alive. The laughter grows louder, and I want to lose myself and laugh with them, to let out a sound of joy when there hasn't been joy for as long as I can remember. I remain quiet, nevertheless.

A sound begins high up in the darkness.

The birds begin to caw and sing, and I can hear their wings flap and fly above us. I can hear the crows, and they seem to be in an uproar. The caws fill the silence, and they make the sounds of laughter disappear. No one is laughing at the sound of hundreds of crows singing out their woes. Something has disturbed them. Without warning another sound begins to fill the air. It is a low keening, a sound of so much pain that it shakes the stone walls around us. When I turn back to look at the crowd, everyone is doing the same thing. They are all looking upwards.

I can't help but let my eyes follow everyone else's. The black sky of the labyrinth sounds as if it's crying and we are all listening as a scream begins to build and grow in pitch. I know it's the Minotaur and I think again *it can be hurt*, but then I wonder what could have possibly hurt it. It lets out another cry and I feel my insides churning at the sound. It reminds me so much of the noise that came out of my mouth after what Janice did. I couldn't make those sounds out loud of course, but all I could hear for the longest time was the sound of wailing that filled my head. I wanted to rage, cry, scream and yell all at once, and my head was filled with sounds that I had never heard before or since. I had no words, then, just an endless syllable that repeated and reverberated on and on in my heart.

This sounds like that. I look up at Mother and see the same feeling shining in her eyes. I wonder if that same sound filled her whole being when father was taken from us. He was a difficult man, but he loved us, and he truly loved Mother, whatever his shortcomings. More than that, she was left alone with me, and I was much younger at that time. I wonder if the sound was screaming within her the entire time, and she was lost within herself, so I had to go to stay with the Oracle. I see the same sound in her eyes as if a sound can even have a physical form. I wonder if Mother will realize what this means.

The screaming wail of the Minotaur goes on for what seems like forever but is really only a minute or two. Normally, the Minotaur would have been here by now and the earth would be shaking around us, our insides trembling along with the ground. The Minotaur will not be coming, and that very fact is incomprehensible. It has always come, but to have it not punish us twice in same number of days is unheard of. Mother senses it, but I wonder if I'm the only person who has realized that the last two times have been different. The last two times the Minotaur let lose its screams had been because it was hurt. That leads me to two other thoughts: how do I find the Minotaur and when I do, how do I hurt it?

The screaming ends on an impossibly high note. It's a sound I remember well because it was the sound that filled my head during those last hours of grieving for Janice. I remember them well. It was during those hours that the shard was created. I remember the feeling of the shard pressing down into the skin of my chest right by my heart. I relished the pain then because it meant that I was still alive. That pain eventually became a hindrance until I could hardly stand.

It sounds like that kind of pain now. The sound begins to soften, then grows still, and the air is left with the sounds of flapping wings and the caw of the crows mingled with the sounds of our heavy breathing.

I look at Mother and she nods and moves toward home, pulling me with her. I hold on to Sunita's hand, not willing to leave her and she follows me with a grateful smile. I look back at the people in the market. Everyone's face shares the same shocked look. I wonder if they have just realized that our lives have changed however slightly, and they aren't sure what to do either.

As we near home, the enclave of our scattering of walls within this maze, I see a shape standing by the phoenix. Even though it is in shadow, I know who it is. It's like the shard that is no longer there hums in the water and I can hear its song, even from here. I do not venture towards it so that I can swallow it again. I ignore the song being sung, loud in the silence that has fallen.

When we get closer, Janice steps out of the shadows. She wears a look both fearful and hopeful. The anger I feel at seeing her is palpable and I let that anger fill the hole where the shard once was. "What are you doing here?" I ask without preamble.

Janice looks shocked at the anger that can be heard in the whisper. "I thought, well, I thought that when the Minotaur screamed that we would go to...the other place again?" Her eyes are all glassy with fear and I'm not moved at all. There is a cool breeze rushing through where there had once been a forest burning for her.

"You thought wrong. Go home, Janice," I say.

Janice looks at Sunita and sneers. "You've replaced me already?" She lets out a small snort. "I don't think much of your taste in women."

"That says more about you then it does about me," I say. "Go away, Janice."

"Aren't we going to hide?" There is a note of panic in her voice. I've never heard that tone from her, not even when she was in an almost catatonic state the night we hid in the owl room underneath the ground. "The Minotaur could be here at any moment!"

Sunita squares her shoulders. "You know that when the Minotaur lets out its roar that we have seconds to hide, not minutes." She gives Janice the same sneer that Janice gave her. "Use your common sense, we'd be dead if it were coming."

The meanness in Janice's eyes intensifies as they flick to Sunita. "How do you know? Are you speaking for everyone now? Or just for Roanne?"

I put my free hand up. "That's enough Janice. We're not taking you anywhere and I am not responsible for your safety. Where is Hugo anyways? That makes it twice now that you've left him to fend for himself while you ran to safety. It must be a really deep love that the both of you share if you're willing to leave him for slaughter." I don't know where the words come from, they leave my mouth as if they're erupting from behind my lips. It's like the shard blocked more than the air that I needed to breathe. It blocked all the words I wanted to say to her for so long. It feels so good to finally stand up for myself, until Janice wheels back and slaps me.

The slap nearly knocks me down, but I maintain my footing. I put my free hand to my cheek. It's the first time someone has ever hit me, and I can't believe it was Janice who did it, that she thought so little of me to slap me. Sunita takes hold of my shoulders to help me maintain my balance. My shock only deepens when Mother steps forward and slaps Janice hard enough to make her fall to the ground.

"Now you *listen* to me," Mother says, anger making it seem like her eyes were on fire in the shadows. "I don't know what you did to my daughter, but she was different after what you did. When I look at her, I see pain in her eyes that wasn't there before you. I don't know what you did, but I do know that you will never ever lay a hand on my daughter again. The only reason I didn't slap you the other night was because you were in shock." Mother's eyes narrowed as she looked down at Janice sprawled on the ground. "I won't hesitate again."

Janice looks at my mother with a steely gaze. I look at Janice's face, so filled with malice and hate, and I realize I never really knew her. I loved her, but I don't love her anymore. Something else comes free in me when I realize this. It is like my lungs have finally learned to breathe again after a long time of not breathing at all or merely breathing enough to keep me alive. Now they breathe freely again, taking in as much air as they can. I look at Janice lying on the ground and remember the time I lay on the ground in front of her, beaten and bruised, the air in my lungs gone from me. I look at her and try to see something of the woman I knew, but I do not find her.

"You should go," I say.

"Your mother hit me!" Janice says. "Aren't you going to *do* anything?"

I shake my head slightly. "I wasn't planning on it."

"You're not going to do anything to *defend* me?" I can hear the whine in her voice even though she whispers the words with a fierceness that makes her sound like a snake.

"She only hit you because I'm too polite to do so. Rest assured that I'm becoming less polite the more time you spend in my company, and I shall have no such problems in the future," I tell her. "Go back to Hugo."

Mother and Sunita move into our enclave, and I follow, turning my back on Janice for the first time. I always thought that I would gladly give my heart to her again, but now I know that if I want to give it to someone else, I will not give all of it away but keep a small part safe for myself.

When I turn my back on Janice, I hear her begin to cry. I take pleasure in it, hearing an echo of the pain I felt after she left me. As I walk away, I try to put notes to the sobs that come out of her in whispers, much like Gabriel would put notes to each step he takes. I wonder if I will ever put words to the tune that is now running through my head or if the tune alone will do. As I walk away, I try to make sure to keep my feet in tune to the music flowing through me.

CHAPTER EIGHTEEN

WHEN the night comes, the darkness is full of music.

First, I hear the birds. The crows are talking to each other much louder than they usually do. The volume of the caws worries me. I've not heard the Minotaur for a few days now. We can always hear it in some way, whether its breath sounding like the wind or its cries like the lighting when storms pass through the labyrinth. It's gotten to the point that I don't even notice it, except now I do much like the rain that falls within the walls. It rains in the labyrinth more than you would think. The librarian Eleanor tried to explain it to me once during my schooldays, but I forget the specifics. It doesn't matter now. All that matters is that the silence is now filled with the music of living.

As well as the birds, I can hear the sounds of people. I can hear laughter and, in the distance from the middle of the labyrinth, someone is singing softly. Sound carries within these walls, so I can hear them clearly. My pallet feels uncomfortable tonight and I'm unable to settle down enough to sleep, so I sit up. There is too much in my head. The story inside the little blue book is still on my mind. Though short, it carries a weight to it.

I have kept it to myself as I do with most things I learn. I take time to process, and then when I'm comfortable, I find a way to shape my words so I may properly share my thoughts. That normally works, but not this time. I know that there's only one person who I can talk to about this, and I stand, brushing off the earth and dust from my clothes as much as possible. I take hold of my bag and check that everything is there. The green and blue books are in there, as well as the fountain pen the Oracle gave me and the journal from Cheryl. I check inside and make sure that the key is safely tied in place; tied by a string through the fibres inside a pocket. I don't know why, but I need to keep that key safe as well as everything else the bag contains.

I quietly slip out of our enclave. I have no wish to wake Mother and Dominic. They are as unsettled as I am with everything that has been going on, and every day that passes without hearing the Minotaur their worry lines become deeper. They are as worried as I am, but only I know what has to be done. I think of that little blue book and the story contained within its pages. I know what must be done but I don't think that I can do it. It will mean going farther than I have ever gone, at least if I've interpreted the story correctly.

I take a jar from the cupboard and put a glowworm inside, taking it with me for comfort. It flutters for a moment and then starts letting off a bright blue glow. I wonder if it feels as trapped inside the jar as I feel inside the labyrinth.

It settles into place glowing softly now. I cup my hands around it as if it's a candle; I've seen those in books in the library. Candles would be dangerous here in the labyrinth, they would give off too much light and attract the attention of the Minotaur...well, they normally would. I don't know what would happen now. I hurry as fast as I can towards the Oracle. I don't want to wake her, but she's the only person to whom I can talk, the only person who might understand. As I walk, I think of the key and its three colours intertwined with the dark metal: the yellow, blue and red. I wonder what the third book will bring and what secrets it might hold. The words in the books burn brightly in my head.

Though I carry the book with me, I do not need to read it to know the words. They burn like candles in my mind; dangerous and hard to extinguish.

I have not been paying attention to where I'm going, but my feet know the way, they have travelled to see her so often before. I do not wish to wake her up, but it is necessary. I don't think I will sleep until I talk to her. I don't know if I will sleep even after I tell her of what I've read. I always knew, even as a child, that reading had the power to change your world. I just didn't expect reading to actually change my world. I was perfectly content not knowing and now that I do, I wonder if the words will be bursting to get out of my head. I will have to make sure that my lips are clamped shut when they try to escape.

I make my way to her section of the labyrinth to find that she is already up. There is sage tea brewing. I can smell its familiar scent, and I find her sitting on the floor in front of her small wooden table, a glowworm in front of her. She beckons me over for a hug and I stay inside of those arms for a moment, relishing the feel of her embrace. She is the one person who I do not mind hugging me. She gets free reign to do so whenever she wants, which isn't that often. She knows how I feel about people being too close to me.

She pours me a cup of sage tea and then sits beside me and takes her own cup. We clink them softly together and we each take a sip. "What seems to be on your mind, Roanne?"

"Is it that obvious?"

"I could feel your mind from all the way over here. That's how I knew that I would have to get up and make you a cup of tea. What is it? What seems to be the problem?"

I shrug, not sure where to begin. I take a breath and focus, just as she taught me to do long ago. "I'm worried."

"I am too. I don't know when I've ever been so worried. The world is very odd at the moment, and nothing is certain, is it?"

I shake my head. "No, it's not."

"So that's at the tip of it, your worry. What is worrying you, Roanne? Is it the Minotaur?"

I nod. "Yes. I've never heard is scream the way it did the other day," I tell her. "It didn't sound angry. It sounded like it was in pain."

"You caught that too, did you?" She clinked her cup to mine again. I picked up my cup and took a sip. "Yes, I thought you might. You've always been good with sounds and what they mean, or words and what was left unsaid."

I feel a flash of pride at those words. She does not give out compliments easily. I often think of the Oracle as my mother and want her approval, but I don't go begging for her approval. I want it naturally, organically. I want her approval to mean something. "Thank you."

"And then again, I'm very skilled at hearing what is unsaid, too. You're just bursting to tell me something. It's why you came here when you're supposed to be asleep, isn't it?"

"How did you know that?" I ask her. This isn't the first time she has given the impression of reading my mind or knowing what I was thinking before I speak. For a while, I thought that the Oracle could read my mind and kept trying to think only good thoughts until the Oracle and Mother started to ask me if I was constipated.

"It's all over your face. Your eyes look ready to pop out of your skull. So come on, tell me what you need to tell me."

I don't know where to begin or what to say. I have too many words inside my head, and I wonder which ones I will let out first. I can feel them fighting on my tongue, pushing and pulling to get out of my mouth. I let the words fight amongst themselves on my tongue and I pull out the little blue book. I will overpower the words I want to say and read someone else's words instead. I hold it in my lap for a moment, running my fingers over the words that were embossed in gold on the cover. The indentations and flecks of gold still remain. The book isn't that long, a few pages at most. I open the book carefully and show the Oracle the first page.

"The Minotaur's Lament," I say. I turn the page. I pause for her to look at the title page. The words are written in a black script that snakes across an aged white page. The title is there with the authors name, listed as Anon, which seems like an odd name to me. I turn the page. There are only a handful in this small book so while I know that this won't take too long, the words fighting on my tongue fight even harder when I try to pronounce any other word.

The next two pages show the picture of a labyrinth and a man in the bottom corner, looking down over all the twisting walls and hallways. The illustrations are all done in black and white. "He looked down at what he had created," I read. I flipped the page, and the pictures on the pages showed an array of clocks, all stopped at midnight. "It all gave him pause," I said. I flipped the page, and we can both see the shadow of a beast covering both pages. "For something lurked within the walls," I said. I flipped the page, and it showed the Minotaur, covering the whole of the labyrinth. Its mouth was open in a scream and one of its hands looked to have morphed from human to half horse, half bird. There were long talons that curved across the page. "A beast with long, sharp claws."

I take a deep breath. I have seen what those claws can do, what they have done to people I know; gouged skin, eyes that used to belong to people I loved or knew that I found in the dirt. I think of my father and how we never found all of him, and I always wonder if he was the Minotaur's dinner that evening. The Minotaur always comes at night because night is all we have. I let another breath out and turn the page.

This page shows a man who has been hit by lightning. Even though his body remains the same except for the glow of the light, we can see his shadow has grown twenty sizes bigger than him and was now the size of the Minotaur. "At the moment of its creation, he wondered what he had done." I turn the page, and we look upon the Minotaur standing atop what looks like a mountain, looking down at the labyrinth, much like the man in the beginning of the story had. "To curse a man to become a beast, with only one way to be undone." My hands are shaking, so the Oracle reaches out a hand and turns the page for me.

My words have stopped, the fight on my tongue becoming too much for me to handle. It comes upon me suddenly, this need to fight stronger against the words and yet it's so important that she understand, that she read the words as I have read them, over and over and over. Only then can we talk of what I need to do. She sees the panic in my eyes and continues the story for me. I turn the page.

The picture shows the man from the beginning of the story leading the Minotaur who has been shackled in chains. The Oracle speaks: "He knew that the only way to set his friend's spirit free," she turns the page now, showing a white sky with the black outline of a Minotaur in the clouds; whether he was the clouds, or they were him was unclear. It didn't matter. The meaning was clear. The Oracle continued to speak: "Was to bring them to a body of water, so that they may truly see."

She closes the book then and slides it back to me across the table. Then she takes my hands and places them around the cup to warm them. "Drink, Roanne. Drink. When there is nary a drop left, then we will speak, but soothe your tongue, your voice, and your mind for a moment. There will be a time for talking, but for now, rest." She pats my hand and I'm amazed by the warmth of her touch.

I nod and take the cup, and I drink until there is nothing left. She refills the cup, and I drink this too, letting the warmth of it run through me. I can smell the sage, and it refills that part of my spirit that was lost in the waters of the dark. I put the cup down and look at the Oracle and she looks at me, within me, and what she sees makes her nod her head. "There now," she says. "You'll be fine. It will be okay."

"How can you be so sure?" I ask her. "Knowing what we now know?"

She makes a sound like *pffft*. "What do we know? That we've read a very good story."

"Well, it fits with what the green book says."

"And what did the green book say?"

"It was all about the building of the labyrinth. The people who worked on it, the materials which were needed, the plans that were followed. We know that a person created this place, maybe a whole lot of persons, and that green book was what led me to the key which led me to the blue book that we've just read." I point to it. I take out the key from my bag. I look at the veins that run through it, the green, blue and red colours flowing through the key that looks like a feather.

"I was there," The Oracle says. "I've seen those books before."

I don't know why I'm not shocked to hear this. "When did you see them?" I ask. She blinks and takes a sip from her own cup of sage tea. She looks down into the cup and I wonder what she is trying to see in there, if she is attempting to somehow scry with her mug of tea. I wonder what it is that she sees. When she finally speaks her words are slow, as if she is pulling them from her memory and this is the first time in a long while her words have seen the light of day.

"Many moons ago, it must have been when I was in my teenage years, I remember my mother carrying them around with her. Before she disappeared, she had grown fretful and distracted. She almost looked like she wanted to scream at something but couldn't find her voice to do it."

"What did you do?" I ask. My whisper is even softer than usual. I don't want to break her concentration.

"What any child would do, of course. I asked her if I could read those books. I was entranced by the gold writing on them. They looked so beautiful, like three jewels that glowed brightly in the labyrinth."

My heart skips a beat. *"Three* of them?"

The Oracle nods. "You must have had an inkling; there are three colours in that key you found."

My head was spinning. I have a random thought. My father built the owl room. Did he also build the hole in the wall which hid the blue book? "Have you ever read any of the books?"

She shook her head. "I was never allowed to. My mother was adamant about that, and I didn't dare disobey her. Aside from that, I only saw the books a handful of times when I was growing up. My mother would carry them in her pockets and flip through them from time to time, but whenever I went looking for them, they were gone." The Oracle had withdrawn inside of herself, and I could see her wandering around her head, chasing the cobwebs which hid the thoughts she did not want to deal with. When her eyes clear, she looks at me again and she is herself. "One night, my mother left with the books and never returned. I do not know where she went or if she remained alive. I remember her kissing my forehead like she did when I was a child and then when morning came, she wasn't there."

We share a moment of silence, each of us sipping the last of our sage tea. I quiet the words fighting on my tongue for a moment. "Did you ever find out what happened to her?"

The Oracle shakes her head. "She was lost to time and space, it seems. Nothing was ever found of her, so I don't think she was one of the Minotaur's victims. She just was there one moment and gone the next." Her eyes cloud with the memory for a instant, then she blinks, and the clouds were gone. "I will tell you two things. You must listen to me. The first is that no one else can see those books."

"Why? What harm could there be?" I ask.

"Because the green book shows that the labyrinth was man-made, that it was made to house us. It was built for some reason, and we were placed here. To what end? And who did the flip book drawings which led you to the key?" She shakes her head. "No, there is too much there. And that storybook is dangerous."

I look down at the cover and rub my hand over where words had been, now only remnants of the gold flakes. "Why is it dangerous?" I ask, though I think I know the answer to that question.

"The Minotaur began as a man," she whispers fiercely. "Think of what that could mean."

The Minotaur can be hurt runs through my head. "I see," I say, and I did. It would mean bedlam in a world of enforced quiet. It would mean craziness when there was a semblance of order when people realized that the Minotaur had been one of us. "What is the second thing?"

"We had better figure out the clues in the second book to see where they lead us. The first book had the flip drawings which led you to the crane where you found the blue storybook. We have to take a closer look to see where this book will lead us or if it has anything else to say apart from the story. The flip drawings were hidden in the green book, yes?" She looks me in the eyes. "What is hidden in the blue book? And how do we find the red one?" The Oracle went to pour herself some more tea, but there was nothing left.

We sat there, looking at the two books and the mountain that lay between us. I didn't know what to say and the Oracle didn't speak for a while. We sat there looking at each other but also looking at nothing, and yet the air between us seemed full of words. I knew that the words on my tongue were growing impatient and wanted to be heard but I didn't know what would happen if I let them out all at once. I sigh instead. *What do we do?* I ask.

She shakes her head and then holds up her hand. *I don't know yet, wait.* She takes the books from me, the green and the blue, and she first looks inside the green book. She reads quickly; a lot faster than I had. Then she reads the blue storybook again. She flips back to one of the pages in the blue book and shows me what I hadn't seen before. She points a finger at the picture where the man was looking down upon the maze. There was a thin dotted line that traced a path towards its destination and then she tapped the walls of the maze within the drawing. I saw something I hadn't noticed before: I could make out a small rabbit. Both the dotted line and the rabbit were drawn with red ink.

"You could only find the blue book after the green book," she whispers. "That is the way of these books. Someone who built the labyrinth had to have made both books, but why let people find them? Why lead people to them at all?" Her voice is even more hoarse than usual, and I reach out across the table to take the hand that had pointed at the page.

"Maybe they wanted to give us a way out?" I ask, hardly believing the words.

She shakes her head again. "I don't think so, Roanne. Why trap us all in here and give us a way out? Where did you find the green book that started all of this mess?"

"It was in the owl room. Mother says that father built it."

Her mouth opens in a small "o" and closes again. "That can't be possible. He was born in the labyrinth like the rest of us." She shakes her head for a third time. "There is too much to think about. Take the books away from me for now. I have to think on what we've learned."

"I can talk to Dominic to see if he knows where we might find a rabbit within this labyrinth."

She smiles without humour. "Hasn't it occurred to you that we are the rabbit, Roanne? Always going someplace but never arriving?" She stands and shows me to the entrance of her enclave. "I must rest and ask spirit what to do."

I stand and put the books in my bag, holding it close. "Are you going to be all right?" I ask.

"No, Roanne. I don't know that any of us will be, however we can find joy in the moment. Go and find your joy and leave this old woman with her thoughts, okay?" She pats my cheek like she used to do when I was younger. "I will be okay. I will talk to you soon."

I give her a short hug and then did the only thing I could think of: I form my hands into the shape of a heart, curving my fingers and bringing them together until my thumbs touch. I hold it up to her. It was the symbol that we used when we wanted to convey deep love for someone else. The Oracle repeats the gesture and despite the uncertainty of what we had just learned, and the vastness of what we did not know, my heart felt lighter.

CHAPTER NINETEEN

I go back to my enclave, the books hidden in my bag with all my other important items, and the bag seems heavier because of the fact that I have to keep everything concealed. I admit that it makes me feel important, but it also frightens me. What does all this information mean? Why would a ledger of information about what it had taken to build the labyrinth be hiding in a room created by my father? What did the story truly mean? Was the Minotaur really a man made into a beast? Could he be hurt? There was also the rabbit and its dotted line path to consider.

What if I follow the line on the map in the little blue book? I try to remember if I have seen a rabbit upon the walls of the labyrinth. I was never reckless enough to venture out into the labyrinth on my own. I was familiar with a select group of visual landmarks and sigils so that I could always find my way to where I called home. I thought of what Dominic had called her. He had said that she was his touchstone. It was like that for me, too. I never wanted to stray far from my mother. I wasn't sure what would happen to her if I did.

I knew explorers that knew the labyrinth though. Dominic had discovered so many part of the maze that were not familiar to me. I would speak to him and find out if he knew where it was.

I know in my gut that the rabbit will lead me to the red book. There had to be one, if not then what did the vein that ran through the feather key mean? I took out the key and ran my fingers over its grooves, hoping in some way that it would tell me what I needed to do. The key remained silent in my hand, and I put it back into my bag with a sigh. I knew that it held answers, I just didn't know how to find them yet. I wondered if Kiles and Riley had seen the rabbit? Or Dominic? I didn't want to ask him because he might mention it to Mother. I didn't want her to have any idea of what I was planning to do. She would worry needlessly; I meant to find the rabbit, no matter what Mother would want me to do. I felt in some small way that my father had left this clue for me. I couldn't explain why I thought this, even to myself. I sit up on my pallet when I hear Mothers' footsteps in the darkness. I make sure my bag is tightly closed and take out the book of Shakespeare. I scan a page and my eyes land on a line from Macbeth: *Fair is foul, and foul is fair.*

Mother comes out of her room, and I can see Dominic shifting in the darkness. Mother bends and puts her hand softly on my cheek "Morning poppet. How did you sleep?"

I shrug. "It was good."

"So good that you got up early to sleepwalk?" She asks, grinning.

I shrug again. "I woke from a nightmare and went to see the Oracle."

Mother's face softens. "You could have woken me," she says.

"I didn't want to wake you, you and Dominic looked so peaceful."

"What was the dream about?"

I have never really lied to my mother but in order to keep everything to myself, I will have to lie now. I realize that I will have to tell Mother what I have found eventually but now is not the time. I give her the one answer that will quiet her questions.

"It was about father," I say.

"Oh, of course," Mother says. She runs a hand comfortingly through my hair. "You must have been frightened."

"I was," I tell her. This is not a lie. The knowledge that the Oracle and I found in the books has left me shaken and frightened of what is to come. Of what I had to do behind Mother's back. *The Minotaur can be hurt*, I thought. *It can be hurt and I will have to hurt it.* It was the first time that I had thought this. The words rattled around in my head and went through me, clacking like stones inside my skin. They are so loud within me that I wonder whether Mother can hear them, they are so loud in the quiet stillness of the dark. She rubs her hand on my cheek.

"You look so tired. Did you sleep at all?"

I try to arrange my mouth into some kind of smile and nodded my head. "I slept some. Just not as well as usual." I put every ounce of sincerity into my voice, hoping that she does not hear the fib.

"Of course, poppet. I know that it can be hard, especially since you didn't know father very well. He really was a…wonderful man, once upon a time. I'm sorry that you knew him the way you did. I think he just lost so many people that he also lost a lot of himself along the way."

I'd never heard her speak of father in this way. Her words took on a hardness. I know that she missed him, but I think she loved her life now a lot more, as much as one could within the maze. "I'm sorry Mother," I told her.

"It's okay, poppet. He became someone I no longer knew, and you never did."

She tucks a lock of my hair behind one of my ears and I reach up to clasp her hand. I hold it there and see her face soften. I don't allow many people to touch me, so moments like this are rare. I know that I've given my mother a gift, this little moment of tenderness, even though it holds no physical form.

Mother wipes something away from her eye and when she speaks next, her voice is slow, and I can tell she's about to cry. "Oh, my poppet, let me make you something to eat, then you can go exploring as I know you want to." Her words are thick with emotion.

She goes to our kitchen and begins to cook up some kale, radishes and turnips. It doesn't taste very good, but I know that it's good for me. Mother says that these foods are high in vitamins and minerals; I'd hate to tell her that they seem to be wasted on all of us wandering in the dark. Still, I let her chop them up and boil them over a low flame. We don't need to speak while Mother is cooking. It's part of the ritual between us. Dominic comes out of their room. He signs "Good morning,"

I shrug and make a motion with both of my hands, wiggling my fingers as I drop my hands down beside me. This sign means "Is it morning or is it night?" I see him smile in the shadows. He goes to help Mother prepare the food. I watch them together and I'm happy that Mother has found someone who, though he leaves her from time to time, always comes back to her. He calls her his heartbeat and it's not hard to see that they share something together. I often wonder if she had any of that with father and can only assume that they didn't. I'm glad that she has Dominic.

When Mother passes me a bowl, it warms my hands, and I look up at her with a smile. "Thank you." I break the ritual of silence in thanks. It seems appropriate as I'm sure she didn't receive thanks from father very often. "Thank you, Mother."

She nods at me and is beaming as she sits down on the ground across from me. We use a small square of stone for a table and

Dominic sits between the two of us. I wonder, if someone were to come in our enclave now, would we look like a family?

We share food together in silence. I can hear Mother's breathing and can hear Dominic moving the pan closer to himself, to better get the food to his mouth. I can hear the sounds of others in the labyrinth, and it occurs to me then that we're all trying to live whichever way we can. Even in the maze, things can thrive, even humans.

I thank Mother and Dominic and make sure that I have all my things in my bag. I tell Mother that I won't go out further than the block of walls marked by the whale on my own or without coming to ask her permission first. She nods and I leave, weaving my way through and around the walls I know so well. I let my mind wander. I see others out walking, most of them headed towards the market. I see Nicole walking with Michael, and a little further on I see Maureen. She is holding a bundle of carrots and even in the darkness they are bright like the sun. I smile slightly as I pass her and she nods, holding out her hand to me with a closed fist, then releasing her fingers. I return the sign, and for a moment, it looks like two eyes in the shadows.

My smile falters as I move onward; I'm wondering if I can find a spot at the watering hole or a new book I haven't read at the library when I walk right into someone. I stumble for a moment, and my bag pulls me off balance. I right myself with my cane as the person reaches over and helps me up; I look right into the face of Janice.

For a moment, my heart skips a beat, and I feel a pulse of pain from where the shard had been. My throat and chest convulse, and for a second, I can't breathe. My head feels as though it is under water. Then the moment passes and I look into her face. I see the shock there, the widening of her eyes as she takes in my own face. I see her lips press together and then release, going thin and then full, like she did when she was nervous.

"I need to talk to you," she says. I was delighted to hear the fear in her voice.

"I don't need to talk to you," I say.

"Roanne, please?" Janice asks. "Can we go somewhere to talk?"

I knew that I wouldn't be able to get rid of her. She has that frantic look in her eyes that I know well. It was the one she wore when she wanted something and wouldn't take no for an answer. It was the look that had gotten me to do so much and to give her almost all of myself. They were the eyes that I would have gladly followed to the moon and back. I nod and walk away from her towards the market. If she wants to talk, I'm not going to go anywhere with her alone. I not going to give her the chance again. I don't want to be vulnerable around her. The fact that a small part of me still wants her after everything that has happened worries me for a moment, but then I swallow to remind myself of the pain she had put me through. The shard was no longer there, but the memory of it was. My throat could still feel the shape of the shard and I guarded myself.

I'm not sure where she thinks we are going, but when I turn towards the market, she makes a sound. I turn to face her, and she looks confused. "I thought that we were going somewhere so we could talk privately?" she asks.

I let out a small snort before I can stop myself. "Do you really think I'd let myself be alone with you after everything that has happened?"

She walks to catch up with me. "We were alone in the owl bunker."

"We weren't. My mother was there," I correct her.

I say nothing more until I am in front of a stall. Razzle's stall is open. He has the most beautiful pieces of metal which he carves into shapes using knives and stones he has found in the labyrinth. There is a small otter, a badger, and even a peacock with a plume of feathers. I stand in front of his stall and look, and Janice stands beside me. Razzle is unable to speak, but he can hear fine. I want to be around someone, to force Janice into an uncomfortable situation. If she wants to talk, so be it, but I won't give her the satisfaction of being alone with her.

"So, talk," I tell her.

She looks uncomfortable, as well she should. I wanted her to squirm. I wanted her to have her own version of my shard, perhaps a needle of some sort that is digging into her skin. I'm not a malicious person, but I want her to suffer as much as I am. It looked like she was, but it wasn't enough. Would it ever be enough? I would have to make peace with what suffering I could elicit.

"Look, about what happened…" she begins.

I wait for Janice to continue speaking. I'm not going to make this easy for her. She fidgets uncomfortably and her eyes begin to shift, taking in the other people that walk around us. She looks ready to bolt. Despite my intentions, I will have to prod her. "What exactly do you mean?" I ask.

"You know what I'm talking about," she says, unable to hide her frustration with me completely.

I place both of my hands on my cane and try and look as innocent as possible. "Do I? What *are* you talking about Janice? What happened?"

There is fury in her eyes where before there had been worry. "Do I have to spell it out for you?" she asks. "You were there, you know what happened."

"Why don't you remind me?" I say, speaking a little louder. A few people have now stopped what they were doing and are watching us.

She looks uncomfortable again. "Can't we just talk about this in private?" She almost whimpers this and I remember how she used that tone of voice to get what she wanted, to get her own way. Not this time.

"No, I want to talk about this *now*," I tell her. I'm careful no to yell, but I pronounce my words carefully so that everyone can hear me. I won't let her hide what she's done. I am through hiding it for her. I don't know what has made me come to this decision, but with so much to hide about the labyrinth, I need to be open about this now, so it becomes one less thing to hold on to. I look at Janice and know that she will never admit out loud what she did, so I must.

"You remember what happened, don't you? It wasn't that long ago. You remember the night we were making out beside the sigil of the weasel and a group of kids came upon us, laughing and jeering." There are some of them in amongst the people here at the market and I could snitch on them too, but this is about Janice and what she did to me, not about anyone else.

"I know what happened, all right?" Janice says.

Panic has begun to seep into her voice and the sound is like what imagine honey tastes like. I want more of it. "I know you do, but do they? What have you been telling everyone? What lies did you tell to cover up what you had done?"

"I didn't tell any lies," she says.

"You did that time. You pushed me away. I fell on the ground, and you laughed at me." The memory makes my throat convulse and I almost choke on the shard even though it's no longer there. "You called me a fucking dyke, a reject. You spit on me, and you even kicked me a few times when I was down, all so that you could put on a show and protect your fragile sexuality."

Janice looks afraid now. Everyone is looking at her with malice in their eyes, and Sunita, who was there and helped to stop the whole thing, holds up a fist and then raises her middle finger. I see a few others follow suit. Janice winces as she looks around at everyone glaring at her. My intent in finally speaking about what happened isn't to embarrass her. I want her to feel everything I felt that night. I want her to feel *something*.

"I think the best part was when you picked up my cane and you started walking around like you were me, exaggerating the way that I walk and telling everyone that you were a *cripple*." I let those words set in. "Sunita yelled at you to stop, tried to hit you and you threw her down to the ground, too. Then you threw my cane down on top of me. The others started to point and laugh at me, and I think that was the worst part. Not your betrayal, but being laughed at, being thought of as someone deserving of ridicule. Afterwards, you hooked up with Hugo because you needed the world around us to know that you were straight, that you weren't into women like I am. You know what the worst part is, Janice?"

She won't look at me but she shakes her head so I know she's listening to me. I don't have to raise my voice to be heard. "The worst thing is that when it happened, I lay there in the dirt for hours. No one found me, no one came to look for me. They left me there; *you* left me there. Sunita stayed with me and held me while I cried but didn't urge me to get up until I was ready." I give Sunita a look and nod in thanks. She nods back and gives me a small smile. "The worst part is that I *believed* you. As I lay there in the dirt, I thought I was a crippled dyke who deserved everything she got. I believed you," I tell her again.

Janice still won't look at me, but there are tears sliding down her cheeks. A few months ago, those tears would have moved me to pity, but now I don't feel anything. "I don't believe you any longer. I know that I'm more than you ever will be, that I'm better than you," I finish.

I begin to walk away from her then. I know that she won't say anything, but I've said all that there is to say. I don't know why I've waited so long to say the words, but now that they are out, I feel lighter. They don't take up room within me anymore. I see Hugo at the edge of the crowd, and he nods to me. I nod back and notice the look he is giving Janice.

Sunita comes to my side, and we walk away from the market. She takes me to a small brook, and we sit there and say nothing. I love Sunita for that. We sit there and listen to the sounds of the brook running by. I imagine the moving water is cleaning the shard which was lodged in my throat, and it now resides in the water. I know where it is, but I have no need for it anymore. I'd like to think that the running brook is cleansing that shard; I can only hope it is, lest the feelings that were trapped in that piece of glass poison the meagre water supply. I put my hands in the water to take a sip when we hear a noise in the distance.

I can hear Hugo's voice and he's shouting. I stand and Sunita and I begin to walk as fast as we can back to the market, Hugo's voice getting louder as we approach. I hear a whispering, and I wonder if there are others talking, but then I realize they are trying to quiet Hugo down, shooshing him to get him to stop talking. People are signing to him, holding up their hands with all five fingers spread out in a clear sign to stop. He continues going.

"You told me she was crazy, that she loved you, but you kept trying to let her down gently," Hugo said. His eyes were wide and looked like they were coated in glass; I wondered if he had been crying.

"Hugo, I can explain," Janice said pleadingly, her arms out to him, but he slapped them away.

"You were so fucking desperate to throw yourself at me, I should have caught on. Part of me wondered why you were holding on to me so tightly, but then another part of me believed that you really liked me even though you'd never even locked at me before!"

Hugo's voice was rising with each word and now he was full on yelling at her, brandishing a fist that punched a stone wall instead of her face. Janice is crying now, she is on her knees holding out her hands to him, pleading with him. Part of me, a very small part, feels sorry for her.

Sunita grabs my arm and holds on to it. I spot Mother and Dominic, and we lock eyes. When our gazes meet, a shiver runs down my spine. This feels like last time. There is something in the air and I can feel it on my skin, taste it on my tongue. I can feel the hairs on my arms standing and I clutch Sunita tighter, and she tightens her hold on me. She can feel it too and I wonder if she's intuitive or if she's reading the unknown language my body is speaking right now. The air is full of an electric current and we are not the only ones who feel it.

"You love her, you've always loved her but you're too afraid of who you are to be true to that love!" Hugo was yelling and crying now. His face looked tormented, as if there was a person inside of him trying to come out by ripping apart his face. Hugo looked to be coming apart. The tears fell to the dirt around him, and I wondered vaguely what kind of plants would grow from those spots, or if the salt from Hugo's tears would stop anything from growing at all. "I love you, but this entire time you've always loved her, and I didn't want to see it or believe it, but I knew. I've always known; every time you look at her there is a sea of emotions. When you look at me, all I get is a blank wall."

"I love *you*, Hugo," Janice says. "I *do* love you! Please!" She sounded like she was trying to convince herself.

At that moment, the current of air that was passing through the labyrinth changed. It became faster and more heated, more *alive* somehow. Then within the wind, a sound began, and Sunita and I held on even tighter to each other as we heard it. It was the sound that we had all been waiting for and believed gone, though I knew that it was only a matter of time. It can be *hurt*, I thought. Well, what can be hurt can also heal. There was an ear-splitting scream that filled the air. The trees shook and a few glowworms remining in the giving tree in the centre of the market flew away to the heavens. The ground around us began to shake and the rumble spread far. I began to hear the screams of the other townspeople from deep within the labyrinth and I knew that it had happened at last.

The Minotaur had woken.

CHAPTER TWENTY

THE air was different this time.

When the Minotaur had let out its scream before, it had been weakened and drawn out, as if it were suffering. It can be *hurt*. It was strong again, but now it sounded angry, as if it had woken from a nap that it hadn't intend to take. I looked at Sunita, Mother and Dominic. Razzle gave me a worried look and began packing things away into his jacket and ran into the darkness to hide. I hoped that he found safety.

When the ground begins to shake, Sunita takes my arm. She pulls me to her and we try to bolt toward Mother and Dominic, my cane slapping against my side. Though we try to get around them, the crowd is too large, there were too many people milling about worried about their own safety. I saw Rob hurry by with Catherine, each of them with a look of panic on their face. We all knew what would happen after the Minotaur's cries. We had seen it countless times before. I wondered if we found the quiet almost too unnerving and we hoped that the screams would come because they meant something familiar would happen.

Mother motions to me and somehow, I hear her voice over the growing noise of the crowd. Perhaps I heard it because I was so used to reading her lips. "Stay safe, Roanne! We will find you. Go to the spider!" I see the panicked look on her face and then she was gone, pulled away by Dominic and the ever-moving sea of townspeople.

Sunita still had my arm in a vice, and I didn't complain. "The spider," she whispers. "The spider, what could be hiding there?" It almost sounds as if she were talking to herself as she moved us through the crowd of people.

"I don't know," I say, but I thought I did. The owl had given us a place to hide; would the spider give us such a gift? If owls brought us wisdom in the form of a little green book, what would the spider give us? "You read my mother's lips?"

"Of course; we all can. She's talking about the walls, isn't she? The ones with the animals and insects?"

"Yes,"

Sunita needed no further information. She is almost walking for me, we move so quickly. I see the animals on the walls, and they stare back at us, silent sentinels to our race for freedom. I begin to see animal shapes that I recognize: bear, wolf, beaver, tiger. I know that we are close, we were almost there. We take another few turns and we hear the air fill with the sounds of renewed screaming. The ground shakes beneath our feet and the sound of screams grows louder. The Minotaur had arrived. I felt the ground shake again, and then Sunita shook, and I squeezed her arm to give her strength.

We turn another corner, and I see more familiar animals: whale, dog, seal, and then there it was - the spider. I could taste panic in my mouth, and it was a physical presence inside of my body. I thought of Kiles and Riley and Hugo. I thought of the Oracle and my mother and Dominic. I prayed that they were all right. I didn't pray to a deity, though; I had long since given up believing that there was anyone there watching us. I just prayed and hoped.

I run towards the spider, hoping that our salvation will be immediate, but I didn't see anything right away. The spider reaches out its eight legs over a web of its own making and stares at us with red eyes that seemed made of jewels. I know that it probably hid something, much like the crane or the owl, something that we had to find in order to access the safety we needed. The ground rocks beneath my feet again and I almost fell over. I feel the Minotaur walking, the vibrations of its steps coming closer. It moves quickly, so I'm unsure how much time we have. It could destroy the market in one slash of its clawed hand and kill those within it with another. The screams sound different from so far away; I could hear the Minotaur's anger, as if it were upset that it hadn't been able to act before and was making up for it now.

"Help me look," I tell Sunita.

"What are we looking for?"

"I don't know, something hidden. I've found a key and a keyhole in one of these sculptures and in another it led to an underground room. Mother and I hid there during the last Minotaur attack."

"So, you don't know what we're looking for?"

"Not a clue."

"Why would your mother send you to look for the spider? What does she know? Couldn't she have given us a clue?"

"The spider was the clue," I say. "She didn't have much time for anything else."

"I know, I know, I'm just so out of my league here. I don't know what to look for." I hear the frustration in Sunita's voice.

I try closing my eyes to see more clearly, using my intuition instead of my actual sight, but the shaking ground and the sounds of carnage make me keep my eyes open. I couldn't close them; I was too afraid, and to do so at this moment might mean our downfall. The Minotaur moves quickly and though I can hear it in the distance, that didn't mean anything. It could be upon someone at any moment. In the blink of an eye, it would be there and then you would be gone. The Minotaur is fear given form.

I look frantically at the spider sculpture, hoping that something will show itself, that the answer would be clear, but there is nothing to be found. I remember the way that I looked for the key, trying to feel the knots and grooves of the feathers of the crane without touching it. I do the same here using both my eyes and my fingers. I have to see without seeing. My fingers trail over the spider's legs, probing the jewel-like eyes again, but I can't find anything. I look at the web that it has spun out of metal and run my hands through its grooves, feeling every stretch of the web until my finger catches on something. I look closer even as the ground shakes again with more ferocity.

The eyes are made of red jewels that seem to hold some kind of inner light. The spider was fashioned out of black iron like the rest of the sigils, but this one was different from a lot of the others. While the majority of the animals depicted were flat, a cutout of their shape, this spider was like the crane; I could reach out and touch it, there was more than just a shadow here. The spider hung out from the wall, and it was detailed. I could see each of the legs, the markings on the spider back and the mouth, full of fangs that looked sharp enough to bite. I look deeper into the spiders mouth and I wonder if it holds a secret. Mother always said that spiders are the secret keepers, it's why they spin their webs so that they can tell a different secret every day. Putting my finger in my mouth, I taste blood, and it seems fitting to me that the spider would take a drop of blood as if it were a toll. I think of the pound of flesh from Shakespeare's Merchant of Venice. There is always some kind of price when you try to gain knowledge, and I wonder what else this labyrinth will take from me. I reach to the part of the web where my finger got nicked and feel something there behind it, close to the wall.

"Sunita, I need your help," I say. "There's something here. Can you reach it from the bottom while I try from the top?"

Nodding, she prods below where I had my fingers, both of us trying to dig out what is hidden there. It occurred to me that this one had been well-designed. One person on their own could not have done it; you need two people. This labyrinth expected you to work to reveal its secrets. I had been hiding everything I knew for what felt like forever, but like it or not Sunita was now involved. I wondered if I would have to involve other people. I thought I would; in order to find the right path, I needed to go further into the labyrinth than I had ever been so that I could find the route that was outlined in the storybook.

Sunita and I dug a little bit more and we could feel the piece of metal moving, sliding, and then it fell into the dirt. I pick it up, and we are looking at a small key. "Always with the keys," I said. It seems to be the labyrinth's trademark. I hand it to Sunita. She rolls it over in the palm of her hand.

"What do we do with it? I can't see anything around here that would have a keyhole," she says.

I, however, am beginning to understand the labyrinth. I know that, like with the feather key, the hole is hidden. We were running out of time and my search for the keyhole last time was done with my eyes, fingers and intuition. I ran them over everything and then as I neared the end of the spider's body, I noticed a hole in the very end, where the spider's web would originate from if it were real. With eyes that shone even in the dark, it wasn't hard to imagine the spider being real. I wondered if the spider would take more than its pound of flesh.

I slid the small key into the hole and turned it. There was a soft metallic click, and the end of the spiders' body opened like a door. There wasn't a key or a book in here, but a spider's web. Made of a fine, sheer metal, I pulled it out and it amazed me how much there was. There was enough to cover more than just one person. This made me wonder again at the game the labyrinth was playing, but only for a moment.

As I kept pulling the web out of the spider, I thought of what the spider symbolized. I had read a book about insects in the library, where Eleanor had seen me reading. She tapped the picture of the spider. *"Did you know, Roanne, that the spider is the ultimate creator? It spins its web every day, only to rebuild it the next morning. They are dealers in illusion, spinning a web only destroys the lives of others. I've always been fascinated by them. Sometimes, they hide within the very web they've created to remain hidden from their prey."*

I wondered if the same thing could be true in reverse. If the prey could hide from the hunter in the same way? The ground shakes and I'm almost thrown off my feet, but Sunita catches me. I wondered how many seconds it would take for the Minotaur to arrive. Without thinking about it, I threw the spider's web over both of us. I made sure that it covered Sunita and myself completely, keeping my cane close.

The spider's web was not transparent, but we could see through the small holes made of metal. We could see the shapes of the walls, but not their details. We could see the shadows, but I doubted whether they could see us. Sunita and I sat within the web, our breath making our webbed cocoon warm, as if we were in sleeping bags. Sunita held my hand, and I squeezed it to comfort her. I didn't want to hug right now. We had to remain alert. Soon there was the sound of footsteps running towards us.

A couple of people had tried to outrun the Minotaur, some of them always did. The Minotaur always found them; it was only a matter of time. I used to wonder why people ran, what they had left to save. Now I knew, they had themselves and we were all together fighting in the dark.

The peoples' shadows came into view, and they fell a little way away from us. I could hear a girl crying and her father trying to reassure her, tell her that it would be okay, that they would be free. I want to say something to them, to tell them to keep running, that the Minotaur was right behind them. I could tell because I could feel the ground shake underneath me, but neither Sunita nor I say anything. I could hear them both crying softly. I would remember that sound and all the others from this evening, I was sure of it.

In the blink of an eye, the Minotaur was there, its shadow too big to see fully. I saw it's legs as it stalked towards the father and the daughter. The father must have known that time was scarce because he started muttering *I love you* to his daughter over and over so quickly that it all sounded like one long word: "*ilcveyo uililoveyouiloveyouiloveyouiloveyou*". The daughter said nothing, but I could hear her crying and mumbling unintelligibly. I watch as the Minotaur's feet approached them, its great hooved feet kicking up dust. There was a sound like the growl of a dog and then the shadows moved and shifted. There was a loud scream from the father and the daughter, and then the shadows shifted again and there was nothing left but the Minotaur.

It looked around, and even though it stood too tall for me to see its eyes I know that its gaze passed us over. It doesn't move to take us, though. It stands there for a moment and then moves back towards the market and the continuing noise. It let cut a scream and began to run away from us. Sunita sat there for a moment, hardly daring to move, until I gently lift the spider's web. All that was left were a limb or two from the father and a large pool of blood.

Sunita and I look at each other and then at the spider's web. It slides from us and retreats back into the body of the spider with a soft hissing sound. Sunita and I look at the blood littering the ground where the others had been only a moment ago. They weren't even three feet away from us. I would have to thank my mother, I thought.

Sunita echoed my thoughts a moment later. "We have to have a talk with your mother," she says. Her voice is filled with relief but also with curiosity.

We sat there, listing to the sounds of destruction raging in the distance. Moving closer to each other, I let Sunita put an arm around me. We wait for the noises to stop, for the sounds of pain and torment to end. Part of me wonders if they would go on forever, when it had only been mere minutes. I would not die today and for that I was grateful. I wondered how many others had died in my place.

CHAPTER TWENTY-ONE

WHEN we return to the market, it is to find destruction once more.

I see Mother and though she looks bloody and shaken, both her and Dominic are alive. I wonder if she took him to the room of the owl or if there was some other place they had gone. I was beginning to realize that Mother was filled with many secrets. I wonder if I really know her at all. What else did she know? I look into Mother's wisdom-filled eyes and now wonder what else she is hiding from me.

I help Mother gather the dead and wonder how many glowworms we would need to set free. I counted at least twenty bodies. As we piled the bodies in the centre of the market, the Oracle came to us. I could sense her as she stood behind me and when I turn, it was to find her smiling at me.

"Thank goodness you're all right," she says to me, enveloping me in a gentle hug.

"Never mind me, are you okay?" I ask her.

"I am fine. I was able to hide in my little hovel under some lumber I found. The Minotaur didn't come near me," she says. Her eyes are heavy-lidded. "It looks like others weren't so lucky. How did you survive, Roanne?"

"It was thanks to Mother and the spiders," I say.

Mother gave me a warning look, but I ignore it. The Oracle's eyebrows raise. "The spiders?" She looks at Mother, who seemed terrified. I didn't know why she was afraid if what she said helped me and Sunita survive. "You weren't supposed to tell her about the spider," the Oracle says.

"I saw no other way. I couldn't get to her in time to bring her to safety."

"Like you brought her to the owl room?" The Oracle asks. She makes a sign then, lifting her hand and making a shooing motion, waving her hand back and forth as if she were trying to get something off of her fingers. "You know that you're not to speak of those things. She has to learn the stories that the labyrinth holds on her own. It's bad enough that you brought her to the owl."

"If I hadn't, she would be dead," Mother tells the Oracle.

"Even so, she has to learn."

Mother makes the same motion at the Oracle, except her movements were frustrated and angry whereas the Oracle's signs had been more fluid and calmer. This was the difference between the two of them. I had seen the sign before. It was a polite way of telling someone to fuck off. The extended middle finger was when you wanted to be more direct. *At least they were being polite to each other*, I thought.

"She's too young," Mother says.

"She's already an adult," The Oracle says.

"Are you both going to stop talking about me like I'm not here and tell me what this is all about?" I ask them, my voice tinged with impatience as much as I try to keep my speech calm. They both look at me, and for an instant Mother seems genuinely surprised that I am standing there in front of her.

"Sorry poppet," she says. The coldness that had been in her eyes fled and she runs her fingers through my hair. "I forgot myself."

"You forgot yourself a long time ago," the Oracle says. "Now are you going to help me move these bodies or are we going to stand here talking about things that don't matter?"

Mother and I both agree, and we continue gathering the bodies. My heart nearly breaks when I see that Razzle had been gathered up and placed on the pile. He hadn't been able to get away from the danger after all. It looks as though he had been spared a gruesome death; he still had all of his limbs in place, at any rate. I saw others whom I knew, but they no longer saw me.

Gregor came up next to me and offered me his cart. "You can take this if you want," he says.

I shake my head. "I don't mind," I say. I was determined to prove that I wasn't weak and that I could do everything that everyone else did. I was used to people looking at me differently because I walk with a cane. I take hold of Mike's body and threw him gently over my shoulder. I stumble a little but right myself with my cane. Gregor smiles and gives me a sign that I recognize, a thumbs up. This was made clearer with the smile he gave me.

"Good, good," Gregor says, patting me gently on the shoulder. This was something that my father would have done or *should* have done. My father hadn't been one for showing any kind of fatherly affection. I squeeze Gregor's hand in thanks. He had no idea of the gift that he had given me, even though it was small and had no physical form.

"Where do you put the bodies?" I ask. I never asked this before, just piled the bodies in one area and Gregor and others would carry them away to wherever they put them.

"It's too far away," he says. "You might not be able to carry the body that far."

"I will use your cart," I tell him. He nods and grabs another almost identical to the one I had my hand on. I know that he built them himself and took great pride in them. I wonder about the world that we lived in where a man had to build a cart to carry bodies. It must be an odd thing to take pride in something well constructed that was made to make death easier to deal with.

I just really want to get away from Mother and the Oracle. I don't want to be around them when they were like this, especially since they were talking about me like I was something weak that needed to be coddled. I have always known that my mother knew more than she had let on, but now the Oracle is the same. I remember what the Oracle said before: *"Well observed, Roanne. I have indeed seen them before. The books always show up when one is ready to begin their own journey. It seems to be the way, at any rate."* What does she know, and did she know as much as Mother?

I placed my cane in the crook of my elbow and use the cart as an aid. It is high enough to support me, and I can push it at the same time. Gustav and I didn't talk, we merely push our carts. I follow him for quite a distance. I have never been out this way before; it was one of the areas that Mother forbade me to go. As we walk, the air is fragrant with sage. It starts as a tickle in the back of my nose but grows to the point where the scent was almost overpowering. I could breathe it in and taste sage upon my tongue. There is something different about the taste and scent of it. It reminds me of when the rain trickled into the labyrinth and the worms in the soil pushed themselves to the surface to avoid drowning. The air smelled and tasted of wet earth filled with blood. I have a moment where I want to turn back, knowing that I will not like what I am about to see. I continue onwards despite my fear.

As we approach, I can see the sage. It has grown wild and stretches six feet into the air. There's a breeze here and the sage flows in the wind, waving at us. I can see that the sage is a thick wall and there's no telling how far it goes back. That would account for the strong aroma. We move even closer, and the earthy scent grows stronger. Gustav motions with his hand, mimes parting the sage. I do so and at first all I see is more sage, but I keep going, pushing my cart into the green leaves. After about four feet or so, I come out upon a landscape that I have no words to describe; they leave my mind and my body, both unable to comprehend what I'm seeing. Gustav sees my face and puts what is supposed to be a comforting hand on my shoulder.

I am looking at first seems to be a large mountain. It spans high into the air, and I can see the shape of it like a rock face full of cliffs and jagged edges, the shadows and the dark masking dangers. I didn't know that there were mountains in the labyrinth, and I turn to Gustav. When Gustav speaks, his voice is a whisper, perhaps out of reverence.

"This is where we bring the bodies," he says to me. "It is their resting place."

I look again at what I thought was a mountain and I see the arms and the legs, the torsos and the heads that I thought to be jagged rock faces and mountain boulders. My mouth falls open and Gustav squeezes my shoulder. I don't speak for a moment, taking in the thousands of bodies and body parts that make up the mountain. Finally, I seem to find my tongue, buried as it is in the back of my mouth.

"I wondered where all the bodies went." I can think of nothing else to say.

I can see Gustav nodding in the darkness. "We can't bury them; the soil is too hard and compacted. They need a resting place. When we take a body away, we release a glowworm. The Oracle says the glowworms are their spirits."

I personally feel that their spirits are no longer here, that as soon as they could the dead sought the solace of the afterlife. I just nod and am content to remain silent when something else occurs to me. "Why do you leave the bodies here?" I ask Gustav.

He points at the highest point of the man-made mountain. "That is where the Minotaur comes from," he says. "This is where he emerges from each time he visits us."

It is odd to hear a slaughter called a visit. "Why do you pile the bodies here?" I ask.

Gustav shrugs. "It was the Oracles idea. It was her hope that the Minotaur would see the havoc they have created and feel remorse."

"Has no one been up the mountain?" I ask.

Shaking his head, Gustav takes the body from my cart, that of Razzle, and places it at the base with the others. "No, we don't go up there," he tells me. "It would mean our deaths."

One thought runs through my head: *the Minotaur can be hurt.*

Gustav places the other body alongside Razzle's, and we begin the trek back through the sage. As the sage leaves brush my face a thought occurs to me, and I know what I will have to do. I will have to find the path which leads to the red book and see what it has to tell me. Then there is one more thing I will have to do.

I will have to climb the mountain.

CHAPTER TWENTY-TWO

I am filled with a grim resolve.

It occupies my body and is stronger than the fear which filled me only moments before as we return to everyone else. I can still feel the kiss of the sage on my face. I thank Gustav and leave him his cart. I see my mother and the Oracle, and they are still standing there talking, anger and secrets upon their faces. I still wonder how much they really know and what they have kept from me. The two books feel like a sea of things left unsaid between us. I know I could just demand that they tell me everything, but I know that they wouldn't.

The Oracle is just as confused as I was about what was in the books, but what if that was all subterfuge? She had seen them before. What if none of it is real? I clutch my bag to my side and quickly walk by everyone still left in the market. There is one person I need to find right now, and that's Dominic. I have a feeling that only he will be able to help me find the wall marker shaped like a rabbit. I know that I will find another key there and it might lead to a third book. It stands to reason that if there are three keys, there are three books, but what could the third possibly contain? I am again filled with fear and a sense of anticipation. I also wonder if I was ever meant to figure out the riddles of this maze on my own, I've had to rely on the kindness and knowledge of those I know, first the Oracle and now Dominic.

I am not sure if he will even help me, but I must try. I walk past Kaylan. She looks like she's been crying. Diane and Cindy try to comfort her, but she's inconsolable. I wonder if the Minotaur took Geoff, the man she loved. I have a fleeting vision of Kaylan's beautiful face when she looked at Geoff. They brought out the light in each other. I wonder if Kaylan's light will be permanently dampened, or will it burn again? If I were able to collect all the light the labyrinth had stolen from us, it would be brighter than the sun.

Sunita sees me and comes to my side. I know that she is as drawn to me as I am to her, but I don't know what this means or if it will lead to anything good. I just know that my heart is ready to try again. We link arms and she helps me walk faster than I could on my own. She seems to understand my urgency.

I spot Dominic in the distance, ducking into the web of walls leading to our enclave. I hurry my step and ignore the Oracle's calls when she and Mother finally notice me. I keep walking, clutching my bag to my side. If I'm able to find the rabbit, I wonder what it will be hiding for me? And why a rabbit? For that matter, why an owl and a crane? I wonder at the symbolism of the animals and a random thought occurs to me: *I wonder what the other animals do?* Followed by *it can be hurt.*

We dip into the shadows of the walls, and I call out to Dominic in a harsh whisper to stop him from walking any farther. He turns and sees me and lifts both hands to trace a smile on his face over his lips. He's happy to see me.

I make the same sign, and he offers me a real smile and a small bow. "Are you well, Roanne? You look distressed."

I nod and motion to our enclave. "I need to talk to you about something." I tell him, walking into Mother and Dominic's sleeping area. It's the most private spot I can think of within the labyrinth, aside from the room where Kiles and Riley brought me where the rocks glow like the sun, but that's too far away and too busy of an area. I pull the little blue book out of my bag and flip to the picture of the labyrinth with the red dotted line leading to the rabbit. Dominic takes the book with reverence and looks at the page. I can tell that he sees it right away when he traces his finger along the line throughout the maze.

"Can you take me there?" I ask.

"Where did you find this?" His tone is one of reverence and fascination.

"I can't tell you that," I say.

"What can you tell me?"

"Only that I need to find the rabbit and that it hides something I want. I think it may lead to something that will end all of this." As soon as I've said it, I know that it's true. Why else would the books and the key be hidden? I wonder what the new book will show me or if it hides something else? I think of the rabbit in Alice in Wonderland. I read it once in the library with Eleanor. The rabbit took Alice on a journey.

Dominic traces the line across the page. I can see him trying to orient himself, his eyes focusing and widening. He is mumbling to himself, and I know that he's trying to find the direction of the drawing within his mind. I wonder if he knows the labyrinth well enough to map the whole thing out in his head. I think about all the drawings he's made, and how far the labyrinth reaches. Will we be able to find the rabbit? Will I be able to find its secret?

More importantly, I can't take the Oracle or Mother with me. I don't like the fact that they are lying to me by omission. I won't hold it against them, but I don't know if I'm ready to talk to them yet. I need to think of what I want to say. I wonder what else they haven't told me. It felt good to have a secret or two all my own.

I felt like the light which reverberated off the walls in the hidden room where Kiles and Riley brought me. I felt like the secrets I carried brought me light.

While Dominic reviews the map in the book, I look at the things in my bag. I don't think I need to carry everything with me; I could leave some of it here. I didn't need a jar for a glowworm or the collected works of Shakespeare. I want to keep the key and the two books, my journal and charcoal. I think it's almost time to tell my own story and I want to make sure that I have the tools with me to do it.

I place the things I'm not taking with me by my pallet with some grass around them for safekeeping. It feels like something is changing but I'm not sure whether it's me or the world around me. When Dominic looks up, his eyes are filled with wonder, and he looks like a child again. I wonder if this is his countenance when he's exploring.

When he looks back at me, there is a smile on his face. "I know where your rabbit is," he says. "It will take a few hours to get there though."

"That's fine," I tell him. "This is important, it will be worth the time."

"And you're not going to tell me what this is about?"

I shake my head. "I can't yet because I don't really know." I don't know what the book will contain. If the green book talks of how the labyrinth was built and the blue book told of the secrets behind the Minotaur, who knows what information will be within the red book. "We should go now," I tell him. I'm thinking of Mother and the Oracle deep in intense conversation. I want to make sure they are distracted enough that they don't notice my departure. I don't want them meddling in what I feel I need to do.

There are footsteps outside of our enclave, and I turn to see Sunita standing in the shadows. "Roanne?" she whispers. "Are you okay?"

I nod and decide that Sunita can come along. I remember something the Oracle once told me: *"You don't need to do everything on your own. There are those around you who love you. Let them help, too."* I decide to take her advice.

"I'm okay," I tell her. "I need you to come with us." I look at Sunita and see acceptance in her eyes. I decide that this is the right thing to do. I shouldn't venture with Dominic alone into the unknown. Though I love him in a way, I don't want to burden him if I must navigate difficult terrain. Sunita has already helped me, and I know she will again.

She nods and gives me a tentative smile. "Where are we going?"

"To find the rabbit," I tell her. "Dominic will take us there."

Dominic nods. "I know where we're going," he says. "I haven't been near the rabbit for a long time, but it was always one of my favourite sigils."

I wonder if the rabbit will tell me how we can escape this place. I think again of Alice in Wonderland and I wonder if it's a smart idea to go after this particular rabbit. That one that led Alice on a wild adventure turned out to be a dream in the end. This labyrinth is no dream, though I've often wished it was. We always wake in darkness and shuffle around here as if asleep, yet if we are asleep, we can never wake.

"What do you mean, sigils?" Sunita asks.

"You must have seen the animals on the walls. I've heard that they were put on the walls as part of an ancient rite or ritual. No one knows what their purpose."

I look at Sunita and I know she's also thinking of the spider and how it saved us from the Minotaur. I told her of the owl room too. I wonder what the rest of the animals do, or if only some of them have a function. It would take too much time to go around the labyrinth testing all of them out, and I have a glimmer of understanding about why Mother didn't tell me. Knowledge is power and she knew that I wouldn't stop until I had gained all that I could, possibly getting me into trouble.

"Do you want to go now?" Dominic asks me.

I nod. "I think it's best."

"I'll try to trace the route shown in your book. I figure it gave us that route for a reason, yes?"

"I think so, too." I tell him. I've always liked the way Dominic thinks things through.

He goes to the food box, pulling out a few carrots and some cooked potatoes. Mother dressed them with some precious salt and pepper. He puts them in a rough burlap sack and hands it to me. "We'll get hungry on the way. I'll try and make this as quick as I can, all right?"

"Okay," I say, and Sunita nods.

He looks at Sunita. "I am glad you're coming, that you will be there for Roanne."

"So am I," Sunita says.

I give him a nod. He says this not because I am weak, but because he knows how close we are. He's glad I've allowed someone to be close to me. I think of Kiles and Riley and my heart goes out to them too. I wonder if they were able to find safety during the last Minotaur attack. I will have to find them when we return.

We start out walking quickly. I try to match Dominic and Sunita's pace, but they eventually slow down a little so I don't have to struggle to keep up. Dominic slips forward to check out the terrain and to give Sunita and I a chance to talk, should we wish. Dominic moves objects and stones from our path, so I won't have any issues on the unknown terrain. The walls aren't as well cared-for here. They're falling down in places, even more dilapidated than the section of the labyrinth where we live. I see animals I've never seen before: hummingbird, bear, something that looks like an eagle or a bird of prey. These are drawings on the stone of the labyrinth walls, and I understand why Dominic called them sigils.

The further we walk, the more frantic they become, some of them are unrecognizable as any kind of animal known to us. There is the odd animal we do know, though: a peacock, a tarantula, a python. I sense we're walking towards the sound of water in the distance, its murmur growing louder with each step we take. It provides obfuscation for Sunita and I to talk with more ease and lessens the chance of being overheard.

"Why are we chasing after a rabbit?" she asks.

I take out the book and show her the pages I had revealed to Dominic. Like him, she traces her finger along the line, all the way to the rabbit. Then she hands the book back, giving me a look with her open dark eyes that I get lost in for a moment. "What does this have to do with the secrets you've been keeping?"

"I haven't been keeping any secrets," I say.

"You've been carrying more than usual in your bag, and you won't let it out of your sight or grasp even though it is heavy enough to throw off your gait," she tells me. "We are all allowed our secrets, but if I'm joining you on this journey, I'd like to know why."

There is no judgement in her voice, only open curiosity. I start haltingly, feeling almost as if I'm breaking some kind of unwritten rule about the secrecy of the books. I remember the fear within Oracle's eyes when she looked at the two volumes as they sat in front of hers. However, after a few moments of speaking, I felt a big sense of relief. I didn't have to do this all alone, and having someone else know about what was going on was a good thing. I had to get over the idea I had that the skies would open up and swallow me whole now that I had spoken. I had to let go of the fear and learn to trust. Alice learns a lot about herself in Wonderland even if it does all turn out to be a dream. Maybe I'm already in Wonderland, and this is some test.

The more I talk about what's been going on inside of me and what I've learned about the labyrinth, the lighter I feel. My steps are easier than before as each word is shed from my lips. I feel the weight shifting in me, and then a pain fills my stomach. It radiates throughout me, and I try not to pay it any mind; I've been in pain my whole life, so pain is nothing new. As the pain continues to grow, I realize that I've felt pain like this once before. With every word I tell Sunita, the pain grows in me, but I keep going until Sunita notices the change in my tone and my gait.

"Roanne, what's wrong?" She tugs gently on my arm and helps me gently to the ground.

"Is she all right?" Dominic asks.

"I'll be fine, I just need to rest for a little while."

"We've been walking for a long time. We're almost there, but you two rest and I will go scout out what the landscape is like ahead of us. I won't go very far. Are you sure you're going to be all right?"

"We'll be fine," Sunita says.

Dominic walks off a little ways and Sunita cradles my head in her lap. "I'm sorry that you had to carry all of this with you," she says. "It's too much for one person."

"It's okay," I tell her.

"No, it's not. I hate that you felt alone in all this."

"Well, maybe I've realized that I don't have to be." I tell her.

The pain reaches a new pitch, and I can feel it rolling around in me. I feel like I'm going to be sick, and I roll off Sunita's lap and get on all fours. I let the pain move through me, its heat increasing as I welcome it once more. I open my mouth to gasp, to scream, to yell for help; I feel like I'm suffocating. I can't breathe as I try to push air out through my lungs and throat. I feel something shift in me once more and it slides into my throat and out through my mouth and then it falls from my lips and I can breathe again, I can breathe, and I take in breath after breath of air.

Sunita reaches for what fell in the dirt while she was rubbing my back. In the palm of her hand is a stone. It's black and looks as if it's filled with stars. I look at Sunita's face and her eyes are full of fear and wonder. I can see myself reflected in her eyes, and I carry the same look upon my face. I take the stone from her palm and tell her about the glass shard. Sunita looks at me with something close to astonishment, holding the stone almost reverently.

"What do you think this means?" she whispers.

"I don't know," I tell her. I really don't. "It's like my body is trying to let go of what I no longer need." I take the stone from her palm and hold it in my hand. It feels warm against my skin, and I wonder if it holds the warmth of the stars within it, but then I remember Eleanor telling me that stars are millions of light years away. Eleanor once let me read a book in the library that said we were actually stardust, given shape and substance. It was a book of poems and though I don't remember much else of the poems in the book, I remember that line. It reminded so much of something Shakespeare had written in A Midsummer

Night's Dream. It made sense to me. We can only sparkle in the dark. Perhaps we were stars, trying to find our way out of the dark?

As I hold the stone, I'm not sure of anything anymore.

CHAPTER TWENTY-THREE

WHEN Dominic returns, we are waiting for him.

Sunita holds my free hand, and my other grasps my cane. I don't feel weakened by the loss of the stone from within me; I feel lighter and more in control of myself. I can feel its weight in my pocket as we walk. I hold on to Sunita because I am shaken by the whole thing. I no longer trust what my body can do. What other surprises does it have? First, a crystal shard, now an obsidian stone? It feels like a long time since I bathed at the watering hole with Mother. That felt like a lifetime ago, one where I had blissfully known nothing. Now I knew too much, and I want to send my thoughts to the rowan tree with the glowworms so that they could shine for all to see.

Dominic has a grim look on his face as he approaches us. I can see the harsh lines on his face even in the darkness. I squeeze Sunita's hand, and she squeezes it back. "What's wrong?" I ask right away.

The look on Dominic's face darkens. "I don't know if I want you to go any farther," he says.

I bristle. "Don't be ridiculous," I tell him. "The rabbit is that way, yes?"

"Yes, it is."

"Then we go onwards," I tell him.

Sunita presses my arm, then holds out a hand to Dominic. "What is it, Dominic? What did you see?"

He shakes his head. "It's not what, it's *who*," he says. He then begins walking back in the direction from which he came. Sunita and I exchange a look and then begin to follow him. I'm not sure what he's seen that has upset him so much. He's the man who has travelled farther than anyone in the labyrinth. He's seen everything, or almost everything, that the labyrinth has to show us. I'm not sure what has him so spooked, but I can't help being a little bit afraid now when normally he's so unshakable.

We walk onward and I clutch Sunita's hand for strength as much as courage. As we walk, I begin to hear what I think is a soft breeze moving through the labyrinth walls. It seems to grow and shrink, fluctuate and whisper as we move closer. Then I realize that I'm not hearing a breeze, but the sound of people speaking to each other. I can make out certain words and phrases and a small part of me is afraid. There are people here; are they friend or foe? I know that Dominic wouldn't have led us forward if it wasn't safe for us to be here, but I can't help but be apprehensive. The fact that Sunita is almost crushing my hand isn't helping either. I try to gently ease her grip, and she offers me an apologetic smile.

When we round one wall, the source of the whispering comes into view. I'm momentarily at a loss for words or even thoughts. There is a sea of people in front of me. They're walking around, going about their day in what looks like an eerily similar parallel to the part of the labyrinth that we live in. They're all milling about their own market square, and I'm surprised by how many people are here. I look at Dominic for an explanation and he motions with his jaw for me to look again. I'm not sure what I'm supposed to be looking at, but when I look again, I receive a shock.

There are people here who I know. I can see Carolyn sitting

with Kimberlee and Su Jay; all three of these women disappeared a long time ago, presumed to have died. I can see Dawn talking to Alexander and Lucy and they're all laughing about something that Dawn has said. It all seems unreal to me, as if we've stepped into a dream part of the labyrinth that was hidden until we found the deepest level of sleep or shock. Dominic motions and points beyond this market square and I can only assume that the rabbit is beyond them. I nod to show Dominic that I understand. As we make our way closer to these people in their market, I can see others who I used to know. I can see Brian giving Gailene a quick embrace and I remember both of them, how they used to argue all the time, they were so unhappy. It seems odd to see them smiling now, laughing about something Gailene said; I can actually hear her laughter from where we stand. It sounds like her mouth finds something funny that her mind doesn't understand. A little further on, I can see Pamela talking with Iskra. Pamela is trying to choose from crystals that are on offer and Iskra is pointing out her prettiest ones. Pamela is smiling brightly as I watch them. Their smiles are real, but they do not match their eyes. Pamela's curly white and gold hair frames her face, making her stand out in the shadows. She looks almost frightened about something, and I don't want to walk into the crowd, but Dominic and Sunita are nearby, and I hope that we can keep each other safe, but safe from what I wonder.

As we move forward, it's like we step over some sort of live wire. The crowd of people haven't noticed us thus far, but when we step over that unseen wire, they all turn as one. Pamela, who we are closest to, exclaims and puts her hands to her mouth. When she lowers them, she is smiling again and for the first time I can see that the smile is reaching her eyes.

"Roanne..." she half whispers. "You've finally come! We've

been waiting for you, and you finally came. I had hoped that you would one day. The rabbit said that it would be so."

"The rabbit said that it would be so," the people around her repeat.

Everyone has gone still and they're all looking at me. It's like they haven't even seen Dominic or Sunita, who now move even closer to me. Sunita puts her left hand at my back and takes my right arm with her own. Dominic moves closer to me on my left side; they have both felt the same threat I have sensed.

I don't know what I will say, but I ask the first thing that comes to mind. "How did you know that I would be coming to you?" I'm shocked at how calm my voice sounds when all I really want to do is run away and hide. I want to trace my steps back to our own enclave and hide behind the walls I know so well.

"The rabbit said it would be so," Pamela says.

"The rabbit said it would be so," the crowd around her intones. Gailene reaches forward to gently touch my herringbone coat and she smiles even more brightly than before and lets out a happy sigh, as if the act of touching of a piece of my clothing has brought her joy.

I look at Dominic and Sunita to see what I should do and Dominic motions with his chin again. I take a step forward and then another one, letting the people there touch my clothing and my skin. They are treating me like I'm some kind of messiah and I don't know what to do but move forwards. They simultaneously move closer to me and away from me, finding room for themselves in the corridors of the labyrinth, their eyes like jewels in the darkness and shadows. As they move away from me, I can see the wall ahead of us and I know from looking at the pages of the little red book that the rabbit is along that wall, just a little further down from us. I take another few steps; no one seems to want to stop us, but I'm still apprehensive.

Cynthia, Sylvia and Dana walk forward as one and they're all smiling at me. Dana is actually crying and smiling at the same time. I don't know why the words come out of my mouth but there doesn't seem to be a way to stop them. "Dana? Why are you here?" I remember her from before; she was always trying to make food that would taste better with the meagre supplies that we had. She steps forward and bows her head slightly and when she looks at me, I can see myself in her eyes, her pupils have grown so large. I wonder if they are all drugged somehow.

"We are waiting for you, Roanne. It was prophesied that you would come and that you would deliver us, but I never thought that it would happen in my lifetime. I thought your spirit would be more likely to show up and to shower us with light, but here you are!" Dana smiles brightly. "I told them that you would come. Are you on your way to the rabbit? Can I take you there?" she asks hopefully.

"It's okay," I tell her. "I brought my own escorts. We alone can know what the rabbit has to say." I don't know what made me think of that, but it seems like something the Oracle would say. I tried to keep my voice light, so it didn't convey how afraid I was. I had spent so long pretending that I didn't exist that to have all these people looking at me like I was some kind of messiah was worrying. My whole body was filled with shivers, and it was a miracle I stayed upright, thanks to the support of Sunita and Dominic on either side of me.

"Of course!" Her smile brightens and it reaches her eyes, but that makes me more afraid than before when her eyes were dead and cold. "Please come and see us afterwards and we will offer you refreshment and discuss what the rabbit had to tell you." She gives me a half bow and backs away into the crowd of people who are all staring at us.

I nod in return, hoping that my heartbeat isn't too loud, and I walk forward. No one in the crowd moves to stop me and we keep walking, Sunita and Dominic holding on to me until we are far from the crowd of people. We turn the corner and there is a long stretch of wall. I can see the rabbit sigil at the end, just like the little blue book showed me. We walk a few steps and Sunita speaks.

"What is wrong with them?" she asks, her voice a soft and urgent whisper. I can hear the fear within her words, and I know that it's echoed in my heart that still beats far too quickly.

Dominic hesitates and then lets out a long breath. He waits a beat and then speaks. "The Minotaur isn't the only enemy within these walls."

"What do you mean by that?" I ask him. "Are there more beasts here that we don't know about?"

"There may be, but that's not what I'm talking about. I'm talking about those people. Sometimes, they can't handle the strain of living within the dark all the time. It plays upon a person's mind, you know? Surely, you've felt it?"

"Do you mean like Susannah? She wanders around looking for her lost dog," Sunita says. "I always take her back home and get her settled, but she usually finds her way to getting lost again."

"Or like Cassiopeia?" I say, realizing what Dominic means. "She talks to the spirits in the walls, telling them that it's okay, that she knows their secrets. She has withdrawn so far inside of herself that she can't see a way out."

"Exactly. That sounds an awful lot like you, Roanne. There is a whole world inside you that no one knows about. I don't mean that as an insult, only that you use that world to help you cope with the world around you. This labyrinth plays so many tricks on all of us; it warps the mind and damages the psyche. We weren't meant to live this way, together but alone, afraid all the time of what will come. This is no way to live," he says. "That's what happened to those people." He motions with his chin back to where they came from. "They are so lost within themselves that I don't know if they will ever find their way out."

I'm looking back at them when I hear the sound of singing. I know it's the whole group of them, singing low with their voices at the ground. If I hadn't just seen them, I would have assumed it was the wind. "Why did they focus on me?"

Something moves in Dominic's eyes and when the words come from his mouth, I know that he is lying. "There's probably no reason for it. Maybe just because you were there," he says. "There is probably no reason for it," he says again.

I look at Sunita and I know that she is thinking the same thing as I am. I can see the realization in her dark eyes. I decide not to challenge him right now. We are so close to the rabbit and I'm more concerned with what we'll find there than the secrets Dominic may be concealing. There will be time afterwards. I want to confront all of them about what they know; Dominic, my mother and the Oracle. I don't know what I will ask, only that I will. Sunita takes my hand, and we walk onward with Dominic leading the way.

When we reach the rabbit, I look up at it. It's made like the other sigils, out of wrought iron. It has blackened with age like the others. Sunita stares at it too, and at first glance we don't see anything. I know that the rabbit hides something that I need to access, something that will help solve or add to the riddle that has filled me for days now.

I try not to get too excited lest I forget how to breathe. I wonder if I was at the end of this journey or if I was merely at the end of one part of it? Where would the rabbit lead me? Down the rabbit hole where I would have to learn more? Or beyond to where I would find out more secrets that I needed to solve? I give my head a small shake. I had to pay attention. I had a riddle to solve. I look at the rabbit for any obvious holes or hiding spots, but there was nothing evident. Sunita and I got really close to it. What I notice at first is that every blade of fur is shaped so that the rabbit looks real, as if it could leap off of the wall and take us on a journey. It looks quite realistic, even though it is made of black metal. The darkness of the labyrinth made it somehow seem even more real and I am struck by how beautiful it was.

As I was running my hands over the fur, I feel a hot bite and pull my hand away. I look and see that one of the strands of fur cut my hand. It bleeds a dark red in the shadows. I reach up to touch it again, easy to find now because my blood dripped from the tip of the metal point.

"Be careful," Dominic whispers. "Your mother will kill me if I bring you back to her injured."

"I am being careful," I tell him. I don't want to think of my mother at the moment, though, and what she isn't telling me. I'll have to go back to her eventually, but it will be on my terms. I don't know whether I will confront her or not.

I focus on the rabbit again and reach towards the one strand of fur that I can now see is sticking out from the others. In fact, it's the only strand of iron fur that seems to be at an angle— every other hair is streamlined. If I hadn't cut my finger on it, I would never have noticed it. I pressed it gently and it moved, so I pressed down more forcefully. There is a sharp click, and we watch as a hole appears in its mouth. Looking at the hole, I can see that there are colours among the black: jade green, sapphire blue and ruby red.

Sunita lets out a gasp. "It's a keyhole!" she whispers. "I wonder if your key will fit, Roanne?"

"There is only one way to find out," I reply, even though I know without a shadow of a doubt that it would. I wonder for a moment if this is what they key had been made for. I reach into my bag and take it out.

"Where did you get that, Roanne?" Dominic asks in a harsh whisper.

I ignore his question and put the key in the lock; of course it fits perfectly. I turn it and hear a clunk within the walls. Looking for a slot that opened within the wall, I was discouraged not to find one. Something had opened the last time I used it with the crane, and I wondered what the point of the rabbit was when Sunita lets out another gasp. "Look, Roanne! Look at the light!"

She points to a line of light that now runs down the wall. I pull my key out and put it back in my bag, and at the same time I see what my key opened. There was a door within the wall. I don't hesitate and pull it open wide. There is light emanating from within what looks like a small tunnel. Sunita and I step in. Looking back, Dominic hesitates. "What are you afraid of, Dominic?" I ask him.

"You have no idea where that leads," he says.

"There's only one way to find out."

He nods and follows closely behind us. Dominic keeps his hand on my shoulder, and I put my one of my hands on Sunita's shoulder. We enter the tunnel as a chain and I don't have any fear inside me, even when the door closes behind us. There is light in this tunnel, I did wonder how there could possibly be light within this labyrinth and pondered whether there might be another hidden room or rocks and walls that glowed like the ones Kiles and Riley had shown me. The light that we were walking towards seemed too pure for that, too much like sunlight. I feel Sunita increase the speed of her steps in front of me and I hasten my own. The tunnel leads us around a small bend and then the light was upon us.

I blink several times, trying to become accustomed to the light in order to see where the key had brought us. Sunita takes my hand, and I feel Dominic's hand squeeze my shoulder when I let out a gasp. I blink again, thinking surely that what I was looking at was some kind of mirage, but everything remains still and real and when I reach out a hand, it touches green leaves. I could smell the scent of the earth around us. I turn my head to take it all in.

We are in a small garden. Sunlight filters in through a few holes that have been made in one of the walls.. I wonder if the people who built the labyrinth had also built it like this. How would they have known that sunlight would shine through?. Or was it the person who created the books? Vegetables and flowers grow here in abundance, and nothing looks small or stunted from lack of light.

In the centre of the garden, there is a wooden pedestal, and I can see the red book atop it, its gold lettering rubbed off, bits of it shining in the light. The book looks like it is covered in jewels. I go to the pedestal and place the book in my bag right away. I won't take the time to read it here; I'll save that for Sunita and myself later. I don't want Dominic to see what it contains. Given what he didn't say before, I don't feel I can trust him now. He's hiding something from us.

I look beyond the pedestal and there is a doorknob. I know that it would lead us back to another part of the labyrinth, so at least we would not have to cross the crowd of others who had blocked our path before. I wonder where it would take us. Again, I feel like Alice in Wonderland and thought about how the red book would change my life, just as the green and blue ones had. I felt like I was falling down the rabbit hole even further.

"We should bring back a few of these plants," Sunita says. "At least a few of the vegetables. Think of what they could do for us!" She is so excited, and I marvel that she could be so excited for properly grown produce. It's a treasure beyond rubies or diamonds and a thrill runs through me.

"I have lots of room in my bag, we can put them in there," I tell her.

I reach for a head of broccoli and pull it free. There are full grown carrots, and fresh, full asparagus. I can see potato leaves and pull a few from the ground; they are free of worms and rot, unlike the ones that we grow. Soon, Dominic and Sunita are grabbing what they can carry. Neither of them has a bag, so Dominic fills the pockets of his leather coat with whatever he can, and Sunita fills the pockets of her dress. There is no way that we can carry everything. I'm sad about that, but it's a fact of life here in the labyrinth. This would be more than we'd had in such a long time and the bounty would be such a gift to so many people.

A thought occurs to me: I wonder if this garden was somehow a reward for getting this far. Maybe we were being given a prize for figuring out the three riddles or finding our way through the clues. I couldn't escape that thought and it warmed me that whoever had built this hidden room and planted this garden knew that it would be waiting for whoever made it through and found their way here. I wondered who that person was. There was no way to tell from the green book or the blue book as there was no character or tone of voice to the words. I put these thoughts out of my mind and loaded as many vegetables as I could into my bag. I'm thankful that the labyrinth is cool so the vegetables wouldn't need refrigeration. This could keep us fed for a few weeks; I thought of the joy that I would see on my mother's face when she saw the bounty that we would bring home. I would have to bring the Oracle something nice, too.

My bag is heavy, and I have an idea. I start to head back to the tunnel. A look of panic flits across Dominic's face. "Where are you going?"

"We need to leave some food for the others that live here," I tell him.

"There is no time." Dominic says.

"There is always time for kindness."

Sunita takes my bag as we quickly head back down the tunnel and I leave a small selection of food at the base of the wall, near where the doorway was. I can only hope that those within the cult of the rabbit find it. There is no way to venture back the way we came. When I come this way again, when I find the rabbit after this, I will make sure that I bring them food.

I look at Sunita, I nod. "Let's go," I tell her.

As I make my way back to the garden,I stop by a rose bush that grows there. The petals hold little droplets of dew. I chose two of them; Dominic cuts off the thorns from the stems with his knife, and I placed them in my bag, folding over the flap to keep them safe. I hoped that my mother and the Oracle will be happy with the gifts of food and flowers, but part of me knows that they will be worried by now. I have no idea how long we'd been gone. Both my mother and the Oracle must be frantic. I shake my head and square my shoulders. The flowers will be a peace offering and hopefully the impetus for sharing what they hadn't told me in the first place. I will have to work my way towards forgiving them—we are all in this labyrinth together. My bag is heavy with enough potatoes, carrots, broccoli and asparagus to last us for weeks. I hope this and the flowers would be a good way to calm the air between us.

We move towards the door behind the pedestal and Dominic turns to me. "Are you going to look at the book now, Roanne?" There was urgency in his voice.

"No, let's go. Will you lead the way?" I ask him.

Dominic nods and Sunita takes my hand in hers. She gives it a squeeze. I find it hard to be defiant with Dominic, as he's been able to bring us here to the rabbit, but I don't want him to know what is in the book. That is for Sunita and me first. After that, we would see. Dominic pushes the door open, and I turn for one last look at the garden, not knowing if I would ever be able to find my way back here on my own or if the door would work now that I had removed the little red book. I had no way of knowing.

Dominic opens the door into darkness and we all shuffle forward. I let the door close behind me. There isn't even an indication that there was a door there when it closes. I turn and look at the wall we had just come out of and saw a turtle sigil. I thought of what the significance was of the turtle might be.

I hear the sound of frantic steps coming quickly towards us. We all stood there holding our breath, and when Mother and the Oracle come into view I am not surprised. A part of me regretted plucking the roses for them because they did not look happy to see me at all.

I wonder what lies they would tell me now.

CHAPTER TWENTY-FOUR

W<small>E</small> walk back to our enclave.

Mother actually made a shooing motion at Sunita. "You will see Roanne again when I let her out of my sight," she says.

I bristle at that. "You're not holding me prisoner. Where am I going to go?"

"Well, where have you been for the past few hours? Where *did* you go?"

"You seem to know where I went, seeing as you both found us so quickly, or was it just a lucky guess at where we'd turn up?" I look to Sunita. "You can stay or go, as you wish, but I'd like you here," I tell her.

"I think it's time for Sunita to go home," Mother says. "We have a lot to talk about."

"As Sunita came with me today and has been a lot more helpful than either of you, I think she should stay," I say. I am trying to keep my anger in check, trying to keep the words I want to say inside because if they erupt out of me, they would come out in a torrent of hate, and that's not what I want. I don't want my anger to dissipate; I wanted it to remain. An idea had formed in my head, and I would need this anger to make sure my idea would come to fruition.

"It's okay," Sunita says. She takes hold of my hand and traces the sign for spider in my hand, letting me know that she would be there. "I'll talk to you tomorrow, Roanne." She gives my arm a squeeze and I wish she would do more. I wished that I could hug her, feel her heart beating against mine. It is what I want right at that moment. I consider slipping the little red book into her hands, but they would see that. I try to communicate everything to Sunita with my eyes, but subtlety is lost in the dark. I know that she understands me somehow, though, even without the benefit of sight and words.

Mother puts a hand on my shoulder and squeezes it in what is supposed to be a reassuring manner, but it feels like a vice grip. It's meant not to comfort me but to control me or at least keep me from getting away. We walk quietly to our enclave. I recognize the walls and the paths that led there, having traversed these pathways so often. With every step, I harden my resolve and my hands grip my bag and cane. I'm not sure what I would do or what they would do. I had never seen Mother so frantic. She was normally my rock and my support. I don't know what she is, now.

She almost shoves me into the main room. It's hard to believe that I had been there only a few hours before when the world had been different. Now, Mother and I are on opposite sides of a chasm. When Mother and the Oracle look at me, I see the panic struggling within both of them and I wonder if the hardness had been there all along or I just hadn't noticed it before. They wear it like a wall. I tighten my grip on my bag.

"Please explain where you went tonight," Mother says.

"I don't think I will, thank you."

"We need to know where you were tonight," the Oracle says, her tone of voice soft compared to the hardness in Mother's.

"I think you already know where I was, since you were there when we made our way through the door."

"You don't know the game you're playing!" Mother hisses

out in a whisper. "Your father started asking questions and then he was gone, taken by the Minotaur. This is what always happens."

"I find it hard to believe that all the victims of the Minotaur went looking for knowledge or tried to solve the riddles of this place," I tell them. I didn't hiss my words, though, as there was no anger in them. Instead, the anger roils within me. It's a torrent that moves its way through me in waves, but I don't let any of that show in my voice. I want to hold on to my anger, but I would not give them the satisfaction of knowing they were the cause of that anger.

"That's not what your mother means, Roanne. Only that the Minotaur seems to know when someone is close."

"Close to what?" I ask. Mother doesn't say anything but looks at me with that frantic expression in her eyes. She looks as though she is fighting to keep the words in at the same time as wanting to let them go free from her lips. I wonder how long she has been keeping something from me. I turn to look at the Oracle and she shakes her head as if she were afraid to speak the words she is keeping in.

Dominic's low voice filled the air. "We're just worried about you," he says.

"I'm fine," I tell him.

"After what Janice did to you, your mother was so worried," Dominic says gently.

"I know she was." My mother had been my rock then, holding me as I shook with sobs, unable to tell her what had happened, too ashamed of what Janice had done to me. There were no secrets in the labyrinth though, so I'm sure it was only a matter of time before she found out. "That has nothing to do with this though, does it?"

"This is different," Dominic says. "This could get you killed."

A soft laugh escapes my lips before I can stop it. "Seriously? That's your defense? There's so much in this labyrinth that can get us killed, the Minotaur for one. We could die from hunger, because as you know there isn't enough food to go around. Or we can die from loneliness, but you'd know nothing about that would you? Gallivanting off to see the distant shores of the maze and yet never being able to find a way out."

Dominic looks hurt but when I look at Mother, I see her smirking a little. She looks a little overjoyed for Dominic to be getting taken down a peg or two. I don't like the joy I see, so I distract her from it. I look away from her and to Dominic once more. I go closer to him and touch his arm. He softens a little and I watch as his shoulders relax.

"I know you're worried about me, but I'll be fine."

"Whatever you are doing, you have to stop this," Mother says. "Before you do something that can't be undone."

"And what would that be, Mother? You obviously know what could happen. Why can't you tell me *anything*? You took me to the owl, and you told me to go find the spider. What do the other sigils do?"

I watch my mother struggle, like watching a war on her face. Her jaw clenches and unclenches, her eyes bulge, and in the shadows of our enclave, she looks demented. I had seen her look this way only once, when father was taken by the Minotaur. She didn't look quite as broken as she had then, but Mother did look as if she were about to break.

Mother lets out a sound of suffering low and primal, the Oracle went to her and put her hand on Mother's shoulder. "We don't have time for this right now. We can tell her enough, but not everything. That way promises won't be broken, Sophie."

Grabbing hold of the Oracle's collar, Mother presses her forehead against the Oracle's. "She is supposed to figure things out on her own. She's so close, but we both know what comes next. I can't lose her, I just can't."

I have no idea what Mother is talking about, but it sounds like she was talking about the journey I had been on and the rest of it that stood before me. "Mother, does this have to do with the books?" I reach a hand into my bag and take the red book out so that I could show her, but she wipes her eyes of the tears that had fallen and reaches out a hand to stop me. She gives me a watery smile, and this made her look even more crazy than before. Her smile did nothing to comfort me, rather it made me more fearful of her.

"It's okay, Poppet. I've seen the books; I've already read them. Everything will be okay. You just need to stop, okay? There is only one way to go on the path you're on, so why don't you choose a new path?"

I figured the truth would hurt her, but not this much. My mother, normally a rock of strength, looks soft and fragile. I didn't think it would be a good idea to let her know that regardless of what she says, I would be continuing on this path. I had already come too far, I couldn't stop now. I thought of the mountain of bodies, and of the glass shard in the water. My throat convulsed around where the shard used to be. I thought of the stone in my pocket and the three books in my bag. I going to need all my talismans with me on this journey, perhaps even the book and pen that Cheryl gave me.

"There is only death for all of us," Mother says. She grips both of my shoulders in hands that feel like talons clawing at my skin. "I've seen it and so have you in the eyes of every person you know within these walls."

"If that's so, why didn't you let me die when the Minotaur came the last time? You told me to look for the spider and I did. Sunita and I were saved because of that. Would you have me just accept death now after trying for so long to keep me alive?"

The Oracle approaches me and takes my mother's hands from my shoulders. "Your mother is just worried about you Roanne, and I am too. I don't know if you understand the journey you're on."

"I *do* understand. I think this could be leading us, leading me, to a way out of the labyrinth."

"How can you know that's what it will say?" the Oracle asks. "Have you read the red book yet?"

"No, have you?" I look at my mother and Dominic. "Have any of you?"

"No," Dominic says. "I've only seen the red book. I saw your mother with it too, once, but I do not know what information the book contains."

Mother shakes her head. "I had it briefly. I was too afraid to read it and know what it said. Can you imagine? Reading the words it contained and being the first person to know of its wisdom?"

"If you didn't read the book, why are you so afraid of my reading it?" I ask them.

The Oracle puts a hand on my mother's shoulder and then holds a finger to her lips when Mother looks as though she was going to start talking again. The frantic look in her eyes has not gone away and I worry for her sanity. Mother looks as if something has broken inside of her and I wonder if this is the first time I might actually seeing my mother as she truly is.

"Your father read the red book, Roanne," The Oracle says. "It was her fault that he read the books in the first place. In a way, the red book took your father from the two of you before the Minotaur took him. He was so distracted about what he had read, it's no wonder that he was taken by the beast. It was like he wandered out to meet the Minotaur, really. Like he was in a trance. I remember it like it was yesterday."

"You just let him walk out to meet the Minotaur?" I ask in a hoarse whisper.

"There wasn't anything we could do," the Oracle says. "The Minotaur simply scooped him up as if he were a toy and carried him away. We never found his body."

Mother lets out a small sob but covers her mouth with her fist to keep the sound from rising and becoming louder. Shaking her head, she takes several deep breaths and when she looks at me again, my mothers' eyes are full of light. Whenever I see her eyes like this in the darkness, they give me hope. I marvel at the way she is able to switch off her grief and fear so quickly and I wonder how she learned that particular talent with no one to show it to her.

"I know you don't remember that day, but I can still see him in my mind. He simply walked out to the Minotaur as if he were meeting an old friend. I watched him look up at the beast and yell something, but I was crying too much to be able to hear it. We never found his body, but we released a glowworm in his memory. I don't want to have to release one in your memory. Can't you let this go?" She asks.

I did think about it for a second, but I have come too far. I know that I can't do it alone, but I will not be asking for their help. They would continue trying to stop me. I plan to find out what is at the end of this journey, no matter where it brings me. I shake my head. "I can't Mother. I think you know that," I tell her.

Nodding, she takes my face in her hands. When I look into

her eyes, I do not see fear or grief, only understanding. "I know. You truly are your father's daughter," she says.

"And yours," I say. "I'm your daughter, too."

She gives me a watery smile. "Go and read your book. I know that I can't stop you, as much as I want to. If I had my way, I would keep you as my little girl forever. The labyrinth has a way of making time seem endless. I know that you must grow and change and make your own choices." Mother lets out a breath. "Even if I don't agree with them."

I look into her eyes and see the truth of her words. The law of the labyrinth is about paying attention to what is said and what isn't said. I give her a soft hug, something I haven't done for a long time and try to communicate everything through that hug, all the words I can't say. I think she understands because she hugs me back. It is the most wonderful feeling, being held by her. I take the memory of this feeling with me when I climb the mountain.

Finally, Mother let me go. "Go, Roanne. Go find your girlfriend and read the book. I don't want to hear what it has to say, but Sunita might."

I hug her again. "I love you, Mother," I say.

"And I love you too, Poppet. We all do. You're going to do what you need to. I pray that the book does tell you how we're going to leave this place. Whatever it says, it will leave you changed."

"Do you think so?" I ask.

"How could it not?" When she pats my cheek, I see the fear in her eyes again. I give the Oracle and Dominic quick embraces and go to find Sunita. We have some reading to do, and I was sure that things would not be the same afterwards, nor that I would want things to remain as they were.

I thought of the flowers that grew here in the labyrinth. In a way, I felt like one of those flowers, able to grow in spite of everything that tried to keep me down. I nod at Mother and go in search of Sunita.

CHAPTER TWENTY-FIVE

I found her in the library.

She was looking through picture books. One is a caterpillar that had eaten through all the pages of the book. She is flipping the pages when she hears me come in and I watch her face brighten. I feel mine light up too, the smile surprising me. I have to deal with this. I had felt attraction before, but nothing like this. The passion that Janice and I experienced together paled in comparison and yet it wasn't all consuming as my love for Janice has been. It breaths air into me instead of stealing it.

Before Sunita can come over to me, Eleanor walks out from behind one of the shelves and gives me a small smile. She is a matronly woman of great humour but could also be fiercely tempered if one of her books came back to the library damaged. She had still not completely forgiven me for a copy of *The Secret Garden* that I had damaged. The front cover had bent and creased when it was in my bag, and she had given me quite the telling off. Every time she lent it out to another person, she told them not to damage it more than I already had. I hoped that she would forget one day, but the books were her life; she lived for their stories. It wasn't a bad life to have, one which was motivated and captivated by words.

"You've returned again I see," Eleanor says. She holds out a hand to me in a come-hither motion and I let her hug me briefly. She shows affection even less often than I do, so I consider myself fortunate that she still wanted to hug me even though I had mangled *The Secret Garden*. "You keep growing, too. I must bring those clothes I found to your mother, she can make something great with them, I'm sure."

"I'd like that," I tell her.

"Now, are you here to collect more books, or Miss Sunita? I'd wager the later rather than the former."

"You're right," I tell her.

"You're both welcome to sit and chat in here. I always find being around books so peaceful and you look like you could use some peace, Roanne. Sit with her and stay a while. There isn't anyone else here and school is out for the day. It would be nice to know that the books have some company." She reaches out and pats the spines of some of the books on the shelves as if they were her children. They were more than that. It was something I understood because of her; books hold the lives of many and gave our minds an opportunity to travel when our bodies remained still.

"I would love that, thank you."

"I will make some sage tea for you both, just mind that you don't spill the tea on any of my books. They so hate getting wet," she says.

"I won't."

"I'll be right back then." Eleanor gives my shoulder a rough pat and turns away to go to the back of the library where a small fire was kept in a stone fireplace, away from any of the books. She takes a pot off the fire and puts some sage leaves inside. Soon the library is filled with the scent of sage, and I immediately relax. She pours the contents carefully into a teapot and brings it and two mugs to a table set away from the books. Setting the pot down carefully, she gives me a stern look. "I mean it, Roanne. No getting the books wet, am I clear?"

"Yes, Eleanor." I give her a smile. I know that she is a lot of bluster and hot air, but she has to be considering she teaches all of the children in the labyrinth.

"All right, then. I got some new books to look over. I need to see if they are worthy of saving. Just come and find me if you need anything."

"I will," I tell her.

She gives my shoulder another awkward pat. When she looks at me this time, I can see everything that she couldn't say. Eleanor is a very private woman, and this includes talking about anything related to one's feelings. According to Eleanor, one just didn't discuss such matters. Her patting my shoulder was akin to a full-on hug for her.

I sit down next to Sunita, and we look at each other for a moment without speaking. The air is filled with the words unsaid between us.

"What did your mother have to say?"

I shake my head. "It was bizarre. The Oracle, Dominic and my mother have all seen the books before, but no one has read what is in the red book. I know their fear is related to what happened to my father, the only person who has read the red book."

She asks her next question slowly, as if not trusting her words or my reaction to them. "Are you sure it's wise that we do, then?"

I raise an eyebrow. "Do you think we shouldn't?"

She gives a light shrug, as if not wanting to commit to it. I can see the shadow of a word covering her cheek. I put my hand over it and felt the warmth of her skin. When I let my hand drop, she is filled with words which I had wanted to forget, but which came to my tongue now. I did not say them, but I would save them for later. Three words have a lot of power; I've learned that the hard way.

"I think we should," I tell her. "I mean, what harm could there be?"

"Well, your father went looking for the Minotaur after he read it and was taken by the beast. Could the same fate be waiting for us?"

"Us?" I ask the word like a wish.

"Of course, we're in this together now, aren't we?"

I nod and try to tell her how I feel by looking into her eyes. It was too dark in the library, so I didn't think she could really see my eyes. I did the only thing I could think of. I held up my right hand with my all my fingers raised, except the third and forth which I kept down. It was the sign for "I love you". Just because I can't say the words yet doesn't mean that I can't show her how I feel. I wait, holding my breath, and when she raises her hand the same way, I let my breath out again.

I give her a smile and dig the red book out of my bag. This book was the thinnest of the three, containing only a scant handful of pages. It is also the smallest and looks to be the most worn. The words on the front cover are in gold, same as the green and blue books, and like them the words on the cover of the red book were almost gone. I can see the imprint of some of the letters, but even the indentation has faded with time. I have no idea how long the books have been hidden within the maze, but it must have been a long time.

I hesitate to open the book. I don't know what this would tell me or how it will change my journey, whether it would finish it or change its direction. I've never been one to back down from a challenge, but something about this book frightens me. I don't know why it scares me. I've always had to fight every day of my life, and I know that I am strong so it isn't a question of bravery, and yet I am afraid.

I take a deep breath and open the book.

I don't know what I was expecting, but it wasn't this. The first book contained rough notes and sketches as well as journal entries showing how the labyrinth was built. The storybook which was written in poetry revealed the secret of the Minotaur., This book is different. It isn't a list or a story or a log; it's a letter, written in brisk handwriting. I thought about reading it myself first, but that wasn't fair. Sunita had travelled with me to get it. I held the book so that both Sunita and I could read it at once.

***

To Whomever Reads This

I commend you. You've gotten this far, but there is farther still to go. I assume that you're intelligent as you found the green book tucked within the trunk of the elephant. It was aptly named Ledger of Events. The elephant never forgets, and I wonder if you will always remember what you read. You know how the labyrinth was built but not how the Minotaur came to be within the labyrinth's walls.

I assume that you're able to keep secrets as you figured out what the pages in the green book held which led you to the crane and the crane held the secret of the Minotaur. They are the mystery keepers and the keepers of secrets and if I can make a guess, you've kept all these secrets to yourself. Do you feel the weight of them yet? I do hope that you were able to share them with someone you trust. Secrets between people tend to eat away at relationships. Holding on to words unsaid can lead to madness. If you are reading this, you figured out the path that was hidden in the blue book. But did you understand the riddle in the poem? I wonder if you did. It took me a while to understand it when I read the first copy of the storybook. There have been many copies of them; I don't know how long this journey has been going on.

Indeed, there have been many copies of this book, too. You ran to the rabbit to find out where it would lead you, didn't you? Will you go down the rabbit hole? Or will you close the book and walk away from what I have to tell you? Don't worry, I'll wait.....

.....I assume since you are still reading that you want to continue?

There is no easy way to tell you this, so I'm going to just come out and say it. You'll have to kill the Minotaur or at least try to. It's what we've been trying to do for eons now, haven't we? We are tired of living in the dark and I know that I am desperate to see the stars again. I don't even know if the stars still exist, but I'm desperate to find out.

The thing of it is, I urge you not to go alone. Many have tried before and they have all failed because we are still here, still held captive. I know that you may have had to rely on help from other people to find this book. It's kind of cruel, isn't it, sending you like a little rabbit on a journey that you aren't able to do on your own? Don't worry, we've all had help along the way. It's the only way to find the book.

I hear you asking, "but how do I kill the Minotaur?" as I did. Well, you read the storybook, didn't you? You know what to do. Show the Minotaur who it used to be or even what it looks like now; both end at the same result. I can hear you thinking surely that's not it? There must be more that I have to do?

You'd be right. I can't tell you what you need to do, or what you might need to sacrifice to get there. You have a decision to make now. Will you continue onward? Will you lead your people to a possible exit and supposed freedom from the walls that surround you? Will you go towards the Minotaur and its end and most likely your own? Or will you do what countless people before you have done and hide the books again out of fear? What will *you* do? This your story after all, and only you can decide how it will end. Just remember that the rabbit is always on a journey of rebirth and regeneration and only you can decide where you want to go.

It's your journey after all.

CHAPTER TWENTY-SIX

W<small>E</small> are both quiet as we leave the library, our cups of sage tea untouched.

All I can hear is the thumping of my heart and the shuffle of our footsteps in the dirt. Words want to pour out of my mouth at the same time as I want to keep them in. I feel so full of words and syllables and consonants. The letters poke at my throat and fill the part of me that used to be occupied by the shard of glass. I need to find that shard. I remember where I was, when I let the anger and the sorrow flow out of me. I will need to gather those close to me; they will be my weapons against the dark.

Changing direction, I walk towards the brook where I let go of my pain after holding onto it for so long. My feet carry me there; my mind needs to know that I have everything I'm going to need. My mind is rolling like a storm, and I think of what else I need to take with me as well as who. The red book said that I should not make this mission alone, for it *is* a mission. I've come to realize that it's been a mission the whole time, the entire journey I've been on has been a mission with one final purpose. I wonder if I am brave enough to take this on, to do what no one else could do. Will I welcome others with me when they might die?

"I can hear you thinking out loud," Sunita whispers.

"Then tell me what I am thinking." I tell her.

"You're trying to think of a way to go it alone."

I scoff and try to sound tougher than I was. "That's not even close to what I was thinking," I tell her.

I can feel her giving me a stern look in the shadows even though I'm not looking at her. "You forget how well I know you, Roanne. You're tough as nails, sure, but even nails will make you bleed. You keep going until you can't go anymore, always trying to outlive and outrun your body by trying to prove how brave you are."

I am speechless. No one has ever been able to see so deeply into me. I doubt even I could have described myself with such clarity. I do the only thing I could think of doing and reach out to take her hand. Sunita squeezes mine and holds onto it. My mind is calmer with her near me, more than it ever had been with Janice. With Janice, I always worried that I wasn't good enough for her, that she was somehow settling for me. With Sunita, I felt the world was full of possibilities if she was by my side. I knew that I loved her.

"What happens now?" I ask her.

"You need to decide who will go with you on this part of the puzzle. I figure that the letter writer knows why you can't do this alone. You've had to solve puzzles and riddles throughout all of this. Do you think there are a few more that you'll have to solve?"

"I'm sure of it," I say. As soon as Sunita says that there will be more puzzles on this path, I know that she is right. Why else would I still have a key that I had only used twice? I wondered if the red book held any other secrets; I had the sneaking suspicion that I would have to use the key a third time.

"Well, then you will need all the help you can get. We know that you're brave, Roanne, but you don't have to do this all on your own. Let us help you."

"But you could die!" I whisper fiercely. "I would hate myself if that happened."

"And *you* could die. Do you think I'd forgive myself?" She shakes her head. "You're not talking me out of this. There are things ahead that you won't be able to do alone, I'm sure of it. Look at the puzzles we've had so far. You've had help along the way, too. Don't forget the Oracle helped you, Dominic helped us. Let us help you, Roanne."

I nod slowly, demonstrating my consent. "I suppose that I don't have a choice, do I?"

"No, you don't." Sunita says softly. She leans forward and kisses me gently for the first time, and for a moment I forget that we were in the middle of a labyrinth, shadows all around us, the lives of others surrounding, us shuffling in the dark. In this moment with my lips to hers, there is only Sunita. I can almost forget what I had done and what we had to do.

I broke the kiss before I lost too much of myself and forgot about the path ahead. Sunita has that effect on me, and I can't afford to lose control. I can see the smile of her lips in the dark and my heart warms. I take hold of her hand again and lead her forward. We aren't that far from the brook and a part of me can feel the water in my throat, as if the shard was still in there, the water filling up my body until it was all I could taste. I begin to hear the water, and I know we were almost there; the sound of water growing louder with each shuffling step we take.

When I see the brook, it almost seems to shine brighter in the darkness because of what it holds. I don't know why I need the shard back; I only knew that, like the stone that had fallen from my mouth, it shouldn't be here and yet it was. It had come from me, and I need whatever power it holds.

I kneel carefully at the waters edge and set my cane beside

me. Sunita stands watching nearby, and I can feel her eyes on the back of my neck. I don't need to look for the shard of glass, it's right there in front of me. I thought it would have moved down into the water and gone wherever the water would have taken it, but the shard had landed between two rocks which held it in place. Reaching into the water to grab hold of the shard, I was surprised by how cold the water was. It wakes me up and enables me to focus, the chill running throughout my body. I shiver and wrap my hand around it. Even though it has been under the water for a long time, it is still warm to the touch. I pull the shard out of the water and hold it in my hands.

Looking at it, it seems almost commonplace, except for the fact that it had come from inside of me and was the manifestation of my pain. I now knew that pain could manifest itself in many different ways. I would need to master all of them. Both the shard and the stone came from my pain. I knew that glass shard was the emotions and words left unsaid. The stone held the pain that I lived with every day when I tried to walk, move or do something that required any physical movement. I dried the shard on my skirt and placed it in my bag. It clinked against the stone and then was quiet.

Sunita was looking at me with concern in her eyes. Holding out a hand, she helped me to stand, and I leaned forward to kiss her softly. I pull back from the kiss and feel my cheeks redden and wonder if Sunita could see how red they had become or if the darkness hid the hue of my skin. She touches my cheek, and I reach up and put my free hand over hers. We stand there and I could feel our hearts beating. I promise myself that I will remember this moment, when it was just us and nothing else, just the touch of the woman I love.

"What did you want to do?" She asks.

She asks me as if I have a choice, as if we hadn't come to the last act of the play that we had been a part of for longer than either of us understood. "We've come too far," I tell her. "I'd like to see this through to the end. It could mean freedom for us, and we could finally see the stars. I need to do this. If there's a chance that we can end this, I want to do it."

She says nothing but merely nods and squeezes my hand. "I know you do," she says. "And I'm coming along for the ride. Who else will you bring with us?"

There is no point in my asking her if she is sure or telling her that I don't want her to come with me. There is a conviction in her eyes that I know well and there is no changing her mind. My heart warms and I love her more. "I've been thinking about that," I tell her. "Do you think that Kiles and Riley would come with us?"

"Those two are always up for an adventure and they love you."

"Is that it?" Sunita ask. "Can you think of anyone else?"

I shake my head. "I don't think so. I thought of asking Janice for a millisecond, but I know that she would never be brave enough to come with me."

Sunita lets out a small snort. "True enough." A look of worry slips over her face and then it is gone a moment later. "What can four of us do against the Minotaur? How can we possibly defeat it?"

"Don't you remember the poem from the blue storybook? We merely have to bring it to a body of water so that it remembers who it is."

Shaking her head, Sunita says, "Do you really think it's that simple? There must be more to it than that."

"We won't know until we get there, and we find it," I tell her.

I feel one fleeting moment of apprehension but also sense that this was the right thing to do.

"How do we go about finding the Minotaur?" She asks me. "It could be anywhere."

I shake my head. "We have to go to higher ground," I say. "I know the entrance. We should go and find Kiles and Riley," I tell her.

"How are we going to find them in here?" she asks.

"Well, they're usually getting into trouble of some kind. I have a good idea of where they might be."

She gives me a smile. "How do you know?"

I grin back. "I know them well. Come on." I lead the way away from the brook and towards one of the male bathing holes. I know which one they prefer. I hold up a finger to my lips and Sunita nods and smiles in the darkness. I resist the urge to laugh and walk quickly, Sunita taking hold of my hand and keeping pace with me. I know the route by heart: beaver, tiger, giraffe, hummingbird, turtle, pelican, anteater, otter, cat, dog, mongoose and butterfly. I can hear the water, but I know that they wouldn't be in the watering hole. They would be taking in the sights.

I hold my finger to my lips again and lead Sunita into the bushes surrounding the watering hole. I press in a little deeper and found a small group of people there: Melissa, Charlotte and Megan standing near Kiles and Riley. They are looking at the watering hole through a covering of branches. We can see the men in all their glory, but they could not see us. We were too far into the darkness and none of the men knew we were there. One of the men stood on the rocks and looked down into the water as we watched him. He jumps, splashing the other men who laugh quietly.

Megan fans herself rapidly, looking as if she might happily

faint. I signed at all of them: "You're all perverts."

Kiles grins and signs, "Takes one to know one."

I smirk and hold on to Sunita's hand while we both take in the sights. The men in the bathing hole are all shapes and all sizes and they are each beautiful in their own way. They bathe together without shame, and because it is the only bathing hole for men within our section of the labyrinth. Kiles and Riley use the bathing hole too, just not while the other men bathe. I had once caught them gazing at the nude men through the bushes. They had smiled and welcomed me and now it seemed they had welcomed a few others.

I motion to Kiles and Riley that I want to talk to them, and they nod, turn and wave at Melissa, Charlotte, and Megan and we make our way out of the trees. I don't say anything for a while and all I can hear is the men bathing and the sounds of our footsteps as they shuffle along in the dirt. The words feel too big in my head, and I wonder how I can ask this of them, to come with me on what feels like a monumental fool's errand. I have no idea what we're in store for and I wonder if it's unfair of me to ask them to follow me like I follow the white rabbit.

I wait until we are away from the trees of the watering hole and near the market before I turn to face them. Kiles can see the hardness of my face and puts a hand softly on my arm. "What's wrong, Roanne? You don't wear that face too often, only when you're really upset about something."

"Why must you know me so well?" I ask him.

He shrugs. "Because we're friends..." he shakes his head. "No, more like family. You're like my sister, even if we do have different parents. So, spill."

I look over at Sunita and she nods, giving me a smile of encouragement. I take a deep breath and look back at Kiles and

Riley who both look at me with concern. They *are* like my family and if I can't tell them what is going on, I can't tell anyone. I swallow my fear and let the words flow from me without trying to stop them. Holding them in hurt, all the consonants and vowels scraping and slicing my throat where the shard used to be.

"I need your help," I say. "I think I know where the Minotaur is hiding, and I think I know how to kill it. I was told not to go alone, that it's not a journey I should do on my own. You are both two of my dearest friends and…I need your help," I say again.

Riley smiles. "Of course. When do we go?"

"Just like that?" I ask him.

"Sure, Roanne, we'll be glad to help."

Kiles can see I'm uncomfortable and retreating back into myself a bit. "Maybe you should start at the beginning? Just the Coles notes version is fine," he tells me.

So, I do. I tell them about finding the green book during one of the recent Minotaur raids, how it led me to the crane and how the blue book led me to the rabbit so I could find the red book. I take out the books and show them and Riley accepts them gently as if they are precious artifacts, and in a way, I guess they are. They both flip through them while I talk, telling them of everything that I've been through to get to this point. "The red book said that I shouldn't go on this journey alone and I don't want to. I need those who I love surrounding me," I say.

"What about your mother?" Kiles asks.

I shake my head. "She's unhinged about this," I tell them. "She doesn't want me to do this, but at the same time there's so much they're not telling me, the Oracle, my mother and Dominic. I don't trust them to lead me down the right path, so I have to do this on my own."

"Except you won't be alone," Riley says. "Out of curiosity, did you read all the pages in the red book?"

"Yes, we both did," I tell them, motioning at Sunita.

"Well, then you both saw this, didn't you?" He turns to the last page in the book and flips to the side we had assumed was blank. He holds the page just so and at a certain angle, we can see a rough drawing of a butterfly. There would have been no way we could have seen it in the dark library. It shows more clearly in the light of the glowworms hanging from the rowan tree in the centre of the labyrinth. We all turn and look back at the sigil of the butterfly, mere feet away from us.

"What do you think it could hold?" Riley asks. "Another book?"

I shake my head, thinking of the key with its veins of red, green and blue. "I don't think so. It might be something else."

"Well, we'll have to go look," Kiles says.

"We?" I ask them, not able to keep the note of hope out of my voice.

"Of course, we." Kiles says. "This is the most exciting thing to happen in a long time. Plus, you're like our sister. If you can't count on us, who can you count on?"

"She can count on me," a voice says.

I turn expecting to see Dominic, but Hugo is standing there. He has a grim look of determination on his face as if he is daring me to disagree with him. "What are you talking about?" I ask him, trying to make my voice sound brave when the sight of him puts a grin of fear on my face. Part of me looks in the shadows behind him for Janice, and Kiles and Sunita seem to have the same idea as they move to stand in front of me so that they are between us. Riley looks around Hugo to see if he is alone.

"She's not here," Hugo says. "Janice isn't coming."

"Why are you here?" Sunita asks.

"I came to find you," Hugo motions to me. "I wanted to make sure you were okay."

I nod. "I'm fine, thank you." I'm touched by his act of kindness. "Where's Janice?" I ask. I'm not sure if this is because I want to know or out of politeness.

He shrugs. "I don't know. I broke things off with her. I can't abide what she did to you. I didn't know that she was that kind of person."

"I know what you mean. I had no idea either," I tell him.

"What are you planning?" Hugo asks. "Are you going to go after the Minotaur? Do you need anyone else to come with you?"

"I assume you heard everything," Riley asks.

"I did. I'd like to go with you and help."

"Why should we trust you?" Kiles asks.

"Because I'm here? The labyrinth has been so different lately and the Minotaur is the cause of that. I know that you have figured out a way to end this and I'd like to take part in that. I'd like to make up for what Janice did to you."

"You don't need to repay me her cruelty with kindness," I tell him.

"Isn't that what we're supposed to do?" He gives me an open look of hope. "Look at what came before and forge ahead to the future? What future do we have in here with the Minotaur? If we can end him, I want a hand in that."

I hold my hand up. I want to make sure that everyone here understands what they are in for, what we're taking on. "I don't know what we're up against. Even though this book told me to go after the Minotaur, I'm not sure how to do that."

"Well, we kind of figured that," Kiles says.

"I have no idea what I'm doing," I says.

"Does anyone?" Riley says.

"You have to understand!" My voice is raised, and I know that I'm glaring at them, but they don't get it. "If you come with me, you could get hurt or even *die*. We *all* could. You have to understand." My voice breaks with a sob that comes out without warning. I let it out and the sound makes everyone go still. "I know that you all want to help, but I don't know what I would do if one of you died because you came with me."

"It's okay," Sunita says soothingly. "We all know what we're in for. We also know that with the Minotaur alive, every day there's a possibility that we could die anyways." She gives me a grim look, and I can see the determination in her eyes. "The fact that we could die if we follow you on journey this makes no difference. We could die at any moment in here anyway." I squeeze her hand trying to communicate my thanks in that small gesture.

"Isn't it time we took a stand?" Hugo says softly. "I don't want to sit idlily by and do nothing. If there is a chance that we could end this, that I could see the stars for the first time in my life, then I'm all for it."

"Besides," Kiles says. He holds up the green book. "Someone built this thing and put us all in it, without asking, and left us here trapped with the beast." He looks into my eyes; all signs of joking disappeared from him. "Don't you want to take back control at least a little? Even if we aren't successful, and from what you've said there are others before us who weren't, don't you want to *do* something? Anything is better than what we're doing now."

I looked at them and they all seemed so ready and so sincere. We were banding together to create something new, and I wondered if this is what the person meant by not trying to do it alone. I didn't have to wonder about whether the others that had tried before us had been successful because we were still here, the books had been hidden again. Something occurred to me then, looking at all of their faces, and I realized that for the first time, I felt like I belonged.

"Okay," I say. I nod to make it more clear to myself, as if that nod was the period on the end of what I had said and I knew that I was making the decision for myself.

"What happens now?"

"We should go right away," Kiles says. "Before any of us lose our nerve. You know where to go?" He turns to me and looked at me imploringly.

"I do." I point east of the market square. "There's a mountain there that will lead higher, perhaps higher than we've ever been." I was surprised by how nervous I felt all of a sudden and wondered if it was wise, or if what we were doing was madness. Sunita gave my hand a soft squeeze again.

"You're thinking so loudly," she said to me. "We're all feeling the same way."

"What way is that?" I feign innocence.

Sunita gave me a small smile. "We're all afraid." I marvel at the fact that she knows me so well. "Is that any different from what we normally live with? I've become so used to fear that I can't imagine my life without it."

"Maybe we can use fear to move us forwards," Hugo says. "That's what I always do."

"What do you mean?" Kiles says. "Were you afraid to date Janice?" He asks with a wicked grin.

To my surprise, he nods. "I was because I could see that her heart belonged to someone else. I didn't know what she was running from, but the fierceness with which she loved me frightened me. I kept going, hoping that I could outrun that fear." There was a haunted look in his eyes that I knew well. It was the look I often saw in my own eyes in the mirror.

"It's okay," Riley says softly. "I often ran away from Kiles because I was so afraid of what I felt for him. The more I kept trying to run from him, the more I was just running towards him."

For a moment, I thought of finding Mother and asking her why she moved the green book that was supposed to be with the elephant sigil. It was never supposed to be in the owl room, and I knew she was the one who had put it there. There were mysteries that still needed solving, but they would have to wait. We had our own adventure to finish. I look at all of them, made sure to meet each of their eyes. I see that everyone shares the same look, one of conviction and strength. There is fear there, yes, but there is also a determination to see this through. The fact that they want to follow me on my journey is a marvel to me. Come to think of it though, it is more than my journey now. It belongs to all of us, not just me.

I nod. "Let's go," I say. "If we don't go now, we won't ever go. We need to find weapons on our way. Any of you know where to find any?" I know there aren't a lot of weapons in the labyrinth, but people often make their own given the absence of anything else. I think of my shard of glass and the stone in my pocket. I know that they could be weapons, too. I don't know why it had taken me so long to realize that.

"We already thought of that," Kiles says.

"What do you mean?" I ask. "You knew that I would take you to the Minotaur?"

"No, but I wanted a way for us to defend ourselves if the Minotaur ever came back." Kiles said.

"We broke pieces off of the sigils we found," Riley says.

"How could you? Those are made from iron," Hugo says.

Riley gives him the tiniest of withering glances. "Yes, but how long have they been in here? You know as well as I do that everything deteriorates over time."

"We just helped ourselves to pieces from here and there," Riley says.

I thought of the feathers on the crane and wondered what kind of weapons those could be. "That's amazing!" I whisper. "Do you have them close by?"

Riley nods and points over at a section of walls in the distance. "In the lava rocks," he says. "We figured they were safe there."

"Excellent. Go and get what you've stashed and meet me at the entrance to the market square." I tell them. "We're going to go find the Minotaur."

"Yeah, or die trying," Hugo says.

CHAPTER TWENTY-SEVEN

WE stand before the wall of green.

Even with the strong perfume of the sage plants, I can smell the scent of death. I know that this is where we all come to die in the end, at least those within the labyrinth. It seems an unfitting resting place for human lives, but there isn't enough space to bury people within the walls. It seems so unfair that we are kept in the dark our entire lives and at the end of it, we aren't given the dignity that the darkness can afford. I think of those fortunate enough to have been buried, given a place of their own beneath the ground. It seems an odd thing to wish for or be wistful about, so I wish for something else instead: *please don't let this be a foolish errand*, I wish. I'm not sure who I was praying to or whether anyone actually heard me.

I look at the people standing with me: Kiles and Riley, each with a long shard of iron they hold like staffs. I look at Sunita and know that she has smaller shards that she has filed down to points. They remind me of the feather key that I pulled from the crane sigil, and I know that they will fly well when she launches them into the air. Hugo stands holding a staff he found amongst Kiles and Riley's stash. The long part is just a slim rod of iron, but the top had smaller shards that extended from a round, metal sphere. It reminds me of some kind of wizard's staff, only twice as deadly. Kiles says it has been part of the porcupine sigil, that the long iron pole has been buried within the wall. I wonder if this is another sigil with a hidden secret. Do they all hold a trick within them? I supposed it doesn't matter now.

We look like a small army ready to take on the world. I wish I knew where I was taking all of us. I know they would follow me, that they would walk by my side, but where was I leading them? I take a deep breath and try to keep the worry out of my voice when I speak and the fear out of my eyes when I look at them. Sunita gives me a brilliant smile that makes me feel a little more brave.

I know that we need to go past the sage, that we have to climb the mountain, but a small part of me wonders what would happen if we just turned around and went back the way we came, back to our homes and our families and pretended like nothing had happened, as if nothing was different. Then I realize that not all of us have families and none of us really have homes. The labyrinth is not a home, no matter how large it was. I take a step forward and part the sage bushes. We had let them grow wild. The sage had grown like a wall that hid the majority of the bodies, but it couldn't hide them all. You could still see some through the leaves, but I tried not to look. Now, though, we weren't just looking; we were joining the dead on their journey, wherever it may lead us.

Sunita takes my hand, and I let her. I'll need all the support I can get. Walking on the bodies of others makes for a very uneven terrain. Kiles takes my other hand, and my cane is tucked into the crook of my arm. I try not to look down, but I have to. I need to step carefully. I feel bad when I take my first few steps as these were people I had known, people I had cared for, before their lives were taken by the Minotaur. However, after a few minutes, the faces of the people who I walked upon ceased to matter. They are a means to an end, and we have to climb higher.

With each step, I can hear the soft clunk of the books, the shard of glass and the stone in my bag. I am unsure what part these tools will play, but I know they are my weapons and my defense against the Minotaur, much like Sunita's metal darts or Kiles and Riley's spears. I also know that I have something else—the knowledge I had gathered from all three of the books. Just like the stone or shard, I have my mind. I have always thought that my mind was my greatest asset, and I hope that it will serve me well on this last leg of my voyage. I know that we are close, but I don't know how far we have to go. All I knew is that I can only advance one step at a time and let a plan formulate within me.

"You're deep in thought," Sunita says.

"I wonder if we're going on a fool's errand," I say.

"Then I guess we're all fools, but at least we're together." Kiles says.

That brings a smile to my face that is taken away moments later when we reach a particularly fragrant pile of bodies. I keep my mouth closed as we wade through a cloud of flies. I have no wish to inhale them. None of us speak as we make our way through the cloud and when we do, we all breathe a sigh of relief. I can see everyone's face relax again. I wonder if we'll all find our way through this.

"Why do you think this is a fool's errand?" Hugo asks softly.

I take a large step and then right my balance. "Many other people have tried to get to the Minotaur before," I say. "What if we're not successful?"

"Well, everyone else tried to get to the Minotaur while it was attacking us, right?" Hugo says. "Of course, they died, but we know more than they did. We got this."

I didn't know if we did, though. I nodded, showing Hugo

that I understood him. Sunita looks at me and inclines her head, letting me know that she knows exactly what I am thinking. We take a few more steps, the terrain is becoming more difficult the higher we go. I think of Jason and his wish to see the stars. I wonder if we've gone high enough to see them; it certainly feels like it.

I may not know what we're doing, but we're doing it together. That's the main thing. Everyone else who attempted to destroy the Minotaur acted on their own. We're going through this together. I can't protect everyone. I know that, and the others understand it too. They know that we might not survive this. We may be heading to our deaths but at the very least we were together. I nod again, and this time it feels like a definitive period on the end of a sentence, as if my body is capable of writing words in the air. I can almost see the words of worry and misery floating in front of me. I can follow the curve of a D and the hard lines of a T. I watch as other letters flow like smoke over my eyes, a halting letter H and an A that was full of curves. The E gives me pause; it looks like it has arms, and it is reaching out to touch my face. I let out a soft breath and watch as the letters float away into the darkness. When those words float away, so does the majority of my fear. Yes, I am still afraid, but now I do not take each step in fear. I am afraid but I walk forwards anyways. Though we might be walking towards our doom, I know that my entire journey had led me here, to this moment. I wouldn't turn away from it now, fear or no.

We continue upward. The steps are difficult, but I have someone on either side of me. They wouldn't let me fall. I don't know what will happen when we get higher, or the ground becomes more treacherous, but I will deal with it when it comes. Sunita gives my hand a squeeze every now and again to let me know that she is there and has my back. I squeeze back and wish that I could kiss her. It would have to wait for another time, though.

"What do you think we'll find here?" Kiles whispers. The mountain of bodies is sacred because of the lives that were lost, so I understood his need to whisper. We have spent out lives whispering or talking without words, after all.

"The Minotaur, I hope," I say. I take another big step to avoid someone's head. "I can't imagine there would be much here. How could anyone else survive up here aside from the Minotaur?"

We walk on further, over the bodies of those long departed. I see a few strands of blond hair and the bloated face of Fallan. He had been taken by the Minotaur eons ago. He'd had his tongue ripped out, and his mouth was left just a gaping hole. A little higher up, I see the smug face of Tharon. I wondered what had happened to him. He was one of the boys who used to tease me in school. I may have dug my cane a little harder than necessary into his face. I look over at Sunita and realize that I could see her more clearly than before. I look at the others to see if they noticed the same thing. Was it becoming brighter?

I see confusion on my friends' faces. Kiles looks up to find the source of the light, and his face fills with wonder. Sunita shrugs her shoulders and there is a look of worry on her face. Riley is looking around us but can see nothing in the bodies. Hugo is walking behind me and taps me on the shoulder. I turn and he doesn't point upward, but forward, in front of us. He points to his mouth and covers his lips in a motion like a zipper. He points to his eyes and then points forward. I understand: stay quiet and look forward.

I don't know what I'm supposed to be looking for or what he has heard. I strain my eyes in the dark, and then I see it: the curling tongues of smoke rising above the hills of bodies which surround us. The smoke looks like fingers, beckoning us forward. I am hypnotized by them and hasten my pace. Hugo taps me on the back again. He holds out his left palm and uses his right hand to mime walking, using the first two fingers to walk across his palm. I watch as he makes his fingers walk slowly. I understand. There would be no rushing, we could be hurt that way. Then he points to the rest of the group, then points to his eyes, then points forward again and then all around us. The message is clear: pay attention and look around. He makes the motion of zipping his lips again. We all nod. He steps ahead of all of us, and we let him. He isn't trying to prove that he was a man or that he was stronger than any of us; if anything, Hugo is putting himself in danger by scouting ahead.

I remember seeing him fight once. There were some kids in school who liked to make trouble, and they often tried to beat up the younger kids just for something to do. There wasn't much in the way of entertainment in the labyrinth and kids got bored. We were all angry at the hand we'd been dealt; some found release in a creative endeavour, others found a more physical way of releasing their anger and tension. Hugo often set those kinds of people right by using the only method of communication they understood; brute force.

I watched him often. One time, there was a boy who was kicking a younger boy as he lay on the ground, trying to protect himself. Hugo walked up behind the bully and slammed a shoulder into the bully's back, followed by a swift kick to his groin. The bully fell to the ground, looking up at Hugo with hate in his eyes, and Hugo calmly explained why he wouldn't be attacking any more children. Listening to him that day, it was as if Hugo were making a comment on the weather. He didn't attack people out of anger; he did it to right a wrong. I understood him a little better that day, which is why I was confused when he ended up with Janice. I can't pretend to be unhappy that he left Janice. He walked on the bodies of those underneath us as if they really were the rockface of a mountain. Hugo's steps were sure, and he was confidant, a far cry from the nervous man he had been with Janice.

He stood at the crest of the hill, directly in front of the fingers of smoke. It looks as if he is letting the smoke bathe his face. He motions us closer and waits until we were all standing with him. He gestures forward and we see where the smoke was coming from. A fire was crackling in the distance. I wasn't surprised that we hadn't heard it, the sound was muffled by the bodies that surrounded us. I looked at Hugo and motioned to the fire in the distance with my chin. Then I held out my hands on either side of me as if I were weighing something.

Nodding, Hugo takes the first step forward. I have no idea what we would find at the source of the fire, but it feels like we are going towards something important. I didn't get the shiver of fear from my gut or intuition and there was no answering feeling of sorrow from where the shard used to reside in my throat. I didn't sense a threat, but what was waiting for us? There was no way that anyone could survive up here, could they? And yet, who else but a human could have started a fire? I had never heard of the Minotaur being able to make flame.

The area here is piled high with bodies, but there has been a narrow path made through. Hugo walks in the front, then Sunita and myself, with Kiles and Riley bringing up the rear. The piles of bodies rise well above our heads and had the fire not been lit we would have passed by the opening and kept going. It feels right to be going along this path, even though I have no idea where it will lead. Sunita's worried look had deepened, and I try to calm her by bringing one of her hands to my lips and kissing it. She gives me a smile, but the worried look is still there.

I couldn't tell you why I wasn't afraid, but there is something in the smoke that helped to calm me. It smells like sage and lavender. I wonder if that was what was making me calm. I breathe in deeply and feel even, balanced. There is a little kernel of fear rolling through me, but I can't deny that I am curious about what we'll find at the fire. I only knew that I am following the little red book's instruction, that I am going after the Minotaur, and that I will find it and kill it. I still didn't know how, but I wanted to make sure that it would die at my hand, no matter the cost.

We start slowly towards the crackling of the fire. It is only after we've taken a few steps that we begin to hear voices. Hugo makes a motion with his hand for us to wait. He goes a little further on and then motioned for us to come forward, a look of wonder on his face. As we do, I notice a change in our walking path. The bodies that comprise the mountain have been covered with what looks like fine earth, almost like silt.

I look over at Sunita to see if she has noticed, but she is too intent on what is before her. The path leads to an open area that has been cleared of bodies, or at least the bodies have been covered by more of the silty sand. The scent of sage is stronger here and it's brighter, not just because of the fire but it almost looks like the air around us is filled with sunlight, That can't be, can it? A part of me is growing more frightened with every step that we take, as if the idea of something good happening in the labyrinth is something to be afraid of, rather than the Minotaur that waits for us in the shadows.

I take comfort in the fact that Sunita is beside me, Kiles

and Riley are behind me, with Hugo in front of all of us. We are heading towards whatever this is together. The crackling of the fire and the scent of sage grow stronger with every step we take. I can smell the smoke and practically feel the warmth of the fire. When we turn around the bend in the path the fire comes into view. There are people sitting around it, and this sight is so strange that I stop walking to stare and Kiles bumps into me. Sunita holds on to me to make sure I don't fall and Kiles whispers sorry. The fireside group look at us with open faces and I sense only kindness from them. I wonder if this will be a repeat of when I went to look for the rabbit and the bizarre crowd of people I found there, but this group wait for us to approach. We do so, and I'm not sure what I expected, but it wasn't this.

For one thing, the area is clean. I look around and there are signs of habitation. They have built themselves a home here. I can see a large cabin in the distance and the ground all around us has been cleaned. I can even see a small garden in front of the cabin. I look at the others in my group and they look as confused as I feel. There would be no need for Hugo to tell us not to talk, because I'm not sure that any words would come out. I wouldn't trust the words that would come from my mouth, but I can feel the letters digging into my throat, yearning to burst free.

We stand there, and I can't let the words out even though they're desperate to push past my lips. A woman stands and approaches, her face lit by the fire. She offers me a smile. "I was wondering when you'd get here, Roanne. It's about time you showed up."

CHAPTER TWENTY-EIGHT

T HE woman moves closer to me, and my heart almost breaks in two from shock. I'm staring into the face of Helen, a woman I thought dead long ago. Helen and I would meet at the market and talk about books we'd read, places that existed only in books that we one day dreamed of visiting. Then, after a Minotaur attack, she was gone, and I never saw her again. That was three years ago.

"How can you be here?" I whisper.

She gives me a kind smile and her eyes shine in the dark. "How can *any* of us be here?" Helen motions at the others. "You remember these folks?"

I move a little closer to the fire to look at them, really taking in their features. I see Isabelle taken from us five years ago, and Ginette who has bee gone for three. I don't recognize the other two at first, but they seem to know me.

The man speaks first. "When I saw you last, you were just a tiny thing, Roanne. You've grown up so well. I don't know if you remember me, I'm Richard. I was friends with both of your parents."

The woman speaks next. She appears to be young, but I can see the age in her eyes and wonder what she has been through to age her so much. "I used to look after you, Roanne. When the Oracle couldn't. You were so young then. You used to hold my hand when we went to market. You kept asking me if I could fly because my name is Raven."

Something stirs in my memory, and I think that a part of me does remember these people. A part of me remembers who they were to me, but it's as if they're made of smoke; there one moment and gone the next. The words want to push out of my mouth, and I don't think that I can stop them, I can't stop them. They rush forward in a harsh whispering hiss. "Where have you been? How are you here? We thought you had *died*, why have you hidden? How can this possibly be real?"

I'm almost hyperventilating now. I am staring wild-eyed at people who were dead a moment ago and now here they are, in front of us, and they're alive. They're alive and I can't even comprehend how this is possible.

Helen steps closer to me, holding out a hand. "I know this is confusing. I wasn't too sure of things myself, but if you let me explain, I'll try to do the best I can. May I?"

She motions for us all to sit around the fire. Ginette brings us cups of sage tea which we're all familiar with, and I feel like we are sitting at some kind of bizarre campfire about to listen to a ghost story meant to frighten children before they head to slumber. Only, this won't be like any ghost story I've ever heard, even though I'm sitting with people who should be ghosts.

There are other words that want to break free, and I can feel soft vowels sliding against my throat and consonants jabbing into my windpipe, but I keep my mouth closed. This is their story to tell. I let Sunita and Kiles help me to a sitting position on the cleared ground, and I wonder what they will say. I wonder what they could say that would make up for their absence.

While I wait for them to speak, I look at each of them for signs of fatigue or age in their faces, and though they seem the same, there is no hint of the ravages of time as found on our own faces. Hugo's face is dirty and looks haggard, Sunita has lines of stress that have aged her beyond her years, and Kiles and Riley look older too, as if they've been through a war and have come out on the other end changed by the experience. I don't even want to know how I look. I wonder how these people who I used to know have remained so healthy. Then I remind myself that it's not my time to speak, that it's their turn. I wonder if I will find my voice so that I can let the words free afterwards.

"I was brought to the mountain first," Helen says. "He had slaughtered those in the village and had taken me away and I assumed he would simply eat me later."

"Does he eat people?" Kiles asks. "How do you know it's a he?"

"The Minotaur has always been a male in mythology," Helen responds. "I assumed. I don't really know if he eats the people that he kills. None of us do."

"What happened after he took you back here?" Sunita asks.

"That's the odd part." She says. "He moved some of the bodies that were here and set me down on mostly level ground. Then he left me for a little while, maybe a day and a half or so. I thought for sure that he would return and kill me as he had slaughtered a lot of people that day in the village. I wondered if there was a way to sate his bloodlust."

There was a faraway look in her eyes. I could almost see her sitting here, waiting to die; the smoke of the fire looks to be making different shapes as if it were playing out the scene in front of us. I wonder if there was part of her that was still there, in that moment that had changed her as much as my moments in the labyrinth have changed me. I could see her looking back into herself, pulling the memory out so that she could look at it closely.

"He returned to bring me food sometime towards the end of the second day. He was so tall that I couldn't see his face, but he set down the fish he had found and a couple of potatoes. Then he breathed into the rocks and fire sprang forth. I'm not sure how he did it, but it wasn't like I was able to ask him. I then tried to make this place as comfortable as I could."

"Is the Minotaur nearby?" Riley asks.

"No," Ginette says. "He's beyond the door and we can't go there. Nor would I want to."

"How did you end up here?" I ask Ginette. This seems a fair question to ask. It doesn't feel like the words will go off like a bomb, even though more words now want to leave my mouth. I feel a little like Dorothy in the Wizard of Oz; she spent a lot of her journey confused about her surroundings, much as I was confused by mine now.

"Same as Helen," Ginette says. "The Minotaur brought me."

"He could see that I was lonely," Helen says. "I would wander around here on my own. If I tried to leave, he would grow angry, and I could hear him screaming from the top of the mountain. I knew it was best for me to stay and not anger him, but I felt so lost and alone. He brought me Ginette soon after. I guess he wanted to keep me happy."

"This doesn't make any sense," Hugo says. "The Minotaur is a monster. Monsters don't do things like that."

"But he isn't a monster," I say. "Not really. He may be a monster now, but he was made into one by whoever made this place." I take out the little blue storybook and show Hugo the page with the poem. Raven gasps when she sees the book.

"You brought the books," she says, with a note of wonder in her voice. "I've heard tell of them before, but I've never actually seen them. They are what led you here, I assume?"

"Yes," I say. It felt safe to say this much. I still wasn't sure how much I could trust these people, given that they'd hidden when others had died.

Raven nods. "The Minotaur brought me soon after Ginette, then Richard."

"Why would he do that?" I ask.

"I think he wanted me to have a little family." Helen says. "He didn't want me to be alone."

"This is impossible," Hugo says. "The Minotaur is a killer. A destroyer."

"Even evil can't destroy all the time," Richard says.

"You almost sound sorry for it," Kiles says. "This is the *Minotaur*. It's killed so many people."

"Yet it spared *us*," Helen says. "It keeps us fed and we're safe from it. We must be grateful for the small mercies that it has shown us."

One of the constants is sharp on my lips as the words surge forth. I wonder if it has drawn blood from my lips. "You speak as though it's a father," I say, trying to keep the volume of my voice low and quiet. I can't trust that a loud sound won't bring the vengeance of the Minotaur, and I would hate to be the reason we all died now, especially when we're so close. "That thing is not a father. I don't know why you're alive but its certainly not because of the Minotaur's *mercy*."

They gave me almost pitying looks. I thought of the munchkin who guarded the doors of Oz before Dorothy was led in or the horse of a different colour. I wonder vaguely what these people are guarding; whether they are guarding the Minotaur. How could they have been waiting for me?

Helen waves a hand through the air. "Whatever you may think, the Minotaur could have killed us at any given time, and yet he gathered us here and kept us safe. He made sure we had food and shelter."

"He made sure that we had each other," Richard says.

"You're all talking as if he cares for you," Hugo says a little waspishly.

Helen gives him a kindly look, her wisdom showing in her eyes. "And what if we are? As I said, he could have killed us but instead he kept us alive. We must be grateful for that. Even monsters deserve love," she says.

I shudder. "Yes, you were all kept safe up here while the rest of us had to run and hide. You're sitting on the bodies of those who suffered in your place."

"It's not like we chose this," Raven says. "The Minotaur decided to keep us safe and to protect us,"

"Have you ever tried to leave the mountain?" Riley asks gently. "Any of you?"

A dark look passes over Helen's face, and she nods. "There was one person who used to be here with us," she says. "You might have known her. Darlene? Do you remember her, Roanne?"

I nod. "She was a bossy woman who thought she knew better than everyone else around her," I say. "She was always telling Mother what to do, how to grow and cook food, which watering spots were the best, the right things to buy and trade at market." Darlene had been a short woman, but what she lacked in stature she made up for with her difficult personality and need to bend everyone to her will.

"Yes, well she ended up here, too. She wasn't well-liked down in the labyrinth and then she was *very* much disliked here, with so few people. Eventually, she grew tired of what she called kowtowing to the Minotaur's wants and needs. She stepped off the path which brought you here and started back down towards everyone else. She didn't get very far."

"What happened?" Sunita asks, almost as if she didn't want to hear the answer.

"I remember it as if it were yesterday," Richard says. "She had been going on about not being told what to do, especially by a monster, and started back down the mountain. An ear-splitting scream ripped the air apart and the Minotaur was upon us. He plucked her up off the ground and ripped her apart as if she were a rag doll. Then he ran down the mountain and caused a rampage there." He shudders. "I still remember the black anger in its eyes, as if all the Minotaur could see was vengeance. We heard the screams from down below all the way up here. It was impossible not to."

I don't say anything after that. There seems to be nothing that we can say. They are prisoners here as much as we are all prisoners in the labyrinth. The thought left me with a sense of growing dread. I wonder if we are being watched right now, if the Minotaur can see us and knows we were here.

No one says anything for a moment. We all just breathe in the silence, and wonder where to go from here. The letters rip at my throat to flee my mouth and I wonder if the letter W has ripped a hole in my cheek. "What do you think we're here for? You all know that I have the books, right? I'm not here to sightsee. I'm here to end this."

"We know," Helen says. "Your mother and the Oracle came to see us."

I was stunned into silence, so Sunita speaks instead. "And what about when we went to find the rabbit? All those weird lost people, they knew that we were coming too."

Ginette nods. "Sophie thought that you might go to seek the rabbit and that it would lead you here. The Oracle said that we were not to help in any way."

Raven grins. "But she's not here, is she? Do you have weapons?"

We each hold up our chosen weapon and Ginette nods. She eyes my bag and smiles. "I bet you have treasures in there," she says. "Something to guard against the Minotaur? Perhaps even harm it?"

There is a serious note to her voice, and I find myself nodding, despite not wanting them to really know what I have. "That's good," Raven says. "You'll need them. But we have one more for you. Do you have the key with you?"

I nod. If they talked to my mother and the Oracle, they probably knew what I had been through to get here. I take it out of the bag and show it to them. It glints off of the firelight. It looks to have been made of a metal that had been burned black. I trace my fingers along the three lines of colour and think of the books in my bag.

"It's more beautiful than it has a right to be,' Ginette says. "Hold on to that. You'll know the moment that you have to use it."

"So, a piece of advice is my new weapon?" I ask her.

She shrugs. "We promised that we wouldn't help. We keep our promises. You didn't think the key just opened *doors*, did you? Tuck that into the back of your mind. You won't need it right away."

I wonder why they were all being so mysterious, but I thought I understood. My mother and the Oracle could be hard women to cross. If my mother or the Oracle suspected that we had had any kind of help, they would face consequences. I knew this with a certainty. I felt like our time with them was coming to a close. "What else do I need to know?" I ask them.

"The quickest way to the Minotaur is past this hill. You will find a gate. It's not locked, but you will have to make your way past that and climb higher up the mountain. You will find the Minotaur at the top."

Helen stands and we do the same. She comes closer and embraces each of us softly. It feels like being hugged by a mother or a parental figure. I had not known comfort from Mother, that wasn't what she gave me. She taught me to depend only on myself. I wondered if she knew what kind of gift her comfort was with what we had left to do.

"Many people have tried to kill the Minotaur, Roanne. Perhaps hundreds of people. However, I didn't think that any of them would be successful until you. I believe you can do this. I *know* you can."

I nod because there is nothing else I could think of doing. "Thank you for the tea," I say.

"You're welcome, Roanne. Now continue on your journey. We'll be praying for you."

We start out in the direction that she pointed. Before we crest the hill of bodies, I turn back to look at Helen one last time. She gazes up at me, her eyes alive with the flames of the fire and her mouth in a grim line. I try to decipher what it was that I saw in her eyes and the closest thing I could think of was hope.

CHAPTER TWENTY-NINE

I'm shaken by everything that we'd been told.

It is odd that they lived here on this mountain of bodies, never able to go back to the ones who love them out of some sort of affection for the Minotaur. Yes, there is the issue of it not wanting them to leave the mountain. To me, it feels like they traded one prison for another: an even worse one at that. The thought occurs to me of never seeing Mother or the Oracle again, but I push that thought out of my mind. I can't think about that now. I have to figure out what we're going to do next.

I told the truth when I said that I meant to end the Minotaur. I think of Jason and his wish to see the stars and I hope that I would be able to grant that wish. When the Minotaur is dead, I wonder how we would get out but remembered to think of one problem at a time. I have to think like that, to assume that I would kill the Minotaur with bravado, otherwise the fear that is eating away at me will find a way to consume me. I realize that I have been carrying that fear, that it has been my constant companion, as I collect the books and information they contain.

I ask myself, what would the labyrinth be without a Minotaur? I wonder how Helen and the others could have any kind of affinity for the Minotaur. How do you find affection for your captor, despite the fear they bring you? I shake my head to clear the words filling my mind.

"Stop doing that," Kiles says.

"I'm not doing anything," I says.

"Once again, you're thinking too loud." Riley says. This isn't only your journey, you know. We've all come along with you."

"Yeah, I can't think of anything I'd rather be doing right now," Kiles says. "I could be running away in fear instead of heading right towards it." He lets out a little laugh. "Come on, if we're going to die, we can at least have a good time."

I look at him, his eyes bright and his smile wide. "How can you be so flippant about this?" I ask him.

"Because I deal with things through laughter. You deal with things by brooding and thinking way too loud. Hugo likes to stare off into space like he's doing now so he can listen to his thoughts more clearly."

Hugo starts at hearing his name and gives Kiles a dark look. "How did you know that?" he asks. "Are you peering inside my head?"

"Hardly," Riley says. "It's something I tend to do to make sense of things. The world gets too loud in the labyrinth, even if it is so damn quiet."

"We're all afraid, Roanne." Sunita says to me. "But we came with you. We've had this conversation before. Share your thoughts, Roanne." She takes my hand and gives it a squeeze. I hold on to it and don't let go.

"Okay," I tell her. "What do you think is beyond the gate?" I ask them.

"Well, the Minotaur for one," Riley says. "How are we going to kill it with a bunch of spears and some darts?"

"Miracles have been known to happen before," Kiles says.

"We'll have to see if we can take him by surprise." Hugo says. There is a wildness in his eyes, and he looks away for a moment as if to check the layout of his thoughts in his mind.

"How did you want to do that?" Sunita asks.

"We'll have to wait and see what is beyond the gate," Hugo says. "Also, if anyone is going to kill the Minotaur it has to be Roanne."

These words were met by silence, all that could be heard was the sound of our footsteps. "Does it matter who kills it?" Riley asks.

"It should be her," Kiles says.

"Now you're siding with him?" Riley says, jerking his thumb at Hugo.

"Stop," I tell them. "Stop this, please." I've just understood what the little red book was telling me. "The red book said that I couldn't do this alone, that if I could, I should take other people with me." Their blank faces stare back at me. "Don't you understand? There's no way that I could kill it on my own. I'm not meant to. The only way to kill the Minotaur is to do it as a group. It's why everyone before us has failed. They always went alone. What can one man do against a beast like the Minotaur except maim it a somewhat?"

They look at me in shock, and I must be staring back at them with my own. I have been so intent on the fact that it would be me who killed the Minotaur, that it is going to die by my hand because it had taken my father as well as countless friends from me. I had solved the riddles, I had found the books and the key, but I finally realized that I would not do this alone. "I need all of you with me. There's no way I can do it on my own." I tell them. "It doesn't matter who delivers the killing blow. All that matters is that we kill the Minotaur." I look at each of them in turn. "Agreed?"

They all nod and Hugo answers, "Agreed."

We walk on without saying anything, and my mind feels less

full of monumental thoughts. Oddly enough, even though there is fear there, I am able to observe it from a distance. I have lived with fear for a long time, after all.

We walk onward. There is a dark shadow looming in front of us and as we move closer, I see it's the gate. It stretches into the shadows and is so tall that I can't see the top of it. I can see the red, blue, and green lines that form a border around the edge of the door. I wonder who took the time to carve a gate that looks as though it belongs in another world, but the answer will have to wait. We have a job to do now. We all take a moment to look at the gate in front of us, knowing that the time to turn back would be now. I look at everyone and no one makes a move to turn back. I push the gate open and is whisperers over the moss that has grown on the bodies beneath us.

We step over the threshold of the gate, and I wait for a moment to see if anything will happen. I can hear wind whistling in the distance, or is it the Minotaur breathing? I don't know, but I have a feeling that we'll find out.

"Do you think this is the only way down the mountain?" Sunita whispers. "What if it decides to go on a rampage and we are right in its path?"

"There are other ways down the mountain," Hugo says. "We don't know how far it stretches or any of the secrets it may hold."

These words make me shiver. "What an odd thing to say," I whisper.

"Why? It's the truth," he says. "The Minotaur has lived here for so long; it definitely knows more about this place than we do. There is always more than one way, look at the labyrinth."

"What about it? There's only one way out of the maze," Kiles says.

"And yet no one has found their way out." Hugo responds.

"There are things we don't understand in these walls, the first of which is the Minotaur." He looks at Kiles and I see the fierceness in his eyes hiding the fear that I can smell on him. "We can't pretend that we understand the Minotaur, no matter how hard we try to guess its motive."

Sunita nods and I find myself nodding along with her. There are secrets that we can never understand. The walls we're encased by have been here for a long time. I should have looked for a date in the little green book, but I was more concerned with the crane and what it hid. I have no idea how long the labyrinth has been here or for how long the Minotaur has existed.

We all walk onward, and no one speaks now. It seems that to talk would break the spell we're all under or possibly alert the Minotaur of our approach. I wonder if it knows that we're here already. Is it on high alert? *The Minotaur can be hurt*, I think. *The Minotaur can be hurt*. This mantra plays on a loop in the back of my mind; I can hear it loud and clear. Except that I don't want us to merely hurt it. I want us to kill the Minotaur.

We walk on, taking care that our footsteps are as quiet as possible. I am walking on my own with my cane. Sunita and Riley wanted to each hold my hands and walk on either side of me, but this path is too narrow for that. I can hear the wind growing and can smell musk in the air, a light scent of sage and the aroma of rot. The scent grows stronger as we make our way around a small hill of bodies, and then we all stop.

I don't think that I can breathe. The air leaves my lungs, and I don't know how to pull more air inside them. We're faced with another, larger hill than the one we just traversed but the difference is that this hill is *moving*.

I can hear a low wheeze in its breathing and though I can't see the Minotaur in its entirety, I know that it's him. I had expected to need to hunt him down, and so this appearance right in front of us seems like a trick, as if there is some kind of practical joke being played on us.

I approach it slowly and Sunita is by my side, holding one of my arms. She grips me tightly and I wonder if it's out of fear or to gain strength. I motion to the darts that she has tucked into the pockets of her dress. She shakes her head and points to my bag. I know she means me to take out the shard of glass but now is not the time. I think of what Helen said before: "*The quickest way to the Minotaur is past this hill. You will find a gate. It's not locked, but you will have to make your way past that and climb higher up the mountain. You will find the Minotaur at the top.*"

Why is the Minotaur down here if we were supposed to climb higher to find it? I wait for it to jump to life, to tower over us, to scream down at us before it devours us all, but it keeps sleeping, seemingly unaware of us. We all stand there with wide eyes looking at it, some filled with fear and some with fascination. I'm not sure what my eyes are filled with. This isn't what I thought would happen, that we would find it lying down near the gate as if it were guarding something. I approach it, ignoring Sunita's hand on my arm, trying to grab me and keep me from moving toward the beast. I'm entranced by the Minotaur and want to get closer to it. I want to take in everything about it while it lays sleeping before us.

From head to toe, its body is nearly nine feet long. I can see its hooves, lethal and black, with matted dark brown fur covering its body. The Minotaur's back is to us, one of its arms is resting on its side and I can see the claws that stretch from its fingers. I wonder if they are bones that have grown out of the skin? The huge head is one of a bull, almost a mountain itself, and I can see the horns, long and lethal, shining black obsidian. I know they're sharp because I've seen people impaled on those horns. I almost wanted to touch them, to see if the horns would make me bleed and whether my blood would be black or red in the darkness.

The Minotaur seems nearly harmless as it rests there, but I know the true nature of the beast. I wonder how to best continue. Do we attack with our weapons, or do we attempt kindness? Do I merely show the Minotaur the shard of glass with the hopes that it sees itself, or do I take a pound of flesh from it as it has taken so much flesh from our world?

I move back to the group and Sunita, Hugo, Kiles and Riley wrap me in an embrace. I can feel their hearts beating and I can smell their fear. I know that my being so close to the beast worried them, but how else are we to understand our enemy if we don't observe it when given the opportunity? The Oracle always told me to observe and learn everything I could about my enemies. I understand their fear, but I had to see it for what it was. I was looking for the human underneath the beast.

"What do we do now?" Kiles whispers. "I wasn't expecting to find it just lying there, waiting for us."

"Neither was I," Riley says. "Is it normal for the Minotaur to lie down like that?"

"How do any of us know what's normal for a Minotaur?" Sunita says.

"I don't trust it," Hugo whispers. "It could be faking slumber just waiting for us to make a move."

"And yet it sleeps on while we whisper," I say. I share what I have been holding on to for all this time. "The Minotaur can be hurt. Remember the screams that came with no rampage that followed? It can be hurt, and I think it's hurt now."

Sunita shakes her head. "I don't see or smell any blood from it. I don't think it's hurt."

I think about what the poem in little blue book said. I repeated the same lines over and over in my head: *He wondered what he had done. To curse a man to become a beast, with only one way to be undone.* "I don't think it's *physically* hurt," I say. "Remember what the storybook said, that it used to be human like the rest of us? What if it's hurt because it remembers what that used to be like?"

She shakes her head. "There isn't enough human in it anymore." She gestures to all the bodies we are standing upon. "No one that was once human would be capable of this."

"I don't know," Hugo says. "I would assume that all the killing is the instinct of the Minotaur. It could be warring with itself, you know? How it used to be versus how it is now. That's what makes sense to me if the thing was once human."

I nod at Hugo's words. He doesn't speak often, but he speaks sense in this case. I wonder what we're going to do with this information now that we have it."

"That's all well and good," Sunita says. "But we still have to *kill* it. I say we strike now while its back is turned to us, while we have the upper hand." She reaches into her bag and takes out one of the darts fashioned from the crane's feathers and I reach out to stop her. Kiles and Riley watch open-mouthed and Hugo has an almost wicked look of glee in his eyes. I can't stop her; I can't stop the motion of her arm as she pushes me away and I fall to the ground, only to watch as the dart flies through the air and imbeds itself in the Minotaur's back.

An ear splitting and unearthly scream fills the air, taking up all the sound in the labyrinth. The scream goes on for a long time, only stopping for a breath before resuming, and I swear I can see the very air in front of me tear at the noise.

The Minotaur has woken, and it is angry.

CHAPTER THIRTY

I watch as the Minotaur slowly lifts itself to its full height.

It towers above us and I should be afraid, but it's the first time I've been right before it; I can feel the power in its almost majestic stance as it turns and takes us all in. It lets out another chilling scream and even though it has the face and head of a bull, the eyes are almost human. I can see a depth within them that has nothing to do with the beast and everything to do with the human fixed inside.

It regards us for a moment and then reaches to its back and pulls out the dart, bringing it to its eyes in order to see the offending object. I can see the drops of blood that fall from it landing wetly on the bodies under its feet. It looks at the piece of metal and then at us, as if it can't comprehend how it has gotten into this situation. It makes an almost mewing sound that starts low in its stomach and is then released it into the air. It sounds mournful and I shiver as the sound grows louder. The din reminds me of the screams it made when no attack came, and we all breathlessly waited for the horror to land upon us.

The Minotaur looks at Sunita and grins with so many teeth, too many for its mouth, and pulls back the dart dripping with its blood and lets it fly. It lands with a wet *thunk!* in Sunita's neck. She clutches at her throat, making no sound aside from a damp gurgling. She stares at me with eyes that are too wide for her face, trying to open her mouth to say something. I tell her to be quiet, to save her strength, but she clutches at me with her other hand and says, "..love..." The shape of the word sounds soggy and I'm not aware that I'm crying until I feel the tears land on my hand. "...love....you..." she says.

"I love you too," I whisper, the tears coming quickly, filling my eyes so that I'm seeing Sunita through water. I lean forward and kiss her softly on the mouth and swear I can feel her lips return my kiss, then she falls from my grasp and lands in a heap at our feet. From somewhere far away, I can hear the Minotaur crying again, filling the air with its mournful call that somehow matches the anguish I'm feeling. I let out my own exclamation of rage and for a moment the air is filled with a haunting of fury.

The Minotaur is surprised by my sounds and stops screaming to look at me. Its head tilts to the right and it makes an inquisitive sound, almost as if purring. My scream goes on for a little while longer and when the sound is finished, it's replaced with a loud furious wind in my ears. I can hear the Minotaur's sounds, I hear Kiles, Riley and Hugo saying things to me, but none of it matters. I take a moment to look down at Sunita, her dark skin now ashen and her body covered in her own blood and the wind of fury quiets until the anger fills me completely. I don't hear anything else besides the wind and water that move within me, and I feel my words quiet for once, no consonants poking at my throat to get out. I open my mouth and let out another cry, but this time it's not a cry of pain, it's a battle cry full of wrath and anger.

I start to charge forward, but there is a movement in the wind to the right of me as Hugo lets his lance fly. It whistles as it sails and the Minotaur swipes at it, sending it clattering damply to the ground as it strikes the flesh of the bodies. Hugo charges forward and pulls his lance free while Kiles launches his own lance through the air. I bend down to take some of the darts that Sunita fashioned, hoping that she can forgive me for touching her this way, when I hear a wet *thwack!* of the lance hitting its target with a scream from the Minotaur. I feel the ground shake and vibrate beneath my feet as I stand and then the Minotaur is right in front of us. Its shriek filling the air around us and the scream that my fills my lungs is out before it has a chance to rupture my lungs or break my bones. This is a scream of seventeen years' worth of fear, anger and fright all rolled into one.

I let lose the darts and each of them finds a home buried deep within its fur. I can hear yelling and screaming, the air around me moving. The Minotaur lets out another screech and grabs Kiles from where he stands, lifting him up into the air. Riley lets out a yell of his own and Kiles tells Riley that he's okay. He's still holding on to his lance, which he plunges it into one of the Minotaur's eyes, provoking a blood-curdling scream. The Minotaur reaches up with his other clawed hand and slams his talons through Kiles, showering us all with blood. It feels warm on my face, reminding me of a summer rain. I can feel it running down my face, and when Kiles falls to the ground, I can feel another scream roiling up inside of me, but Riley lets out his own first and my scream joins his.

I don't know what I need to do, what I *can* do, but before I can let out another caterwaul, I hear someone calling to me. "Roanne!" the voice says. "Roanne!"

That voice breaks through the screaming, and I stop mine so that I can focus. Riley has crouched down beside the man he loves, cradling him as if Kiles were a baby. Riley looks to be crying tears of blood, his face is so streaked red. At first, I think it's Kiles who has spoken but he has his head bent low, whispering something to Riley. Blood is pooling on the ground, leaking from him to colour the earth, resembling dark wet tar.

"Roanne!" The sound comes again, and I almost don't look up, even though the Minotaur is screaming, trying to pull the darts from its fur and the lance from its eye, and we are bathed in more blood. His claws come within an inch of taking off my head and I do not back away in fright; I'm too afraid to move. The fear is like a wave inside me that somehow keeps me still and yet it makes me want to move with it, to lose myself in the water flowing within me because somehow drowning from the inside out would be easier than dealing with the death that is around me now.

I want to let the water erupt from my throat and fill the labyrinth so that my sadness can take everyone else away but then I hear the voice again, calling out my name. "Roanne! Use the stone! Use the stone!"

I try to place the sound of that voice, but I can't. In a haze of anger and sadness, I reach into my bag and pull out the stone which fell from within me. I remember Sunita's hand rubbing my back as I expunged the stone from my body, the rabbit still so far away and evading capture. I look at it in the dim light of the labyrinth, the shadows taking on an opalescent quality, much like the stone itself. It shines black like a mirror in the half-light and holding it I can feel the pain that was within me given physical form. Clutching the stone, memories flash before my eyes: yelling at my mother, Janice taunting me, hitting me with my own cane, believing that I was broken, and the slash of glass against one of my wrists, the blood pooling to the surface preventing my ability to cut further. I see the face of my father as he looked at me with growing incomprehension as I became a stranger to him, and he became a stranger to me. I remember all the times when I was frozen in place and unable to move, unable to find a way forwards.

The Minotaur lets out an anguished sound and with lightning speed, reaches down and grabs me around the waist. It lifts me high into the air and I can see it's remaining eye more clearly. I watch as it reaches with its other hand and pulls the lance free from the injured eye and while I'm looking at the one whole eye and one dark eye, without thinking I slam the stone into the eye socket formerly punctured by Kiles' lance. The Minotaur lets out its loudest roar yet, and it sounds as if the very fabric of time is going to let go and take us all into blackness. The Minotaur doesn't release me but remains stuck in place, held there by whatever is in the stone. I wonder if it's replaying my memories inside its head, or if it's somehow reliving its own, forced to watch everyone it has maimed and killed. It's held in stasis, frozen by whatever it's seeing. I wonder if that is the true power of the stone and wonder if true stillness can only be found when we confront our emotions.

I look around and see Mother standing with the Oracle and Dominic by her side and I know that it was she who called out to me to use the stone. There is frantic look on her face as if she is about to descend into madness once more. I wonder idly how she knew that I carried the stone with me and make a mental note to ask her later. She sees me looking at her and nods as if giving me permission, but I don't need it, nor do I need to be told what to do. I reach into my bag and pull out the shard of glass. I think of the last few lines of the poem I read in the little blue book: *He knew that the only way, To set his friend's spirit free, Was to bring him to a body of water, So that they may truly see.*

I know there isn't a way to bring the Minotaur to a body of water, and I would not try to bring it to one of the swimming holes where it could maim or kill the people waiting down below in the labyrinth. I will not be responsible for the deaths of others. I wield the shard of glass that came from my throat, and it glints in the half-light. It came from the water and spent time underneath its surface, so it's the closest thing we have to a body of water in this mountain made of corpses. There is a frightened look in the Minotaur's good eye as I bring it close to the one that is unblinking, frozen in place.

I watch as the Minotaur's remaining eye widens to take in its own reflection. Its eye enlarges in fright and wonder, I can see emotions running across its face, bull or not. It lets out a little whimper of wonder and I don't think I've ever heard the Minotaur make such a diminutive noise. It sounds almost human.

I notice the ground is approaching and it's a moment before I realize that the Minotaur is shrinking, growing smaller moment by moment. The noise it's making changes from a mew to a low, long wail. It is not a wail of pain but one of realization. I can see the hair falling away from the Minotaur's face and see patches of actual skin showing through the bull's fur. I can see its eyes changing from a dark black tar-like sheen into a green hue, the irises flecked with browns and golds.

"Drop the shard, Roanne," my mother calls out. There is urgency to her voice. "It's begun; you can drop the shard. Let it go."

However, despite her words, I hold on to it. I want to see this through. I think of the key, the important part that it had to play. Ginette had asked me if I had the key. What would it open? What secrets still had to be found?

We tried maiming the Minotaur to no avail, but for some reason this little shard of glass is making the transformation possible. It will become a man who we can hopefully kill, or maybe the injuries that he sustained will finally kill the Minotaur. I can only hope this is so, that all our efforts weren't for nothing. Riley doesn't look at me, he still cradles Kiles who has bled out, pale and unmoving. Only Hugo is left to witness as the Minotaur changes from beast to man.

It happens slowly, the hair receding little by little on its face, the head becoming more and more human. I watch as the Minotaur's lips shed the fur which covers a bull's skin, revealing the pale skin of a human. I watch the ground come ever closer as the obsidian heels become human feet, one toe appearing followed by another. All the while, the sound from the Minotaur is like a keening, as if mourning the loss of what it once knew and resisting the change that is coming, refusing to accept the inevitable.

The Minotaur finally lets me go and I fall gracelessly to the ground as it becomes more human, taking shape again as if being birthed into its true form. As I see the man revealed, I can't believe that I didn't realize who it was the moment I saw his green eyes, having stared into them so often when I was growing up. Those eyes looked at me as they put me to sleep, as they gave me advice on how to live my life, as they reprimanded or punished me. Those were the eyes that I loved to look into because they were like finding a piece of home, no matter where I was.

I stand there holding the shard of glass, looking into the face of my father.

He stands naked in front of me, but I'm not concerned about that. What concerns me is that the ground seems to be moving again, as if part of it is falling away.

The keening sound becomes a name I know well, for it is my own. "Roanne!" my father bellows. "Roanne no, gods no. Please no!" There are now tears sliding down my father's face as the distance between us grows. "Roanne, no, no no."

My mother and the Oracle approach me, with Dominic following behind them, but I notice a look of fear in their eyes. I can feel the strap of my bag tear off as the world continues to fall away from me. My mother has tears flowing from her eyes and I reach out a hand to wipe them away, but then I notice the shiny sheen of a claw breaking through my skin.

"There must always be a Minotaur," my mother whispers. Those words come out of her mouth, and I can feel the shards of the words catch in my own throat, feel the pain that those words are causing my mother as she looks up at me. "There must always be a Minotaur, and we can never be free," Mother says, and I can hear the pain in each word. It seems like they are ripped from her throat. "Soon, you will forget who you are, my beautiful and wonderful Roanne." The tears slide freely down her face now and she does not wipe them away, does not embrace my father who also looks up at me.

"It wasn't supposed to be you," the Oracle says. She is crying now, and I can hear the sorrow in her voice, the pain that echoes my mothers. "Never you."

I can feel my body changing shape, becoming something made of myth and legend. I look down at myself and I don't recognize my body or the hooves that have replaced my feet. I try to say something reassuring to everyone who is now looking up at me, but all that comes out is a scream, a rage so huge that it defies words and yet I'm sure everyone can understand my pain because everything has already been taken from them too.

I look at the world around me that has grown unfamiliar, filled with hues of yellow, green, blue, and violet but it's muted with the dark and shadows I know so well. I can see movement in the shadows, and I know that these are people I used to know, but I can no longer comprehend who they are, and in another moment, they will be lost to me. What I am becoming has stripped me of my humanity and I do not know what the future will bring. With my last remaining bit of human thought, I look down at the people milling about me like ants and I try to say I'm sorry, I'm sorry, I'm sorry, but all that comes out is a keening wail of rage. The howl of rage leaves my mouth, it fills my ears and my body, and I feel alive with that sound of wrath in my ears.

And then Roanne is gone and only the Minotaur is left.

The Minotaur lives on.

ABOUT THE AUTHOR

J AMIESON WOLF is a number one bestselling author—he likes to tell people that a lot—and writes in many different genres. He has been fortunate enough to win several awards for his writing, including the Best LGBTQ Book of 2019 from the Love Romance Café for his novel *Love and Lemonade*. His short story, "The Descent," was included in the Prix Aurora Award–nominated collection *Nothing Without Us*. Jamieson is also an artist and has been fortunate enough to have his work hang in the Art Gallery of Ontario.

He lives with spastic cerebral palsy and relapse-remitting multiple sclerosis. Jamieson is a disability advocate who runs a blog called "Two Steps at a Time," where he writes about what it's like to live with CP and MS. Jamieson has also written pieces for the Spoonie Authors Network and has spoken on panels about disability and accessibility.

He currently lives in Ottawa, Ontario, Canada, with his husband, Michael, and their cat, Anakin, who they swear has Jedi powers.

You can find Jamieson at http://www.jamiesonwolf.com.

www.ingramcontent.com/pod-product-compliance
Lightning Source LLC
Chambersburg PA
CBHW031940010726
47493CB00007B/2017